LINDA SAMMARITAN

SPEAKING THROUGH THE SILENCE

By Linda Sammaritan

To my sister, my forever best friend.
Your presence in our family taught us to be
kind, compassionate, and strong.
Your kindness, grace, and perseverance
surpasses us all.

To God be the glory!

Acknowledgments

The teen years are times of transition from child to adult in every generation, and where there's change, there is uncertainty and fear of failure. I'm grateful for the adults in my life who allowed me to explore where my talents and personality would take me. So, thank you to my parents, grandmother, and teachers who watched me grow and stumble and grow some more, always ready to pick me up and brush me off whenever I performed a spectacular act of humiliation!

Lady Lits, Heartland Writers, Indianapolis Writers Meet-Up, and Scriblerians, you've seen me through the whole series now. World Without Sound would never have reached publication without you.

To my new friends at bookstores and libraries, especially Debbie L., thank you for supporting me. Your encouragement has forged a new boldness in this fledgling as she leaves her safe nest of anonymity and takes flight into the wild blue yonder of publishing. I gain more confidence everyday as I learn to "put myself out there" with a genuine smile, eager to meet strangers who share my affinity for reading a good story.

Thank you, Cynthia Hickey and Winged Publications, for taking a chance on a young adult trilogy in the genre of realistic fiction. May we all be blessed with hungry readers, and may we be a blessing to everyone who loves to read.

While *Speaking Through the Silence* is a work of fiction, many of the episodes are based on true incidents. Thanks to Mom, Doug, Steve, and Tricia for providing family memories alongside my own.

Finally, to my husband, my children, and my friends who let me know how proud they are to "know a real author!" Yes, you say that in jest, but you let me know in all seriousness how much you recognize the effort and perseverance that goes into writing a book. Thank you for understanding. I love you all.

Author's Notes

A Note to the Deaf Community and 21st Century Readers

The World Without Sound series begins in 1965 and ends in 1970. At that time, the medical and educational establishments were convinced sign language did more harm than good, believing deaf children would never learn to communicate with the hearing world.

These were years where the schools demanded "speech only" education. Hearing parents, deaf children, and many teachers ended up feeling even more defeated in an already-frustrating situation. It wasn't until later in the Seventies that ASL was considered an acceptable alternative, and my sister's school taught both sign language and speech. I believe the combination was labeled "total communication," although today, that term includes cued speech, SEE, and other sign languages.

While I have noticed some contention on both trains of thought to this day, I believe ASL is more accepted as a viable means of communication than it was fifty years ago, and our deaf children grow up with far less stress.

Chapter 1:
Temper Tantrums (August 1968)

Six, nine? Or nine, six?
I don't know. They look the same!
They make me so mad!

My little sister lined up four cards, one right next to the other. Three nines and a six lay on the family room's carpet to display her latest collection for our game of *Go Fish*. Krista was good at recognizing numbers, but since she wasn't quite three years old, nines and sixes looked pretty much the same.

I shook my head and pointed to the mismatched card. Krista's proud smile disappeared. I spread the cards further apart so she could see them clearly, but she wouldn't look at them. Instead, she stared daggers at me.

After gathering the four cards, I returned them to her. She fired them at my face.

"Stop it." I signed the word for *stop* and offered the cards to her again. "Do you want to play, or not?"

Krista accepted the cards with hooded eyelids and

a tightening of her lips. Mad, but not out of control. She locked her gaze on mine, and with perfect control, threw the cards at me a second time.

Here we go again. All I'd wanted was to do something fun with her while we waited for dinner. Without breaking eye contact, I shook my finger at her. *Bad.* I signed the word and flung my hand straight toward her. "You are bad."

"Yeeeeeeee!" Her voice rose like the screech of a tea kettle on full steam. She picked up the rest of the deck and threw it at me.

Being deaf didn't give her an excuse to be a brat. I grabbed several of the cards and threw them back at her. I was entering my freshman year in high school, and she had me behaving like a kindergartner.

When Krista lunged for me, I grabbed her around the waist with one arm and lugged her over my hip to the back door. No easy feat. She might be skinny, but with the metal ankle-to-thigh braces sheathing her legs, lifting her felt like carrying a loaded garbage can to the curb. My free hand turned the handle, and I hoped those lethal legs didn't kick through the new storm door. They shouldn't. After my thirteen-year-old brother Paul punched through the glass last month (long story—he deserved to be locked out), Mom replaced it with acrylic. Nobody wanted more blood splattered all over the house. *Or* another ambulance run.

My parents and Grandma waited for an explanation on the deck as I dumped Krista beside Daddy lounging in one of our newest lawn chairs. If anyone could get her to behave, he could.

"We were playing Go Fish, and all of a sudden, she's throwing the cards everywhere and screaming at me because I told her a nine and a six are *not* the same number. Which she already knows."

I slumped on the picnic bench, finding no pleasure in the ocean breeze while Krista continued to jabber and screech at me. She was really hard to deal with sometimes. She couldn't see our words, and doctors told us we weren't supposed to use sign language. How could we get any kind of message across? I had learned *some* sign language—the doctors could go fly a kite—but I didn't study it like I studied Spanish. Which meant I didn't know enough to help Krista all the time.

Even when I signed, like with the card game, she still lost her temper. Terrible Twos reigned supreme.

With Krista still shrieking at me—no words—just high-pitched, angry squeals, Daddy grasped her shoulders and turned her around to face him. He raised his eyebrows and gazed directly into her eyes. She dissolved into tears and hid her face in his lap.

She and I were totally alike when it came to Daddy. We couldn't stand to disappoint him. And it wasn't just the fact that he'd only been home for two weeks after a year spent fighting in Vietnam. I still hadn't stopped saying in my head, "Thank you, God," every time he pulled into the driveway.

Daddy rubbed Krista's back in soothing circles, something that used to calm me down, too. "Go get the cards that started the trouble," he told me.

I made sure the adults heard my martyred sigh as I pushed off from the bench. With fifty-two cards scattered all over the den, I searched every corner to find the four I needed. When I returned, Krista was cuddled into Daddy's chest. She threw a sullen look my way, then shifted her position so her back was turned to me.

I held out the cards. "Nine of hearts, nine of spades, nine of clubs, six of diamonds. She thinks they all match. At least, that's what I think she thinks."

Daddy grouped them so their corners were right next to each other. Obviously, three numbers had a circle at the top and the fourth a circle at the bottom. He tapped Krista. She looked up, noticed the cards, and burrowed her face against Daddy.

He flipped Krista so she was forced to sit with her back against him, then held the cards in front of her. He pointed to the corners.

She whimpered.

"Honey, if she starts in again, can we leave this for another time?" Mom was sick of tantrums, too.

Grandma stepped inside with her magazine and iced tea. She hated loud noises.

Daddy handed the cards back to me. "Hold two in each hand."

I muttered under my breath. "This isn't gonna be pretty."

"Debbie." His voice held warning.

I thrust the cards close to Krista's face.

Daddy pushed them a few inches away and leaned forward so Krista could see his lips. He pointed to each nine. "What number?"

With a pout, Krista held up five fingers on one hand and four on the other.

Daddy nodded and pointed to the six. "What number?"

The pout tightened to a grim line. She held up five fingers on one hand and *four* fingers on the other.

"A nine?" His eyes opened wide in surprise. He

swiveled his head in an exaggerated motion as if he were examining all the cards carefully. "Nine. Nine. Nine." Pause. "And nine?"

What a ham. Krista stared at him, not impressed with his antics.

"Debbie, put the nines in one hand and the six in the other, then bring the cards closer to my face."

I stood to one side keeping the cards a couple of inches from Daddy's nose. He leaned even closer so one eyeball was almost on a number nine. He looked at Krista. "Nine?"

She nodded. The pout was gone from her eyes. Her lips remained tight, but the corners began to curve up.

Daddy leaned so close to the number six card that his face touched it. He pulled back and looked at Krista, his eyes wider than ever. "Nine?"

He returned to peering at the six. A little snort escaped from Krista. Daddy's head snapped to face her again, and a startled giggle erupted.

"Nine?"

She started to nod, but he raised his eyebrows in a "think again" expression. Krista leaned closer to the six card. Circle on the lower portion of the number. She glanced at Daddy, back to the number. She darted a look at me, then back to the six, then back to Daddy.

"Nine?" he repeated.

Krista hung her head. Slowly, she lifted five fingers of one hand and the thumb of the other. And I had called my baby sister "bad." *What was my problem?*

When she raised her head, she found me kneeling beside the chair, my arms opened wide. She slid off of Daddy's lap for a hug. The only way she knew to say,

"I'm sorry."

Mom stood and picked up her glass, plus Daddy's. "This is why we need to find a school. She's got to learn to communicate without all the tears. It's exhausting for all of us, and it's not fair to her." She headed for the door. "Dinner will be ready in ten minutes."

Chapter 2:
Which School?

Lady in a gray
Dress. Her house smelled like crayons.
I think she liked me.

Once the plates were served and grace said, my younger brothers, Paul and Wade, launched into a play-by-play report of their neighborhood football game. It sounded a lot like it had last night and the night before, but Daddy tossed them questions as if it were all new to him. Mom and Grandma had their own quiet conversation at the other end of the table. Krista grimaced at her dinner and pushed the spinach to the edge of her bunny plate.

I drifted into daydreams of the first day of school. It would be so much better than eighth grade. I didn't have to worry about my father at war anymore, Ronni was my best friend, and now that I was in ninth grade, Bill might notice me. Especially if I made the cheerleading squad. Ronni and I planned to try for it. And if I didn't make it, I'd still be on the bleachers watching Bill play football.

Mom's words pulled me out of my daydreams. "Deaf children need an early education if they're going to be able to understand language, to speak and read it. A lot of families with deaf children Krista's age send their kids to residential institutions." She leaned on her elbows and massaged her temples like she had a major headache. "Some parents actually sent them last year. Couldn't handle the temper tantrums."

Wade, who'd been demonstrating his quarterback passing abilities with a wadded-up paper napkin, fumbled the 'ball,' dropping it on his plate. "They sent their *two*-year-olds to live at school? They *left* them there?"

Wade must not have been around when Mom and I talked about those families last year. Or maybe, having recently turned eleven, he'd developed the ability to follow grown-up conversations.

I rubbed the turquoise and sea-green beads of my necklace between my thumb and two fingers. My parents wouldn't send Krista away, would they? Sure, she had daily tantrums, but that was no reason to get rid of her!

Daddy halted Wade's fears. "If we can't find a school close by, we'll move to be near the school she attends."

"But then I'll have to make new friends all over again," I said. Seventh grade had been awful enough. Now, they wanted to move again, and it wasn't even an Air Force move? "Let *me* teach her."

I was planning to go into special education in college, and besides, hadn't I already taught Krista her letters and numbers?

"You don't know how." Daddy set his coffee

down a little too hard. Some of it sloshed over the lip of the cup. "None of us knows how."

Mom gathered crumpled napkins and all the dirty plates that she could reach from her seat. "Krista needs special teachers to show her how to use her voice box to talk properly. They would teach her how to read lips."

"We could learn sign language," I argued. "And all of us could teach her. Then she wouldn't have to read our lips." Mom and I did not see eye-to-eye about this. I'd been practicing some ASL words even though she didn't want me to.

Mom sighed. "How will she ever get along in life if she can't read lips? Anyway, the deaf schools don't use sign language, and they won't teach it."

"But maybe we could all learn it as a family. At least she could communicate with *us*."

Grandma dabbed at her lips with a napkin. "I'd be willing to learn sign language."

There! Someone was on my side. And Grandma was over seventy years old. If she could learn, all of us could.

Mom stood and lifted the stack of dishes from the table. "I'm too tired to think about it now. I just wish Commack would let us know one way or another."

The Commack School for the Deaf was the closest day school where kids could go home every afternoon instead of live at school. Close, as in a forty-five-minute drive from our house. If Krista got accepted there, we wouldn't have to move, and Krista wouldn't have to live at school. But if they said no…

Daddy pushed back his chair. "Tomorrow, I'm going to take Krista to visit the director of the school. I know Sister Ignatius wants to help this crop of kids from the rubella epidemic. Maybe she hasn't seen those with multiple handicaps in action." He tapped the top of Krista's head with one finger, passing her on his way to the kitchen. "Once she sees how Krista compares with other deaf kids her age, I think the sister will redouble her efforts to add classroom space."

All right, Daddy! Go for it! Doing something had to be better than waiting for an answer in the mail.

When Daddy and Krista returned from their visit to the deaf school, he joined Mom, Grandma, and me for another glorious summer afternoon on the deck. Sunshine and salty wind.

"You should have seen your sister." He grinned at me as he accepted a drink from Mom. "Sister Ignatius gave her some letter cards and asked if she could say the letters." He paused. "Well, she couldn't do that, but I told her to *make* her name with the letters.

"She spread the cards out on the floor, found the K right away, and went to town. Only problem was, there were only twenty-five cards. The T was missing. Krista got to K-R-I-S- and didn't know what to do. She kept searching for a T.

"Sister Ignatius wrote T on an index card and handed it to her. Krista put the T next to the S then found the A. The sister clapped for her."

"*We* always knew she was smart," I said. "Grandma and I have been practicing letters and numbers with her all year."

"Then you know what Sister Ignatius did?" Daddy started acting out his story, making each motion as he talked. He had to set down his drink before he spilled it. "She gets out a Polaroid camera from a closet in her office. She sets the cards upright on her desk against some books, so they look like a sign. K-R-I-S-T-A. She stands Krista next to the sign and takes a picture.

"In two minutes, she shows me the snapshot. There's Krista, full length with leg braces, hearing aids, and glasses. Sister says, 'When I see the governor next week, I'm showing him this photo. A three-year-old who's deaf, half blind, part lame from cerebral palsy—excuse my bluntness, but he'll get it if I say it that way—and she knows her ABCs better than most kids her age. How can he tell me these kids aren't worth the extra effort?'"

Daddy smacked the flat of his hand on his knee. "That nun is some lady."

I hoped he was right. But "that nun" didn't say Krista was accepted into the school.

Chapter 3:
Visitors Day

Deh-bie, Paw, and Way
Disappear in 'ool. Hmmm. Will
I disappear, too?

K rista got accepted!
An official letter from Commack School for the Deaf arrived. The acceptance came with a whole packet of papers for Mom and Dad to sign, plus a lot of school rules and the bus schedule and where to get uniforms and… I didn't remember what else was in there.

They invited us to Family Orientation Day on September first, and school would start on Tuesday. Talk about a whirlwind!

We drove up a narrow lane edged with red rose bushes in our family station wagon, the Big Blue Boat. An extra-long ranch house with a white wooden sign in front sat next to the crowded parking lot. Fancy red script announced, "Commack School for the Deaf." Matching bright red shutters against white shingles seemed to say, "Welcome."

Kids of all ages climbed monkey bars, lined up at two slides, and filled every swing in a playground next to the building. Trees dotted the property, and a lush, green lawn spread between the long house and a second, smaller, white one. Maybe the nuns lived there. If I were a nun, I'd want to live in a little white house with this beautiful view.

As soon as Daddy switched off the ignition, Paul and Wade raced for the playground. I wanted to meet Krista's teacher, peek into her classroom, and find out how the nuns teach deaf children to talk. As a future special education teacher, this could give me a head start.

A nun in a gray habit that only reached to her knees greeted us on the front steps to the veranda that fronted the long house. Her face had a few lines, but with her hair covered by a wimple, it was hard to tell her age.

"Welcome! I'm Sister Michaelina. I'll give you a tour of the facilities and answer any of your questions. Then feel free to enjoy the refreshments we're serving out by the playground." She bent down and smiled directly at Krista. "And who is this charming little girl?"

"This is Krista." Mom watched for Krista's reaction. Were we here with an angry brat or a delightful sprite?

We had tried to explain that she'd go to her own school just like Debbie, Paul, and Wade. But we weren't sure if she understood. She only frowned when we said, "school." She scowled when I signed the word, too.

Krista smiled back at Sister Michaelina, who stood

and offered her hand. To my amazement, Krista took it. Like she'd known this stranger all of her life.

They stepped through the bright red front door. Mom, Daddy, Grandma, and I followed. Sister Michaelina swept her arm like a model on *The Price is Right* as she showed off their front room, spacious and simply furnished with straight-back chairs like a doctor's waiting room. Magazines were strewn on a few small tables. One corner of the room held a toy box. An open window in the wall across from the door allowed visitors to see into the next room. It seemed to be the office. Two ladies dressed in regular clothes sat at counters and jotted notes on papers.

"This is our welcome area." Sister Michaelina pointed to the toy box. "We want little ones to feel comfortable here. Both the new students and any of their younger siblings."

She opened a door in the far-right wall of the room. "We'll start the tour by looking at the older students' classrooms. Up until this year, we had first through eighth grades in this wing, one class per room. You'll see how we've changed things around so we can fit four new classrooms into our school.

As we walked down the corridor, doors from each classroom stood open. Sister Michaelina stopped at the first door to our left.

"This will be our kindergarten room. It's the former eighth grade." She entered, and we followed like a line of ducklings. Krista made a beeline for the play kitchen. I glanced at Mom who hadn't taken her eyes off Krista. Back in July, we'd visited a nursery school in Hampton Shores, and Krista loved the play kitchen so much she threw a tantrum when it was time to leave.

That teacher decided she couldn't handle the extra time it would take to teach a deaf child.

Sister Michaelina didn't force Krista to leave the room when the rest of us did, unlike that other teacher. "Don't worry. She'll find us when she's ready, or we'll pick her up on the way out of this wing."

We continued down the hall where each classroom contained the next grade in ascending order. By the time we stepped into the fifth-grade classroom, Krista trotted in to join us, a grin on her face and a toy teapot in her hand.

Mom started to remove the teapot, but the sister said, "Krista can return it herself when we pass the kindergarten room on our way back up the hall."

We toured the sixth and seventh grade classrooms. Back at the kindergarten door, Sister Michaelina gestured to Krista to put the teapot back. Krista put on her stubborn face.

"There's more for you to see." The nun made a come-along motion, and Krista followed.

The sister stopped, looked at the teapot, looked at the play kitchen, and looked at Krista. Holding up one finger, she said, "First, the teapot. Then we see more."

Krista could see the word "more" and understood what it meant. She already knew she was supposed to put back a toy that wasn't hers. I held my breath. I think Mom did, too.

Sister Michaelina lowered herself to one knee and faced Krista. "Do you want to see more?"

Krista nodded. The sister looked toward the play kitchen. Krista walked to it and placed the teapot on one of the stove burners. Her nasty attitude had magically disappeared. Already, this school was performing miracles.

I sucked in a deep, relieved breath as we crossed the entry area and passed through a different door next to the office window and into a second, shorter hallway. It had one classroom on the left.

"This will be our eighth grade," the sister announced. "It used to be a storage room behind the office."

Except for no windows, it looked pretty much like my classrooms in Hampton Shores but smaller, filled with eight desks, bookshelves, a chalkboard, and hooks to hold coats in the winter.

Sister Michaelina turned left at the corner of the hallway, then right through a pair of double doors and into a gymnasium. Nothing fancy. Lunch tables had been shoved toward one wall.

"This is our combination gym and cafeteria," she said. "We also have special activities for the whole school in here."

"Like what?" I asked.

"Like our Christmas play. And we have other seasonal celebrations. Sometimes, it's a big game day."

Cool. But how did all the deaf kids in the school know what was going on? We couldn't even get Krista to understand a birthday party.

Our tour continued. A second set of opened double doors led outside to a second playground that couldn't be seen from where we had entered the building. Several little kids crawled over equipment obviously made for the youngest students.

We crossed the gym toward the lunch tables.

"We have a kitchen." Sister Michaelina opened a door next to the farthest table on the right and showed us one of those refrigerators that holds cartons of milk. It was filled and ready to go.

Daddy lifted Krista so she could see inside it. She picked up a carton and looked at him with a question in her eyes.

"You drink it." Daddy put the milk to his lips.

Krista cocked her head to one side and examined the sealed carton.

Daddy pointed to one corner. "You open it and drink."

"Feel free to open it and show her," Sister Michaelina said. "We have plenty."

Daddy set Krista down and pulled open the carton. Krista peered inside. The nun popped a straw into the container, then motioned for Krista to drink.

Cautiously, Krista placed her lips on the straw. Her eyes widened in surprise, and her mouth worked the straw with confidence. When she'd had her fill, she handed the carton back to Daddy and smiled. "Mih!"

"Yes, milk is in the carton. This is a little carton for lunch. Like the big carton at home." He brought his hands close together to show *little*, then drew them apart to show *big*.

Krista knew the words "lunch" and "home." She nodded her head in understanding.

Before we left the kitchen, Daddy placed a nickel in a small basket next to the milk refrigerator. Sister Michaelina led us back across the gym, and we continued down another hallway of more classrooms.

"This wing has held our speech therapy room, kindergarten, and two preschool levels in the past. We had hoped to use the additional four rooms as the school grew." She chuckled. "But we didn't expect the flood of applications for this year." She pointed toward the far end of the hall. "The end room is still for speech, but we've taken those extra rooms and converted them into four more classrooms for this especially large class due to the rubella epidemic."

We entered the first classroom on the right. Lots of shelves with toys, another play kitchen, and three little tables with four chairs tucked into each. All preschool classes must contain the same furniture.

But the walls. Two were white, the other two painted green. Not that pale, sickly gray-green like the military hospital where Krista had her heart surgery. No, in this room, morning glories and clematis climbed a painted trellis, dotting the white walls with blue and purple. Red and yellow tulips created a border near the floor. Clumps of pink rosebuds were scattered across the midline. Funny baby animal posters were tacked onto the spring-green walls. *This* was what Krista had needed at the hospital.

Sister Michaelina noticed my enchantment. "Entertaining, isn't it? We're calling this the Spring Room. We've painted each new preschool room with a different season. It will be another way to teach little ones vocabulary."

Brilliant. I needed to tuck that idea away for my own teacher days.

Of course, Krista ran straight to the kitchen while the nun showed us other areas of the room. "Spring will be Krista's classroom, and I will be Krista's teacher."

Great. Krista already liked her teacher. The forty-five-minute bus ride to school wouldn't be so terrible if she got to spend her day with such a nice lady.

Sister Michaelina strolled toward a corner

containing a rocking chair, a large easel, and a rug. "Like any other school, the teachers lead the children in calendar and weather activities. They learn numbers and letters, and we start phonics." She pointed to the letter cards posted over the chalkboard on a white wall.

How could they teach the sounds of letters to someone who couldn't *hear*? I didn't dare blurt out my question, though. Back when we lived in Syracuse, my friends who went to Catholic school said you couldn't ask questions. If you did, the nuns smacked your hand with a ruler.

Sister Michaelina continued. "Phonics here isn't the same idea as what all of us grew up with. Deaf children can watch the sounds and feel the sounds. They practice in the classroom, and each student sees a speech therapist twice a week for a half-hour lesson."

She dipped her head in apology. "I wish we could give speech lessons every day, but we don't have the space or the manpower."

Daddy pointed to a wide mirror set into the wall between classroom and hallway. "Is that what I think it is?"

The sister smiled. "Yes. That's a two-way mirror. Parents can stop by any time and watch their children in the classroom environment. Of course, the speech teacher and other staff are also free to watch student progress, and the children aren't distracted by visitors."

How had I missed that? I hadn't thought twice about being able to look into the classroom before we reached the door, just assumed the students could see people passing by. I ambled out to the hall and turned toward the tinted window. Peering through it, I observed Krista turning her attention from the kitchen to a shelf filled with puzzles.

Another nun with a family in tow walked down the hallway. She nodded a greeting, then continued to the next classroom. I followed at a distance, then peeked inside. Obviously, the Summer Room. Its walls were white, half blue and half green. Painted on the white were trees, corn fields, sunflowers, marigolds, and more roses in all different colors. Squirrels, rabbits, and raccoons played among the flowers in the green spaces, and the blue half held clouds and birds, a beach, and a distant plane.

I just *had* to peek into the other rooms. The Fall Room had all the colors you would expect for the season. Trees with colorful leaves, asters, and zinnias. Then pumpkins and Indian corn and apples. The Winter Room sparkled. Snowflakes and icicles covered in silver sequins had been tacked to the walls. Trees with bare branches. The white, gray, and silver were relieved by the rich dark green of evergreens. I wanted to take notes. Someday, once I was a teacher, I would paint spruce trees on my classroom walls and pin decorations on them. And I would make sure the room dazzled my students, just like this room did.

The last room, the original preschool room, was a circus. Literally. Each of two red walls held a circus tent, the flaps drawn open, to reveal all kinds of circus acts in the rings. Lions, elephants, fancy horses, trapeze artists, clowns, and a ringmaster. Krista was going to love this place.

I slipped back into the Spring Room. Mom and Sister Michaelina picked up puzzle pieces while Daddy reorganized the toy kitchen with Krista's help. Once again, no temper tantrum. Did Krista already understand she would get to come back and play?

The sister stood and straightened her skirt. "At this time, I'd like to keep Krista with me, so I can do a few pre-assessments. The rest of you can go outside to the picnic. We have drinks, snacks, even some hot dogs grilling if you're hungry."

Daddy grinned. "I'm sure the boys have found the hot dogs."

He shook the sister's hand, and Mom did, too.

Sister Michaelina walked us back to the main entrance. Once we were on the veranda in view of the playground, Mom bent down to Krista, so she could read her lips. "You play with the teacher." Mom pointed to Krista, then to the nun. "And I will be here when you are finished." She pointed to herself, then down to the porch floor for "here."

Krista could see "play" and "finished." She shifted her gaze from Mom to the nun to Mom again.

"Okay?" Mom asked, eyebrows raised in question.

Sister Michaelina's beautiful smile and dark eyes reflected kindness. She probably loved all of her students. She didn't look like someone who would smack children's hands with a ruler.

Krista looked nervous but allowed the nun to take her hand. They went inside. When they returned ten minutes later, Krista was all smiles. She reached for my bag of popcorn.

"What do you think?" I tapped my finger against my forehead then pointed toward the building.

Krista popped a kernel into her mouth, then smacked her palm against her chest. *Mine.*

Chapter 4:
High School

*Before I saw my
'Ool, I thought 'ool was bad. But
It's fun! Now I know.*

The cheerleading try-outs form had been stapled to the bulletin board next to the gym doors. I rubbed the beads of my necklace while Ronni added her name under "Junior Varsity." Should I join her or not? I was such a klutz. Who else ever broke their foot in ballet class?

Melissa and Leigh had signed up. *Great.* I had to compete against them for cheerleading, too. In seventh grade the three of us had the same classes. We were all in choir. I thought they were my best friends. Once I came back from California, they made sure to let me know that was no longer the case. They didn't want me around.

A picture flashed into my mind. Me at the bottom of a deep, narrow well, while far above, Melissa and Leigh danced and cackled and fired popcorn kernels from the concession stand at my head.

Ronni stepped away from the bulletin board and pushed me toward it. "C'mon. It won't be any fun without you."

Last year, Ronni was new and friendless. I had needed a friend, too. Since then, we'd done everything together. One of the best friends I've ever had, maybe even better than Francie in fifth grade. I owed her this.

"What if you make it and I don't?" My voice came out whiny.

"Then you'll come to the games and watch me cheer, and afterwards, we'll hang out like we always do." Ronni's honesty and kindness would never allow her to say something hypocritical like, "Of course, you'll make the squad."

Ronni loved gymnastics. I didn't.

Her million-watt smile brought light to the world. My off-white teeth would never be in the running for a Dentyne commercial.

People warmed up to her right away, but they barely noticed me.

I let go of the beads, and with shaking fingers placed the point of the pencil on the sign-up sheet. *Who was I kidding?* I was more likely to make a fool of myself than make the squad.

Ronni hip-bumped me to one side. Before I realized what she'd done, my name appeared on the sheet in her handwriting.

"There. You're trying out. You've got rhythm, your voice carries across an auditorium. What are you afraid of?"

"I can't do splits. I can barely do a cartwheel. And I'm huge next to girls like Karen Marino."

"Barbara Connors weighs at least twenty pounds

more than you, and I've never seen her do a split either. She's a *varsity* cheerleader!"

Ronni had a point. Maybe athletic ability wasn't everything. But…Barbara was perky. An enthusiastic kewpie doll. I looked more like a serious Patty Playpal.

Ronni tugged me down the hall, winding her way through the rest of the crowd aiming for the front of the cafeteria line. "We're late for lunch, and I'm starving."

How could she be starving at eleven in the morning? If I ate her standard breakfast of pancakes, eggs, and bacon every day, I'd weigh more than Mama Cass.

While she relished mouthfuls of Spam Surprise, I pulled out an orange from my sack and three nickels from my pocket.

Her nose wrinkled. "That's your whole lunch?"

I held up the nickels. "My calorie splurge is on a can of root beer from the machine."

She shook her head. "You'll get zits. One swig of any kind of soda, and my whole face breaks out."

"Soda doesn't bother me, but don't feed me chocolate."

As I peeled the orange, Ronni regarded me with a sly smile. "I see Bill's been waiting for you after homeroom every day."

The little zing of anticipation returned, the one that tingled through me every morning since school started. "Yeah. He walks me to Spanish, then crosses the hall to English."

Ronni scanned the crowded cafeteria. "Good thing he doesn't have the same lunch period. I'd need a new lunch buddy."

I raised an eyebrow. "You could sit with us."

"Naw. You know what they say. Three's a crowd."

Three *would* have been a crowd when I saw Bill leaning against my locker at the end of the day, well-muscled arms folded across his chest.

This cool sophomore was waiting for *me*?

He pushed off from the locker and brushed red-brown bangs from his eyes. It was those chocolate eyes and the auburn hair that first snagged my attention last year.

His lazy smile set my heart a-flutter. "I guess you don't ride a bus. They all rolled out a while ago."

"I walk." Which allowed me a little extra time after gym class to dry my hair instead of a dash to the bus with it dripping wet. At the moment, I was extremely grateful for the fresh swipe of deodorant, too, as I fumbled with my combination lock.

"I was wondering…" He glanced down the hall before returning his gaze to me.

Heart flutters accelerated to wild bongo drums. *Was he going to ask me out on a date?*

"A bunch of us guys are going to the movies on Friday night. The early show. I was wondering if you were planning to go with your friends?"

Was he kidding? No herd of girls ever pulled me along to the movies or anywhere else. How could I play it cool? I leaned back against the wall of lockers, looking relaxed, I hoped. "Ronni and I might be going. We haven't decided yet."

"Well, I gotta get to football practice." He ambled down the hallway and called over his shoulder. "Hope I see you tomorrow night."

I opened my locker, a smile tugging my lips. Bill liked me. *Me.* This would be my first date. Or was it? Did meeting him at the movies count? Or was it only a date if he picked me up at home? I'd have to ask Ronni.

Krista loved her first week of school, too. On Friday, she showed me her papers. Lots of coloring, plus a page with a huge capital A across the center and a small apple near the bottom right corner.

"That's easy," I told her, "You know the letter A already." I pointed my index finger to my forehead, fingerspelled "A," and pointed at her.

Krista flashed a smug grin. She stuck her little nose in the air and pranced away to share the papers with Mom, probably for the twentieth time. How she appeared so light on her feet with those heavy leg braces I'd never understand.

I dropped my books on the bottom step of the stairs and ambled into the kitchen looking for something to eat. Mom stood at the stove, tongs in hand, turning hotdogs on the broiler pan. They tasted better from the grill, but outdoor cooking was Daddy's responsibility. With him working all week on an Air Force base in New Jersey, Saturday was the only night we could chow down on grilled meat. Anyway, broiled hotdogs sounded a lot better than Mom's experiments with casseroles.

She looked up when I opened the refrigerator door. "Can you wait five more minutes? I'm feeding everyone early so I can get ready for Couples Club."

Couples Club consisted of a bunch of married couples at our church. They had a group date night every month, usually at one of their homes.

"You're going without Daddy?"

She slid the pan back in the oven. "He'll meet me there."

Mom set a cucumber on the cutting board. "Please set the table, then call your brothers. They're in the woods."

I grabbed silverware from the drawer and placed forks and knives on the kitchen table, each landing with a little tap. Before I could follow step two of my instructions, she asked, "Are you and Ronni still planning on going to the movies tonight?"

"Yup." Butterflies in my stomach fluttered in mad circles.

"Do you think Ronni's parents can pick you up? I know we can't get back in time—unless one of us leaves the party early."

"We thought we could walk back to her place. It's only two blocks. Or maybe one of the guys who drives could take us back."

The knife Mom used to slice the cucumber dropped to the cutting board with a clunk. "Absolutely do *not* get in a car with any teen drivers. Male *or* female." She gave me her are-you-an-idiot glare.

I responded with my best I-am-totally-innocent stare. "So, it's okay if we walk back to Ronni's house?"

Better not ask about Bill walking with us.

She resumed slicing the cucumber. "I guess so. At this time of year, it'll be light enough." She paused from her salad preparations. "If Ronni's parents can't get you home by eleven, call us at the Warners."

"What if Ronni wants me to stay the night?" I was kind of counting on it.

"You'll still have to stop by the house, unless you plan on carrying pajamas and a toothbrush to the movies."

Oh. Right.

Chapter 5:
First "Date"

Deh-bie looks pretty.
She kisses me before I
Go to bed. "Nye-nye."

Ronni and I didn't bother with jackets on such a warm evening. Besides, who wanted to hide a perfect outfit under a coat? Taps on the horns from passing cars signaled their appreciation.

My new bell-bottom jeans fit snugly around my hips, and the tie-dyed shirt with sleeves flaring at the wrist made me feel like I should be heading for a Bee Gees concert. The turquoise beads around my neck finished the outfit. Ronni looked just as cool with psychedelic jeans in magenta, blue, and white, and a white peasant top to match.

When we arrived at the theater, high school kids stood around in small groups on the broad sidewalk out front. I spotted Bill's hair shimmering under the marquee lights, and the butterflies started their crazy dance again. His quarterback buddy had a girl tucked under his arm, but the other guys on the team seemed to be without female company.

Ronni and I joined the ticket line. After talking it over yesterday, we'd decided I'd better take money with me. If Bill offered to pay, great. If not, and it looked like Ronni guessed right about that, at least I'd be prepared.

I kept glancing his way, but he didn't seem to notice me as I shuffled forward in line. As soon as I turned away from the ticket window, there he stood.

"You made it." He grabbed my hand and pulled me toward the doors.

"Yeah, I came with Ronni." I waved madly for her to join us.

Bill spun around in surprise. "That's Ronni? The little squirt from last year?"

"Yeah, that's me." Ronni ambled up to us, her blue-gray eyes examining him with cool poise that came naturally to her. "I had a growth spurt."

His red hair gave him the ability to blush magnificently. He stuttered something about not meaning it as an insult, then turned to me. "Let's go in and find a seat."

The three of us walked in together. Probably not what Bill had planned, but then again, he hadn't let me in on his plans. He stepped into the very back row, the unofficial make-out row. I always thought it was reserved for couples who had been dating a while. Two pairs of seniors had already cozied up at the far end, which proved my theory. As Bill waved me in, Ronni continued for two more rows down the aisle before cutting left into the center seats. I followed *her*. The back row looked thrilling, but too soon for me to be there. Besides, I would never abandon my best friend.

A minute or two later, Bill rejoined us—with a buddy. "You mind if Ken sits with us?"

Ken played right tackle for the team, a big guy, and a sophomore like Bill.

Obviously, Bill was playing matchmaker, but Ronni still only had eyes for Roger Bechelman, who had never noticed her. She shrugged at Ken's presence and shifted one more seat to her left. Ken hopped over my knees like he was on an obstacle course. Pretty graceful, actually. He didn't even spill his popcorn.

So now we sat boy, girl, boy, girl, which meant I couldn't make some comment to Ronni in the middle of the movie without leaning across Ken. The comfort of the beads between my thumb and fingers calmed down the butterflies.

I pulled the necklace away from my chest and studied it. Since when had I started treating it like a beloved rosary, always fingering the beads as if in prayer?

My juvenile delinquent friend in California, Nora Jean, had given the necklace to me as a going-away present. Cheap, glass beads. The only treasure she'd ever owned. Even though Ronni was my best friend now, I wore Nora Jean's beads almost every day. I never wanted to forget the wild girl who would throw a punch first and ask questions later. She'd allowed me to see the fiercely loyal heart that lay underneath that tough-girl disguise.

As soon as the coming attractions started, Bill took my hand again. I'd expected his touch to send electricity through my entire being. Like I'd read about in books. Warm, strong fingers intertwined with mine, but…no strong current traveled past my wrist. Maybe the romance parts in novels were pure fiction, too.

I glanced left to see if Ken held Ronni's hand. Nope. He munched on his popcorn, one arm around the bucket while the other hand fed his face.

The main feature started. *With Six We Get Eggroll.* I loved Doris Day movies. Bill dropped my hand and put his arm around my shoulders. The further into the movie, the closer he pulled me toward him, until the metal arm of the seat cut into my side. When Brian Keith kissed Doris Day, Bill's free hand caressed my chin. He leaned toward me, and his lips pressed against mine. *That* generated a spark or two.

He flashed his gorgeous smile, and I sat back in my seat, my ribs howling for relief. I sneaked a peek Ronni's way. The bucket of popcorn sat on the arm that separated her and Ken. They both dipped into it at the same time. How romantic.

The movie ended, and the lights came up. People took their time filing out of the theater including several sophomore girls who cast envious glances our way. Once we were back on the sidewalk, Bill pulled me into an embrace and kissed me one more time with the crowd milling around us.

I hoped none of the adults knew my parents.

"I had a nice time." He squeezed my hand. "See you on Monday."

And he walked away.

We'd been so close during the movie, but—no offer to walk me home? I scanned the crowd for Ronni. She loitered nearby, smiling up at Ken and nodding her head. He walked away, too.

As we headed back to Ronni's house, neither of us spoke a word for an entire block.

She finally broke the silence. "Not the evening I expected."

"Me neither."

"Liar. You were hoping to get all kissy-face with Bill." She spit out his name as if it were a dirty word. *Was she mad at me?*

"I liked the kissing part, but if he liked me enough to kiss me, wouldn't he walk me home? Or in this case, to your house?"

"So, you can see he's a jerk."

What would be the correct response here? Yes? Maybe? He's not *that* bad?

My lack of an answer fueled her temper. "Oh. You don't *care* that he's a jerk."

I had to run to keep up with her. "I don't know. It's just that he's cute. He's on the football team. He's popular. And he likes me. *Me*. A nobody freshman while he's a sophomore on varsity. I am totally out of his league. "

We reached her driveway, and she spun around. "You've got that right. You are *way* out of his league, pure gold while he's a dirty, old penny."

"Yeah." I had to admit a little disappointment. "He does seem to be a cheapskate."

But *me*? Pure gold? Fool's gold was more like it. *Ronni* was pure gold, a friend who would stick by me no matter what.

I dragged my feet through the gravel, creating little rock mountains. "How did you like Ken? Any kind of future there?" She seemed so mad. It would be better to change the subject.

"He asked me to meet him at the dance next Saturday."

Her sneering tone warned me to tread carefully. One wrong word…

"What did you tell him?"

"I said, 'Maybe.' What is it with guys in this town?" She picked up a handful of pebbles and fired them one at a time across the road to the driveway opposite hers. "Don't they ever come to the house, meet your parents, and take you to the dance or the movies or wherever? Maybe I won't even go to the dance."

"But you'll miss so much fun."

"What fun?" She let another pebble fly. "Like paying for my own ticket? Getting myself to and from the dance? Flirting with Ken or Roger? You can't even talk to people over the music."

"But if you don't go to the dance, I'll have to go by myself."

She dropped the last few pebbles and stared at me, dangerously still. "You mean to tell me Bill didn't even ask you to the dance?"

I shriveled inside. "He said he'd see me Monday."

Ronni looked away.

I glanced down the block. "I think I should go home, and not stay the night."

She took a small step toward me. "I'm mad at him, not you."

"I know. But I need to go home and think some stuff over."

"Are we still going to practice cheer routines tomorrow?" She sounded so sad.

"Yeah. You know me. Things always look better in the morning." I moved toward the road. "See you."

"Aren't you going to call your parents to pick you up?"

"No."

I trudged the five blocks home, crossing through people's yards and taking the dusk-lit trail through our woods. Mom always worried for my safety, but no one ever skulked among the trees between our house and the house behind us.

Paul and Wade were still up watching television when I slipped through the back door.

Paul smirked. "So, did the wonderful Moon Doggie Bill show up?"

Had he just compared me to Sally Field on *Gidget* and Bill as her surfer boyfriend? I'd take it as a compliment. "I never said anything to you about Bill."

"But you said plenty to Ronni, and I've got ears."

Wade grinned and made obscene smoochy noises.

"Are you gonna tell Mom and Dad?"

Paul shrugged. "What's to tell? You went to the movies with Ronni, and you came home. I never saw Bill around."

"Thanks."

"You mean he *was* there?" Paul sounded impressed.

"Yeah. We sat together."

He raised his eyebrows. *What?* He'd better not put on his man-of-the-house role. He drove me bananas bossing me around all of last year while Daddy flew missions in Vietnam. No way would I accept another lecture from my little brother. But he didn't say anything more and returned his attention to the TV. I headed upstairs where Grandma peered into the hall mirror as she smeared cold cream on her face.

"I didn't know you were home. Are you picking up your things and going back to Ronni's?"

"No. We're calling it a night."

She regarded me with pale blue eyes, but like Paul, made no comment.

I slunk into my room and gently closed the door. Krista slept in the bed across from mine. Ten o'clock on a Friday night, an hour before my curfew, and my evening was done. I changed into pajamas in the dark and slipped between the sheets. The second time a boy had kissed me in my whole life, and both were kind of disappointing. Shouldn't I be more thrilled? Instead, I felt let down. If Ronni was right about Bill, and if his kisses didn't thrill me, why did I still want to be his girlfriend?

Saturday morning found me back at Ronni's. Our spirits lifted with the sunshine, last night's storm between us blown out to sea. Krista tagged along. She loved Ronni, and the feeling was mutual.

We shoved lawn chairs to one side of the back patio, which left us space to practice our cheerleading moves. Ronni slipped the cheer instructions under a rock to keep them from sailing away in the breeze.

"Let's start with the chants." She went into her rigid cheerleader stance.

Chants were easy. Lots of clapping, bellowing out the words, and smiling. Krista clapped with us, sort of. She had her own rhythm going on in her head. When we finished a chant and hopped up and down, fists pumping in the air, Krista copied us.

Ronni hugged her. "You are so adorable!"

Krista squeezed her back, a wide smile on her face.

Yeah, she was a cutie *almost* all the time.

We moved on to the more complicated, choreographed cheers. A dancing elephant could have done better than me.

"No. Watch me again." Ronni stepped to the right, closed with the left foot and clapped.

As soon as I got that, my right foot had to step forward, and my arms needed to slide back. Then close with the left foot, swing my arms forward, and clap. Right foot back, arms back, close with the left, arms forward, clap. All the time we had to continue the chant, "We are, we are, the HURR-i-CANES. HURR-i-CANES." To make things worse, the syncopated chant made it difficult to match my words to the same beat as my step-claps. *How could Ronni be so patient with me?*

Krista followed Ronni's motions carefully. After a few minutes, she could step forward and back in time with us. Pretty soon her arm movements matched Ronni's. A deaf kid who wouldn't turn three for another two weeks was a better cheerleader than her fifteen-year-old sister.

Almost an hour later, I could perform the entire set of cheers perfectly. Krista had long since succeeded—even with leg braces. She kicked a plastic ball around Ronni's backyard.

Mrs. Hanks invited us to stay for lunch. After peanut butter and jelly sandwiches, chocolate milk, and orange slices, Ronni and I ran through every cheer on the pages one more time.

Krista rubbed her eyes and climbed into her stroller. Time to go.

As we turned the final corner to home, a beat-up, yellow VW Bug passed us, stopped, then backed up.

Bill hung out of the passenger seat. "Hey. I thought you lived on this road."

He'd been looking for me!

Ken offered a shy wave from behind the wheel.

"My house is the new cedar shingle across from the park."

"We'll go around the block and meet you there." Bill turned to Ken. "Okay?"

Ken nodded and jolted forward. Maybe the stick shift was still a little new to him.

I power-walked the rest of the way home, providing Krista with a bumpy ride. She clung to the sides of the stroller and looked back at me like I'd gone crazy.

Ken's car pulled up and parked in front of the house as I reached my driveway. Perfect timing.

Krista scrambled out of the stroller and hurried inside. Either the big boys scared her, or she wanted to show Mom all the cheers she'd learned.

Bill hopped out of the car, but Ken stayed inside, the motor running.

"Well, now I know where you live." He smiled again.

"Yeah, this is it." *Brilliant line, Debbie.*

"Nice place. Pretty big." He gave it an admiring glance.

"It needs to be. Seven of us live in it."

"Seven. Wow." He plunged his fists in his pockets and let his eyes roam anywhere on the property except directly at me.

I couldn't have managed intelligent conversation if my life depended on it. Apparently, Bill had the same problem. One of the coolest guys in the school, and—

he was shy.

He gazed down the road. "I was wondering if you planned to go to the dance next Saturday."

"I'm not sure. I'd like to." Would he get the hint? *Ask me already.*

One last smile. "Good. Hope I see you there." He slid into the passenger seat. "Talk to you Monday."

Ken jerked the little Beetle into reverse, then first gear, and putt-putted down the road.

Bill had wanted to find out where I lived. He had *searched* for me. Ronni wouldn't be excited that he still hadn't asked me to the dance, which was a bummer for me, too. But. He had a week to prove her wrong. I did my own version of the Watusi all the way into the house.

Chapter 6:
To Be or Not to Be...A Cheerleader

Jumping and clapping
Is fun. Debbie and Ronni
And I jump a LOT!

Dozens of girls milled around in the gym, hoping for one of the sixteen spots on the cheerleading squads. A lot of them were upperclassmen, but I counted fourteen freshmen.

A handful of teachers perched on the bleachers, holding pencils and clipboards. Mrs. Anniston, the gym teacher, rose from her spot on the bottom row and blew her whistle. With her short red curls and long, lean body, she had probably been a cheerleader herself once upon a time.

"Good afternoon, ladies. We're pleased to see so many eager faces. Let me go over what you can expect for the next couple of hours. We'll start with the entire group in four rows of ten each, running through the cheers we assigned to you."

Several girls started to shuffle into position.

Mrs. Anniston blew her whistle again. "I haven't told you to do anything yet. Why don't all of you sit down until I finish with instructions."

Dozens of derrieres settled on the floor.

"Now. As I said, you'll be in four rows and do the two cheers you were given. Returning senior cheerleaders will lead you from the front."

The seniors beamed with self-importance.

"Notice, I said they *lead*. However, they are not guaranteed a spot on the squad. Like everyone else, former cheerleaders must earn their positions."

For some reason, that made me feel like I might have a chance.

"After those two group cheers are finished, you'll get five minutes to practice a cheer of your choice with your partner. If you don't have a partner yet, we will assign one to you."

In a sudden panic, I looked at Ronni. When she signed my name, did she also write us down as partners? She grinned at me and nodded. We were good.

Mrs. Anniston kept talking. "At the end of those five minutes, everyone is to move to the black line on the far side of the gym and sit. We will start with varsity and call up each pair to perform their cheer, and then we will request another cheer of *our* choice. We will be looking to see how well you can coordinate your movements with another person, how well you can keep the beat of the cheer, how well your voice carries. Facial expressions and coordination will be noted as well. Obviously, a perky smile and enthusiasm are important."

She smiled like she expected us to laugh at the attempted humor, but most of us were too nervous to make a sound. Even Ronni.

"Any questions?"

"When will we find out the results?" One of the older girls toward the back called out.

"We'll have the list posted on the same bulletin board where you signed up by first lunch hour tomorrow."

No point in bringing a lunch at all. I'd be sick to my stomach all morning just waiting for that list.

"Anything else?"

The gym remained silent.

"Then move into four rows now. It doesn't matter which row you find yourself in. We can see everyone clearly from our vantage point."

Ronni and I found ourselves toward the left side of the second row, pretty confident about this first part. We'd practiced those two cheers for hours last Saturday. I'd even performed them for Mom and Krista. Mom pronounced them perfect.

As we began, I pasted on my widest smile, off-white teeth and all, and bellowed out the words to the cheer. My arms swept outwards in rigid formation with seventy-eight other arms. My legs danced their step-slide-step-and-stop. Once to the left, repeat to the right. No mistakes during either cheer. One girl in front of me moved to the right while everyone else moved left. I cringed for her.

Next, five minutes of final practice. Ronni bounced in anticipation. "We're gonna do the slicing FIGHT cheer, right? It's our best one."

"Okay."

We repeated the whole thing with its fancy, karate chop-style motions several times. It had taken me a while to get each motion matched to the correct letter of F-I-GH-T, but I mastered it. I even executed the final lunge good and sharp.

The whistle blew. Time was up. Ronni and I found space on the black line. Melissa and Leigh strolled by.

Melissa smirked at us. "You two don't jump at the same height. It looks lopsided."

Why wouldn't she leave me alone? If we both made the squad, cheerleading might not even be fun. And if she made it, and I didn't… better not go there. My life would be as miserable as the summer after seventh grade.

The whistle sounded again, and Mrs. Anniston called two names. As the hour passed, Ronni and I observed, analyzed, and whispered our evaluations of each pair. We could see the difference between the experienced cheerleaders and some of the less capable, but we had no idea how the teachers would rank those in the middle.

Leigh and Melissa were called before us. Wouldn't you know, they chose the same FIGHT cheer we did. Melissa's voice sounded kind of whispery, not loud enough to be a cheerleader. Probably all that practice making sure her voice *didn't* carry so the teachers couldn't hear her constant, snide comments.

"Ronnie Hanks and Debbie Hansen."

My heart somersaulted at the sound of my name.

Ronni grinned at me. "Let's do it."

Standing side by side in a "ready" position, we began. "We're gonna F-I-GH-T." The chopping motions were perfect with every repetition of the phrase. "Fight, team, fight!" Ronni lunged left on the first "fight." I lunged right on "team." We both came forward together, fists to the sky, on the final "fight." We did it.

The teachers scratched marks on their forms while we waited for further instructions. Mrs. Anniston looked up from her notes. "We'd like you to do 'Who's Got Spirit?'"

Ronni's bright smile faltered. This was the one where I didn't always get the timing, and we both knew the risk. "Ready?" she asked me.

"I've got it."

I *did* have it. I could hear the rhythm, feel the syncopation, but my body didn't always cooperate.

Stomp, stomp, clap, clap. Two times through and, "Who's got spirit?" Stomp, stomp. "We've got spirit." Stomp, stomp. "Show us spirit." Stomp, stomp. A new design of karate chop slices done three times total as we spell, "S--P--IR-I-T. We've got." Jump with right knee forward, left leg straight back. "Spirit!"

Other than a slight wobble when I landed back on my feet after the jump, I nailed it. Not one wrong move on the karate chops. Every one of my limbs cooperated. Even if I didn't make the squad, at least I didn't let Ronni down.

Back at the black line, Ronni hugged me. "You did great!"

I hugged her back. "I'm sure you're going to make it after that."

Not even Melissa could wipe the smile off my face. A couple of handsprings and a round-off would've felt so good, if only I had the ability.

By lunch hour on Tuesday, my smile was nowhere to be found. My name wasn't on the list. Ronni stood next to me, silent, as others brushed by on their way to the cafeteria or to read the results for themselves, whether they'd tried out or not.

Ronni's name was fifth on the JV squad.

"Congratulations." I forced my lips to turn up at the corners. "I knew you could do it."

She examined my face. "Are you okay?"

No. But no way would I have her feeling guilty. "Yeah. And I'm really happy for you." True statement. "You were one of the best out there." Another true statement.

She flashed that million-watt smile. "I'm so glad you're not mad."

I shrugged. "We both knew I might not be good enough."

"Try again next year."

I shook my head. Why would I want to humiliate myself again? Strong voice but not strong enough. Nice smile but not all that perky. Good sense of rhythm in my mind, but lousy coordination in my body. I needed to accept the fact that I had brains and musical ability, but athletics of any kind was not in my future.

"Look." Ronni tapped the squad list with her pointer finger. "Most people on the list are sophomores. Once they move on to varsity, more spots will open up, and you were good out there yesterday. Good enough for next year."

I raised my eyebrows.

"Really," she insisted. "I'll teach you all the cheers I learn this year."

"Thanks." I finally offered a real smile. "I'll need all the practice I can get."

"And you know what else you should feel good about?" Her eyes slid to the side, making sure no one was in hearing distance.

I leaned toward her. "What?"

She whispered, "Melissa's name isn't on that list either."

We giggled and I smacked her shoulder. "You're terrible."

"You're laughing too."

"I'm terrible, too."

We headed to the cafeteria. Several kids called out congratulations to Ronni, and she lapped up their attention. No pang of jealousy sliced into me. I really was happy for her. Hungry after all, I joined her in line for the full lunch. The school's fish sticks weren't all *that* disgusting.

Gym class was pretty bad, though. Girls fluttered around Leigh, who had made the squad. They patted Melissa on the shoulder and murmured their sympathy. Nobody offered *me* any comfort. I wished Ronni was in there with me.

Then again, how long would she *really* be with me? She was bound to move on with this new group. They'd practice together, ride the bus to away games together, go to parties together. I'd be like Ronni's old teddy bear relegated to the back of her closet. She didn't want to throw the raggedy thing away, not yet, but she never fished him out of the closet either. That would be me—an old friend no longer needed.

After class, I carefully teased knots out of my wet hair. Between the shower and the never-ending, sweat-scented humidity of the locker room, tangles were inevitable in wavy hair. Mary Franketti, who stared into the wall mirror next to mine, ripped through her thick curls, too. That had to be excruciating.

She laughed at my pained expression in the mirror's reflection. "I got used to it years ago." Her grin exposed a mouthful of braces. "I wish my mom would let me straighten it."

"Don't straighten it." There I went putting my foot in my mouth. "I mean, you've got the most beautiful hair I've ever seen. It's…it's…glorious."

Her brows rose in disbelief. "Really? Thanks." She winced as the brush snagged another knot. "But it sure would be easier to have straight hair."

One final swipe with my comb, and I was satisfied. I started for the door.

"Debbie?"

I turned back toward Mary.

"I'm having a party Friday night. You want to come? You and Ronni?"

My first invitation to a party in over a year. Of course, I wanted to go. "Thanks. I'll tell Ronni." She'd want to go, too.

"And you can bring guys if you want." She worked on a particularly massive tangle. "Are you going with somebody?"

Good question. "Not really."

She winked. "Only sort of?"

"Bill Neagley and I were at the movies together last weekend."

"Sure. Ask him."

Hmm. A girl asking a guy out? The disapproving faces of Mom and Grandma floated in front of me as I trudged down the empty hall.

And who did I find leaning against my locker? Bill. Who might not be interested in me anymore since I wouldn't be a cheerleader.

But once I was close enough, he took my hand. "You okay?" His dark eyes reflected real concern as he bent over me, and a lock of his hair fell across his forehead.

With my free hand I brushed it away from his face. "I'll live." I forced a smile. "I'll just cheer you on from the stands instead of the sidelines."

He returned the smile, but his eyes remained serious. "My sister didn't make cheerleading the first time she tried out, either. Then she made it for the next three years."

His encouragement banished my fear of getting dumped, and my heart melted under his gaze, a milk chocolate heart with liquid caramel at its center, smooth and sweet.

"Ronni says I should try again, too."

"You want to meet me again at the movies on Friday?"

Ronni's words returned in full force. *What is it with guys in this town?* No mention of the dance, but he'd *meet* me at the movies. Then on Friday night, maybe he'd ask to *meet* me at the dance?

My fingers fumbled with the locker combination. "Mary Franketti invited me to her party Friday night."

Since he hadn't asked me for a date, I just couldn't ask him to take me to the party.

"Yeah? Who's Mary Franketti?"

"She's in my class. Long, dark, curly hair. Hangs out with Damon Alspaugh and some other people I don't know." The only reason I knew about Damon was because of his movie-star looks—the raven-haired, brooding hero.

Bill's eyes widened. "The potheads?"

I hadn't thought about that. Mary didn't have that strung-out, hippie look, but many of her friends did.

Bill didn't wait for an answer. "I wouldn't go there if I were you. What if the police raid the party?"

Any hope for an offer to come with me flew out the window. "The police could raid the football team's parties too." They were infamous for a lot of beer drinking. "Don't you take the same risk?"

He shrugged. "You get caught with beer, you're suspended for a couple of games. If you get caught with marijuana, you're off the team, and if they want to get nasty about it, put you in jail."

Maybe Mary's party wasn't such a great idea after all.

"Meet me at the movie instead, okay? And then I'll see you at the dance on Saturday, too."

How could I resist that gorgeous smile?

Chapter 7:
Why We Can't Have a Dog

Wamma does not like
Dogs. Or cats. Or anything
With fur. She will scream.

At the dance during one of the band's breaks, Bill told me he owned a rottweiler.

"Aren't they awfully ferocious?" I pictured a huge, snarling, junkyard dog.

"Naw. Ranger's an overgrown teddy bear always wanting to sit on my lap."

"I'd love to meet a giant lapdog."

Was it too obvious that I was looking for an invite to see him again? Ronni wasn't around to ask. She'd stuck to her guns and refused to attend the dance.

Bill downed the last of his punch from the paper cup. "Maybe I'll take him for a long walk to your place."

For a moment, my heart pit-a-patted at a ridiculous pace, then slowed. *Maybe* he'd take the dog to see me? Pretty much like, "I'll meet you." Ronni wouldn't approve.

Bill grinned. "Ranger would be so tuckered out he'd collapse on the grass and take a nap. No reason to be scared of him."

Did he think I was a wimp? "I'm not scared of big dogs. My uncle has two German shepherds, but rottweilers have a reputation."

He shrugged. "Unless you attack me with a knife or something, Ranger will just lean into you asking for a scratch behind the ears."

The music started up again. Bill offered me his hand. On the dance floor, my mind remained on dogs, not Bill. I'd love to come home every day to my own puppy—any size—and scratch him behind the ears.

As a family, we'd never had much luck with pets. Doh-Doh the beagle got sick and died when I was a toddler. I don't remember him. We owned a cocker spaniel when I was six. Considering his nasty habit of pinching our friends with his teeth, he should've been named Nippy instead of Skippy. Mom and Daddy found a new home for him—an old lady with no kids. We owned Candy the collie when I was eight. She chased bikes and ran away a lot, so Daddy gave her to a local farmer where she could chase rabbits in acres of fields. In the same year, Patches, my gray kitten, got run over by our school bus one morning.

I managed to own two goldfish for four years. They even made it through our move from Syracuse to Hampton Shores. A friend "took care" of them when we joined Daddy in California before he deployed to Vietnam. Four months later when we returned? Dead fish.

Mom decided no more pets. She said she couldn't take care of a dog and Krista too. Besides, Grandma hated pets. If a single hair from any animal, including my brothers, drifted onto her clothing, it gave her the shivers.

Earlier this summer, we visited Aunt Matilda, Grandma's cousin. There's nothing more boring than going to some old person's house where you have to sit and be quiet for three whole hours. Or more.

Grandma sat on Aunt Matilda's sofa, perched in her typical, royally-erect posture. A low coffee table in front of the couch held her glass of iced tea. While my parents and Aunt Matilda settled into other available, deep-cushioned seats, the boys and I sat on three kitchen chairs brought into the living room. Hard wood, no padding of any kind, so add bruised behinds to an endless afternoon of "remember-whens." Krista nestled on Daddy's lap, making me wish I were three years old again. At least *one* kid was comfortable.

A subtle motion snagged my attention when a tortoiseshell cat stretched out on top of the sofa behind Grandma. She didn't shoo it away, which meant she didn't know it was there. I turned my head toward Paul sitting on my right. *Had he noticed?*

No. His glazed eyes stared beyond the window. He was in his own world trying to stave off the torture of talking grown-ups. He sensed my attention though and shifted his gaze to meet mine. My eyes slid left. His dark eyes followed. Electric anticipation zapped between us. He passed on the message to Wade using the same mode of telepathy. Wade woke up from his bored stupor and silently rogered, "Message received."

We waited, cool as cucumbers on the outside, quivering with suspense on the inside.

Grandma and Aunt Matilda reminisced all the way back to their childhoods. "Remember when Hans and Leo decided to pelt the neighborhood bully with rotten tomatoes from Papa's grocery store? What was that boy's name?"

Aunt Matilda cackled. "Rupert Heimschekel. When I sat in front of him in class, he used to yank on my braids so hard that some hairs were plucked right out of my scalp. That hurt something fierce."

Grandma clucked her tongue. "I don't understand what can make a child so mean."

"Probably the name *Rupert Heimschekel.* Other boys teased him so about that. No wonder he terrorized kids before they had a chance to terrorize him."

"Perhaps." Grandma relaxed her position and leaned against the back of the couch with its cat pillow.

I held my breath.

With a smothered shriek and amazing agility for a woman her age, Grandma sprang from the couch, leaped over the coffee table, and landed lightly on her high heels, the hem of her skirt swirling to rest below her knees. She didn't even knock over her tea.

"Oh, dear. Oh, dear. I'm so sorry." Aunt Matilda lifted the offending animal from the couch. He draped himself over her arm, reminding me of Violet and her cat in the Peanuts cartoon. He wasn't the least bit concerned about the upset he'd caused.

Paul, Wade, and I didn't crack a smile. Remarkable self-control. Grandma and Daddy traded places for the rest of our visit, which lasted until Grandma finished her iced tea. A lady must never gulp her beverage.

Then, just a couple of weeks ago, the whole family was invited to an end-of-summer party next door at the Jaspers' house. It rained. Thirty or more people crowded into the three large front rooms of the house. The dining table bore the weight of appetizers, fried chicken, salads, and desserts. Not the kind of get-together children are usually invited to, but since we lived so close, Mrs. Jasper had said all the kids could eat dinner at the party instead of Mom fixing something separate.

The Jaspers owned a big old basset hound named Barney.

So, there we were. Four bored kids watching a bunch of grown-ups stand around and chitchat before returning to the smorgasbord and sprinkling another few tidbits on tiny plastic plates.

Paul, Wade, and I hung around the food, continually heaping up those little plates until we finally filled our stomachs. Krista wandered from us to Mom and back to us. She visited the candy dish of M&M's over and over, ignoring the more delectable desserts of coconut cake, peach streusel, and apple pie.

Wade poked me in the ribs. "Look at that." Keeping his hand below the level of the tabletop, he pointed.

Barney the basset hound stood on his hind legs, forepaws braced against the table's edge. He had discovered the barely-feasted-upon salmon mousse. His long tongue stretched toward the pinkish, brownish, jellied concoction molded in the shape of a fish.

I couldn't choke down that stuff if I were starving. Barney demonstrated his delight over the doggy delicacy with a slurp that removed a good inch of the salmon's tail.

I stepped forward with the intention of forcing the dog away from the table. Paul pulled me in the opposite direction.

"Don't," he hissed in my ear. "Let's watch. Besides, he might get mad if you try to make him stop."

Barney stopped on his own. Seeming to savor the mouthful, he ambled back into the kitchen. Not a minute later, Grandma returned to the table. Grandma loved salmon. She loved all kinds of fancy party food. Maybe it reminded her of the receptions she and Grandpa used to host when he owned an international import-export business. Carefully placing three crackers on her plate, she approached the mousse, and with the curlicue spoon, she scooped little blobs from the salmon's head and dropped the stuff on each cracker.

Wade laughed so hard he had to turn away before Grandma asked what tickled his funny bone. Krista pointed at Grandma. The look on her face showed her concern that Grandma didn't know about the dog. I hadn't realized Krista had picked up on that aspect of Grandma's personality.

I grinned and put my finger to my lips. "Shhh. Don't tell Grandma."

Krista's eyes widened in shock. *Not tell Grandma?* In confusion, she watched Wade laugh. Paul stepped in front of her and copied my motion of finger to lips. *Would she go along with us or tattle?*

A broad grin lit her face as she got the joke. The lady who considered all animals disgustingly dirty had just shared her plate with one of them.

A few minutes later, the scene repeated itself. With

an added twist. Barney wandered back to the table, heaved himself up, and enjoyed a hefty helping. Grandma also returned.

"One last bite of that delicious mousse," she called over shoulder, then she turned toward her destination.

Barney, meet Grandma.

A bloodcurdling scream halted the party. Everyone ran to investigate as if a dead body had been discovered in the dining room. Paul, Wade, Krista, and I faded back toward the walls.

Grandma continued to shriek, most unladylike, her words spurted in a high-pitched stream. "The dog. Shoo! Stop! Shoo! Eating. Shoo! Help! The dog! Mousse! Help! Shoo, shoo, shoo!"

Barney ignored her and concentrated on his feast. If we'd been home, the boys would have been rolling on the floor. Once again, we mastered our reactions.

Poor Mrs. Jasper. She rushed at the dog, but a basset is difficult to move, especially when he doesn't want to. The woman lifted the mousse platter out from under his jowls and hurried to the kitchen. Meanwhile, Mom pulled Grandma away from the table, and a furious, whispered discussion followed in one corner.

The other guests, realizing no tragedy had occurred, drifted back to the living room and resumed interrupted conversations. Mrs. Jasper rearranged the platters to make it look like the salmon mousse had never existed. Grandma refused to eat dessert.

Krista looked at me, pointed to her ear and then to Grandma, and she opened her mouth wide.

"Yes," I said. "Grandma screamed."

Krista tapped her ear with vigor. Then she pointed to Grandma again.

I tapped at my ear and signed "Grandma." "You heard Grandma scream?"

She nodded her head quickly.

"Wow." I mouthed the word.

She smiled, then shaped her lips into a *"wow"* back at me.

Krista's deafness was so profound only the loudest sounds could be heard, either extremely high like a whistle or extremely low like the drumbeat at a rock concert.

She couldn't hear the human voice. But she heard Grandma.

After such an ear-shattering episode over a pet, there was no way on *earth* I would be getting a dog.

However…

Prayers make it all the way to heaven.

Chapter 8:
Kitten and Puppy

Little cat scratched me.
Bee flew inside. Will he sting?
Will the puppy bite?

One of the girls in my class handed out flyers for free kittens, so after school, I walked almost a mile to see them. I was more of a dog person, but since dogs needed so much attention, maybe a cat would be better for our family. Cats pretty much took care of themselves.

Tonya led me into the near-empty garage where a wide carton sat in the center of the cement floor. I peered into the box, just tall enough for a mama cat to jump out but too high for kittens to climb the walls. Yet.

Five kittens, all wearing coats with varying amounts of black fur, scrambled over one another. Definitely not nap time.

There! The black one with white paws and sapphire eyes. So beautiful. How could Mom resist?

I carried him home in a large box and sneaked him

into the laundry room while no grown-ups were in sight. He trembled and mewed pitifully while I lined the box with rags. Poor baby, away from his mother for the first time.

Krista wandered in as I placed a little bowl of milk in one corner of the box. If I could get her on my side, we had an even better chance of persuading Mom to let us keep this little jewel.

She peered down and reared back in surprise.

I couldn't wipe the smile off my face. "Kitty."

Krista frowned. She couldn't read the word *kitty* on my lips. She only saw my mouth move from "ih" to "ee." I made the sign for *cat*. She rolled her eyes at me, insulted that I thought she didn't know what a cat was.

His bright, blue-eyed gaze flitted from me to Krista. Adorable. I would take my time naming him. Who wanted something so obvious as Socks or Boots?

"Isn't he cute?"

Krista couldn't see *cute* either, and I didn't know the sign for that. The teachers at her school had told us that any words with a *k* or a hard *g* can't be seen. We make those sounds at the back of the throat. So *cute* only looks like "oooo" to a deaf person.

I stroked the kitten's back with one finger. The little guy cringed at my touch.

"Soft." I smiled at Krista.

No return smile. Didn't she like cats or couldn't she see the word *soft?* *S* and *t* sounds are almost invisible, too. All she could see was "ah-ff."

Oh my gosh. Krista's name had the hardest consonants to see. *K, s,* and *t.* And an *r* wasn't much better. *How would she ever be able to say her name?*

I shook off the distracting thought and stroked the

kitten again, then pointed to Krista. "You can pet him, too." I used the same finger to gently stroke Krista's arm from elbow to wrist.

She stared suspiciously at the furry stranger. Her hand descended slowly into the box. As she got close to the kitten's head, one forepaw flashed out to stop those little fingers.

Oh, the tears. It was just a tiny claw mark, a pin prick, but she acted as if he'd fatally sliced her open. Krista ran out of the laundry room, me following close behind, and wouldn't you know it, Mom walked through the front door at that exact moment. The little crybaby showed her the mortal wound. I could forget enlisting her as an ally for my cause.

"What's Krista trying to tell me about this little cut on her hand?"

"It's no big deal, Mom."

Krista tugged Mom into the laundry room and showed her the box. She bared her teeth and clawed at Mom's hands, dramatic motions of a killer cat attacking.

Mom noted the contents of the box. "Wherever it came from, take it back."

"But---"

"Take it. Back."

She walked out.

No debate. No negotiations. No deal.

Stupid, stupid, stupid. What had ever made me think a kitten would be allowed to grow up in my house? And Krista! My own sister! Who knew she'd react to a kitten like Grandma would?

I trudged the mile to Tonya's place, lugging the box that felt a lot heavier than it did earlier. Then I walked all the way home empty-handed. The kitten never even got a name. I guess I wasn't meant to be a cat person.

I wouldn't be bringing home any doggie surprise either. Returning a puppy would totally break my heart. If we were *ever* going to get a dog, God would have to deliver it to our doorstep Himself.

The back door creaked open while I read my latest Edna Ferber novel.

"Come on, boy. Come on in." Paul used a high, baby voice.

Too curious to keep reading, I closed my book and headed for the laundry room. Paul held the door wide open, an invitation to the black, wire-haired puppy who sat outside. His ribs protruded like the skeleton of a ship's hull under his coat. His tail swept the deck, but he made no move to come in.

"Where'd he come from?" My words sounded gruff. Maybe I didn't want to get my hopes up. I stepped onto the deck and offered my hand to the puppy. He sniffed it.

"I don't know. Ricky and P.J. and I were playing in the woods near the base, and he showed up. Then he followed me home."

Right. "Did you give him food or something?" Even if a dog decided to follow the boys home, why choose Paul and not one of the others?

"No. We didn't have any food on us." With the door still held open, he leaned toward the puppy and tried again. "Come on, buddy."

The dog didn't move. Meanwhile, a yellow jacket flew into the house.

Paul scratched the top of his head. "I think he's scared. Wherever he came from, maybe they didn't let him go inside."

I waved away a second yellow jacket. "Shut the door before we have a house full of bees."

Paul let go of the handle, and both of us kneeled to pet the puppy. After a moment's tension, his body relaxed as I massaged behind his ears.

Paul added a vigorous rubdown. "When we were ready to leave, we tried to turn him toward Flanders. We thought he came from there, but he wouldn't go. We even started walking in that direction, but he just sat and watched us."

The puppy groaned in ecstasy and sank to the deck on his back. I stroked his throat, and Paul gave him a tummy rub.

"As soon as we headed to Hampton Shores, he got up and followed us again. We figured at some point he'd split off from us and go back where he came from."

"But he never did."

"Nope, he never did."

The message flashed between us. *Maybe we can keep him.* Paul wanted a dog as much as I did. And Wade was the biggest dog-lover of us all.

The station wagon's engine rumbled in the driveway then cut to silence. Two car doors slammed. Paul and I held our breaths. Either they'd come through the back door of the garage to use the deck or walk along the flagstone path in front and go in the house that way.

The door to the garage didn't open. That gave us maybe two minutes to come up with a persuasive argument.

Through the open window, we heard Mom set something heavy on the kitchen counter.

I whispered to Paul. "I'll hold her off as long as I can." I sauntered inside. "Hi, Mom."

"Hello." She pulled ears of corn from a grocery sack and placed them on a plate. "Go outside and husk these, will you? They're not farm fresh, but they look pretty good." She handed me the plate and the empty sack. "It's such a beautiful day. Dad's going to grill hamburgers. Probably the last time we get to use the hibachi and eat on the deck until next summer."

So, Daddy would be firing up the grill within minutes.

I lifted the plate of corn like a London guard carrying the crown jewels on a satin pillow. "I'll get these right back to you. And then I'll set the table." That way I'd keep her inside.

"Why, thank you." She assigned me plenty of chores, but I rarely volunteered for any.

After stepping outside, I waited until I was close enough to whisper an answer to Paul's silent question. "Ten minutes or more for Mom, but Dad'll be here any second."

Right on cue, Daddy opened the garage door. He trotted up the three steps to the deck intent on his beloved hibachi grill, then stopped short. "Whoa! Who's this?"

Paul held up his hands in a desperate *stop* gesture. I put my finger to my lips, and with my other hand pointed to the open kitchen window. Daddy got it.

He squatted down in front of the puppy, who rolled to a sitting position, ears pointed forward, alert to the new stranger.

Wade emerged from the path through our backyard woods. As he loped across the grass, he noticed the three of us sitting on the deck. "Whatcha doing?"

Paul shook his head. My finger tapped my lips again.

Wade's mouth dropped open. He rushed to the puppy who madly wagged his tail. He seemed to feel no need to be watchful when it came to little boys. Wade rubbed the dog's head, wrapped his arms around the emaciated body, and buried his face against the dog's shoulder.

After that satisfying hug, he lifted his head. "Thanks, Dad."

Daddy snorted. "Don't thank me. I don't know where he came from." He glanced from me to Paul. "You have some explaining to do."

In a low voice, Paul rehashed his story. "…so, you see, it's not my fault the puppy is here. Can we keep him?"

"He probably belongs to somebody and got lost. We can't just take someone else's dog."

"What if nobody claims him?" I rubbed the top of the dog's head. "Would Mom even let us keep him? She doesn't like dogs."

"Mom likes dogs." Daddy slowly offered his hand to the puppy, then smiled when the little guy licked it.

His answer didn't convince me. "She didn't like Candy or Skippy."

"She liked them, but she couldn't control them."

Mom stepped outside. "How are you coming along

with the corn?" And then, "Oh."

I'd forgotten about the corn, and as soon as she saw the puppy, she forgot about it, too.

Paul rushed to explain. Wade hugged the dog as if Mom would toss him into the street that very minute. Daddy walked to the grill and got to work. *Coward.*

Mom called after him. "Grant, you're not thinking of keeping this mutt, are you?"

"Only until someone answers our ad."

"What ad?"

Daddy fussed with the charcoal and the lighter fluid, keeping his back to Mom. "We'll put an ad in the paper and contact animal control. He should be off our hands by next week."

My dreams of a little black puppy in the house popped like soap bubbles. Feeding the puppy. Running around town with the puppy. Snuggling with the puppy. *Pop, pop, pop.*

"You want us to keep him for a whole week?" Mom's voice rose with each word. "What if no one answers the ad?"

Daddy turned from the grill to face her. "Then we'll see how he fits in." The expression on his face reminded me of the hungry puppy.

Mom rolled her eyes.

Paul played up his own puppy-dog eyes. "He's starving, Mom. Can we give him some milk?"

She heaved a sigh. "I suppose if we're going to keep him for a week, we'll need to feed him. Come on."

As she turned to enter the house, Krista came flying out. "Peeeee!"

The puppy scrambled to his feet and dove under the picnic table. The rest of us stared at Krista.

"You have to pee?" Mom asked. "Go to the bathroom."

Krista stopped short to read Mom's lips. She frowned in confusion and pointed to the house. "Pee!"

"Yes. Go to the bathroom" Mom repeated. "Inside the house."

Krista shook her head and stomped her foot. Her bladder was not the problem.

What sounded like *pee?* I ran through possibilities in my mind. Peek. Pete. Pea. Bee. Beat.

"Bee?" I looked at Krista and pointed to the house. "There's a bee in the house."

Krista nodded her head twice. "Pee."

The poor kid needed a quick response, not a lengthy speech lesson on the difference between B and P. "Yes." I shook my fist to sign *yes.* "A bee flew in a little while ago." I used signs for *fly* and *house.*

Mom huffed in exasperation. "Bees and dogs." She held out a hand to Krista. "We will find the bee. Make it go out."

She spoke slowly so Krista could see what she said, but probably all Krista read was "bee" and "out." Enough to get the idea across. Would that be her whole life—picking out words from silently-moving lips and trying to puzzle out the meaning?

Paul and Wade trailed them inside. Moments later, the boys returned with a bowl of water and a second bowl of people food—leftover rice and half of a pork chop cut into little chunks—the food Krista wouldn't eat last night.

They placed the food and drink in front of the dog with all the awe of ancient worshipers sacrificing to the gods. The puppy sniffed the offering, gobbled the meat and rice, then gulped the water before licking both bowls clean and flipping them upside down.

With a grin, Wade watched the puppy's antics. "What kind of dog is he?"

"He's a mutt," Daddy said. "Looks like he's mostly terrier, but maybe black lab, too?"

"He sure is skinny."

"He may have been on his own for a while." Daddy flipped out a hand to pet him, but the puppy cringed.

Daddy frowned. "And he might have been mistreated. Looks like he's afraid I'll hurt him."

Wade dropped to the deck to hug the dog again. "So, if somebody answers the ad, we have to give him back? Even if they're mean to puppies?"

"Unless we can prove they've been mean, we have to give him back."

Wade was silent a moment. "What if nobody answers the ad?"

"Like I told Mom, let's see if the dog fits into our family."

Translation: can we win Grandma over, and will Mom like him enough to keep him?

Chapter 9:
Black Jack

*A little black dog
Came to my house. Stay away,
Dog. Do not bite me.*

We coaxed the dog into the house when it got dark, and Paul piled up rags to make a bed for him in the laundry room.

Grandma stood in the kitchen ready to make a run for it if a rabid puppy tried to attack. "Close the laundry room door so he won't wander the house all night."

She didn't want him sneaking into her room. God forbid if he licked her while she slept. Her screams would have my dad tearing up the stairs with a baseball bat, ready to beat an intruder senseless.

Mom showed no affection either. "Leave a bowl of water in there and put down some newspapers. We don't know if he's housebroken."

Paul did all the work while Wade and I took turns holding the puppy. Krista watched the preparations and eyed the dog but didn't try to touch him. Maybe she remembered the kitten.

Before Paul closed the door, Mom peeked in and sighed. "He'll probably keep us awake all night howling. He may not want to be alone."

In the morning, the boys and I found him sound asleep, curled up on the rags. The newspapers remained dry. If he'd howled during the night, none of us heard him, which had to give him a better chance in making us his forever home.

I stroked the puppy's shoulder. "What shall we name him?" He stretched and yawned but didn't open his eyes.

"Why name him anything?" Paul grumbled. "We'll probably have to give him back to some guy who beats him."

"Don't say that!" I fixed him with a glare. "I don't know about you, but I've been praying for a dog for I don't know *how* long. If this is the one, then God is going to let us keep him."

Paul's eyes widened. "You *prayed* for a dog?"

"Why not? With Grandma in the house and all of Krista's problems, it'll take a miracle to get a dog, right?"

Wade reached over to stroke the top of the puppy's head. He spoke in awe. "And you think God sent this dog?"

"I don't know. But he didn't follow Ricky or PJ, did he?"

Our voices must have finally stirred him awake because the little guy opened one eye and thumped his tail twice against the floor. Then he went back to sleep.

I had expected him to greet us with wriggly puppy excitement, but the poor baby must've been exhausted from the day before. And who knew how long he'd been out in the woods fending for himself.

Mom entered the laundry room, craning her neck to see over our heads. "You need to take him outside, Paul."

"But he wants to sleep."

"He'll go back to sleep when you bring him in." She raised one eyebrow. "And the papers will stay dry."

"If he makes a mess, I'll clean it up."

"You certainly will." She opened the storm door.

Out of arguments, Paul leaned down and lifted the puppy into his arms.

As he started down the steps of the deck, Mom called out, "Paul, you can't go out in bare feet. It's freezing out there."

"You said you wanted him outside. I'll be fine."

I stepped onto the deck in my slippers. The surrounding trees glowed yellow and orange under a rising sun, and clear skies had brought down the temperature, so the dew was slick under my feet, almost frozen. In spite of Paul's macho "I'll be fine," he performed a hot potato dance on the frosty grass while the little guy did his business.

The cold must have invigorated the puppy, too, because he ran off into the woods behind the house.

Paul yelled, "Blackie!"

There was no sense in following him. "Blackie" didn't use the path.

Maybe Paul would agree to a different name. "Blackie" was too blah. But ultimately, the name would be up to my brother. He'd found the dog and had done all the work so far, so he'd earned the privilege.

Paul ran into the house. As he passed Mom, he made sure she could hear him mutter. "I should have had him on a rope. But no, I had to take him out *right away*." His voice rose in a falsetto, mimicking Mom. "The papers will stay dry."

"What happened?" Daddy walked into the kitchen as Paul stalked out of it.

"The dog ran into the woods," Mom said.

Wade glared at our mother. "Mom made Paul take him outside, and he ran away." He strode out of the kitchen almost knocking over Krista.

She looked back at him, then turned to the rest of us, eyes questioning.

"It's nothing." Mom yanked open the refrigerator door and grabbed the pitcher of orange juice.

If it were nothing, she wouldn't be pouting over it.

"No dog." I signed both words.

Krista peered into the laundry room. I followed her. "Dog went outside to poop." I pointed to the door. She could see the word "poop" on my lips. "Dog ran away." I made two fingers run along the washing machine. "Into the woods." I pointed to the woods.

Krista shrugged a "So what?"

Fully dressed, Paul and Wade passed by us on their way outside. Paul shoved the door open, and Wade followed.

Mom held the door. "Half an hour. Then you have to get ready for church."

Wade glowered at her. "What if we can't find him?"

"You have half an hour." She clutched her robe closer to her chest against the breeze.

Paul scanned the woods. "What if he comes back while we're at church?"

"We'll leave some water and food on the deck.

He'll know what to do." Mom picked up the dry water bowl and handed it to him.

Wade made sure to look properly serious. "I think God would want us to stay home and keep looking for him."

"Yeah." Paul took on a lofty expression, too. "Doesn't the Bible say man is to take care of the animals?"

"You're absolutely right. So leave food and water on the deck." Looked like Mom had the final word.

The boys trotted into the woods.

Ten minutes later, I spied the puppy sprinkling one of our trees in the side yard.

"Here, Little Buddy!" I held up a bowl of the instant rice we had fed him the evening before. The puppy raced up the deck steps and plunged his snout into the bowl as soon as I set it on the boards.

"Little Buddy" didn't really suit him either. I considered the possibilities as he devoured his breakfast. He was sweet-tempered, independent—he wouldn't have traveled so far from his old home if he weren't—and he was lucky to have found us. Maybe…Black Jack. Like the Jack of Spades, like the brand of black licorice gum. Sweet and lucky, with a bit of an adventurous pirate in him.

Black Jack.

Would my brothers agree?

They did.

After a week of no responses to our ad, Daddy and the boys had taken Black Jack to the veterinarian to get his shots. We'd all placed our bets about how old the puppy was and just what kind of dog was he? Mom and Grandma thought he was about a year old and a thousand kinds of mutt. Wade said part Scottie and part black lab, nine months. Paul argued that Black Jack looked more like a schnauzer but might be part black lab. Seven months. Daddy was sure the puppy was closer to six months old and contained several kinds of terrier, especially Kelly Blue. I just called Black Jack a wire-haired terrier and put my guess between the boys. Eight months old. Krista, of course, had no clue.

Daddy returned from the vet's office loaded down with proof that we were now Dog Owners. A big bag of puppy kibble and another giant sack filled with dog stuff—food dishes, a leash, a chew toy, and a doggy bed.

"What did the vet say?" I asked. "Who guessed the closest?"

"Dad did." Wade said. "The vet says his teeth make him to be six months old, and he really is a Kelly Blue terrier. But not completely."

"Yeah. Wade and I were right, too. He's part black lab." Paul snagged the puppy before he ran under the table near Grandma. We had promised to restrain Black Jack from approaching her, and we would train him to stay downstairs away from her room.

"But he's not totally healthy." Wade pulled a pill container out of his pocket. "He's got worms."

Ewwww.

Grandma emitted a little squeal then put a hanky to her mouth.

"Paul, put that dog outside and wash your hands with lots of soap," Mom ordered. She turned to Daddy.

"This animal is not staying in the house until he's healthy."

Paul snapped his fingers for Black Jack to follow him while Wade sputtered protests. "It's cold outside. He can't sleep outside."

"Sure, he can. We'll put a couple of old blankets on the garage floor to snuggle into." Daddy fished the dog bed out of the giant shopping sack. "And once he's finished his medicine, he can move into these comfy digs."

"It's still pretty cold out there." I imagined a skinny, shivering puppy abandoned in a dark, musty-smelling garage.

Paul heard me as he let the back door slam behind him on his way to wash his hands at the kitchen sink. "Who knows how many nights he slept outside before I found him? He'll be okay."

Oh, so now *he* found the dog, instead of the dog found *him*. What a know-it-all.

Chapter 10:
Road Trip

Long trip in the car.
It gets hotter and hotter.
When will we get there?

Daddy mopped rivers of sweat from his face with a handkerchief while we waited for the gas station attendant to finish with another customer.

"What's taking so long?" Wade's face had turned a bright pink.

"We're in the South," Daddy replied. "They take things slower around here."

"Then why did I have to get back in the car after I went to the bathroom?"

"My mistake, bud." Daddy turned to ruffle Wade's hair but only succeeded in creating wet, blond spikes which made him look like some kind of crazy cartoon character. Even Krista laughed.

Wade shoved Daddy's hand away and slumped into the corner. His rude reaction didn't dampen Daddy's great mood. We were less than ten miles away from the ranch and the "Great Family Reunion." The interstate highway had shaved off a little time between New York and Florida, but it still felt like forever to get to Aunt Nell's.

The only way we could gauge our progress as we traveled south was to test the air when we stopped for gas, restaurants, and motels. Each break proved to get warmer and warmer. Now, it felt like the hottest part of a North Atlantic summer, and it was only the first week of April.

I couldn't share Daddy's excitement over Uncle Hank, Aunt Vivian, and their kids joining us for spring break. A whole *week* with my cousins? One big, happy family? Maybe Timmy wouldn't be a merciless tease. Maybe Nadine wouldn't be as snooty as she was last Christmas. I could hope.

Meanwhile, Aunt Nell's son, Roy, *wouldn't* be there. He joined the Army last year. A great one for practical jokes but never mean-spirited, I'd always had a secret crush on him. Roy would've run interference with Timmy and maybe flirted with Nadine just to get a smile out of her.

The attendant in the gray-streaked T-shirt approached the driver-side window. "What can I do ya for?"

"Fill 'er up," Daddy said.

The man nodded. He stuck the nozzle in the tank, then used one of those wiper-things on the windshield while Daddy fished out his wallet. The pump dinged to indicate "full," and the man ambled back to us, wiping his hands on a rag as black as whatever was under his fingernails.

Krista had noticed, too. She caught my eye,

wrinkled her nose, and pointed. I grabbed her finger, quick, before she embarrassed us all. She frowned at me. Stopping a deaf person from using her hands to communicate was as bad as clapping a hand over the mouth of someone trying to speak.

"It be three dollars and forty-one cents." The man held out a palm speckled with grease.

Daddy thrust a five-dollar bill toward him. "Thanks for the great job of getting all the bugs off my windshield. Keep the change."

The man tipped the bill of his limp baseball cap and strolled away.

Hmm. "How come you gave him such a big tip?" I earned fifty cents an hour babysitting the kids down the street, and this guy got three times that amount for doing his job for an extra five minutes.

Daddy switched on the ignition and turned to look at me. "I figured he could use a little extra. It's not easy trying to feed a family on a station attendant's wages."

Paul looked back at the man as we pulled onto the road. "How do you know he has kids to feed?"

"Either he's got kids, or he's got parents who need help. Most people do."

"Are you going to give Aunt Nell extra money, too?" Wade asked.

"Why would I do that?"

"She's poor, too."

Mom laughed. "Aunt Nell and Uncle Kes have plenty to live on."

"They do?" Wade puzzled over that for a moment. "Oh. They have plenty of *land* to live on. But I don't think they have much money."

Mom and Daddy exchanged a quick glance, their

amusement not quite repressed.

"Why do you think they're poor?" Mom asked. "Aunt Nell is a nurse and Uncle Kes owns a cattle ranch."

Wade shrugged in defeat, but Paul spoke what the three of us were thinking. "Their house sure isn't as nice as ours."

"I guess you're right about that," Mom said. "It could use a scrubbing from one end to the other."

Living on the ranch for a few days was always a dubious adventure. The property—including the house—should have been named as a wildlife preserve for insects and rodents and reptiles. This was only my fourth trip to Aunt Nell's in my whole life, but each visit held at least one memorable episode to teach this town girl about life in the rural South.

"Which reminds me," Mom added. "We have to stop at the grocery store in town for a gallon of milk."

"But Aunt Nell has milk straight from the cow," Paul said.

Mom's lip curled in disgust. "And it's not pasteurized. No, thank you."

"Can we eat the farm eggs, though?" he pressed.

"You get the eggs out of the nest and wash them good, and I'll consider it."

Paul shook his head like Mom was the biggest party pooper in the world, but I agreed with her. Give me already-washed eggs from the store any time. The more I learned about life on a farm, the more I appreciated my life *off* of it.

I was only four when Aunt Nell introduced me to her ranch. Twin calves had been born that week, and she named one of them Debbie. I was thrilled until my education in ranch life continued on the second visit at age seven. I'd wanted to see Debbie again, now a full-grown cow.

"Oh honey," Aunt Nell had exclaimed. "Uncle Kes sent Debbie to the slaughterhouse a long time ago."

My uncle had *killed* my namesake? I'd cried for an hour—as well as every time I thought of poor Debbie that week.

At least the mouse stories were funny.

"Remember when we came here, and I was seven, and Daddy woke up with a mouse nibbling on his hair?" I asked.

The boys cracked up. Mom didn't.

Paul picked up on the direction of my thoughts. "And last time we were here a mouse got stuck in the guitar in their room."

"A mouse serenade in the middle of the night." Daddy smiled at that one.

Mom only shuddered. "I can't believe we'll have to sleep in that room again. And this time we'll have Krista in there with us. How can we protect her?"

Daddy laughed. "Mice don't eat three-year-olds. And if we have another one trying to escape from a guitar, Krista will never hear the performance anyway."

Mom's deadpan response. "*This* vacation had better be mouse-less."

Daddy rolled up to the gate leading to the ranch. "C'mon, boys. I'll show you how to unlatch this contraption."

Paul and Wade didn't need instructions. They tumbled out of the station wagon, lifted the doohickey that held the gate closed, and with a mighty push and the screech of rusted metal, swung the gate wide open.

"First one to reach the front door gets dibs on where he gets to sleep," Paul yelled.

They raced down the dirt and grass path that Aunt Nell called a driveway, but her house was nowhere in sight. I thought of the lane as a century-old road, picturing a horse and carriage traveling sedately under a canopy of live oaks.

Daddy returned to the car, passed through the gate, and stopped. "I should've mentioned they needed to stick around and shut it behind us." Not a bit riled, he exited the car again and closed the gate to the tune of its original screech.

We proceeded to bump down the "driveway" s-l-o-w-l-y, avoiding the worst of the holes and humps in the quarter-mile trek to the house.

Aunt Nell and Aunt Vivian, both dressed in shorts and plaid cotton shirts, stood on the sagging porch, waving madly as we pulled up. Although a bit husky for Ellie Mae, they looked like they'd stepped off the set of *The Beverly Hillbillies*. Meanwhile, Paul and Wade rolled on the ground with three dogs.

Mom threw a baleful glance in Daddy's direction. "We'll all be going home with fleas."

Black Jack didn't have fleas. I missed him. Why couldn't Black Jack have come on vacation with us? What a great place for a dog to play. But Mom said there was no room for him in an already-packed car.

The poor dog had been banished to a kennel for ten days while we had fun in the semi-tropics of Florida, and Grandma visited cousins in Virginia. She'd made sure to take her own vacation. That way, she didn't have to take care of a dog.

Uncle Hank and Uncle Kes ambled around the

corner of the house. They joined Daddy as he pulled suitcases and bags from the back of the station wagon. Krista clambered out of the car, and Aunt Vivian was right there to swoop in on her. Krista didn't seem to mind. She kissed Aunt Vivian's cheek.

What would Bill think of this place? His entire family lived in New York. He lived *next door* to his cousins. The two families spent a week at the Jersey Shore every summer. How uncool was that? We already had better beaches in the Hamptons.

Bill agreed.

Here, in the center of Florida, exotic Spanish moss draped every tree. We could walk for miles through forest or open pasture and still be on Uncle Kes's land. But I never wandered far. Poisonous snakes could cross my path at any time. Timmy had warned me about that last Christmas.

Just in case he *wasn't* pulling my leg, I had resolved to stay close to the house. And you never knew when you might meet up with a bull, which happened to me when I was seven. *Never* climb over a pasture fence.

Aunt Nell circled the car and hugged me. "Debbie! You're all grown up. You've turned into a beautiful young lady."

Happiness bubbled inside me. Even though Aunt Nell lived in this uncivilized wilderness, she and I were a lot alike. She played the organ for her church while I could strum guitar or play piano. She had a beautiful singing voice. I hoped mine ended up as good as hers. And like me, she loved to read. When I was little, I'd seen a photograph of her as a girl surrounded by piles of books. We looked so much alike, I thought it was a snapshot of me and tried to remember where I got all those books. Mom had to point out the date on the back of the photo—1922.

Aunt Vivian came up for a hug, too, with Krista slung on her hip. She made carrying a three-year-old with heavy leg braces look like it was no more work than lifting a bag of groceries. She bellowed. "I can't believe all of us are here at the same time!"

I took a step backward to protect my ears. Did she think yelling all her words would help Krista hear them? Mom handed me my travel bag of books and crossword puzzles. "You're in Roy's old room."

Aunt Nell led us into the house, Mom by her side. "Krista has a cot in the guest room with you and Grant. And all the boys are in tents or hammocks in the front yard. If we get a big rain, they can put their sleeping bags in the pool house."

While the main house was dilapidated, Aunt Nell had a swimming pool in pristine condition and a large pool house with cement floors where she served up the family meals. Both the pool and the floors felt gloriously cool on hot days.

I passed through the parlor, more like a Texas trophy room with the stuffed heads of two deer and the horns of a steer attached to the wall. The parlor was the only room left for Uncle Hank and Aunt Vivian to sleep in. Back in January, Aunt Vivian hadn't been too happy to receive Aunt Nell's letter decreeing the arrangements.

"We're ten years older than you and Grant," Aunt Vivian had complained to Mom on the phone. "And we'll be on that cowskin pull-out bed."

Mom had been properly apologetic. "If you don't

mind tending to Krista at night, Grant and I can switch with you." She made it sound like Krista still woke up for a feeding, which was ridiculous, but Aunt Vivian didn't know better. She'd hired a nanny for her kids.

Aunt Vivian decided the parlor sofa bed was better than sleeping with a toddler. Or sleeping in the pool house.

Chapter 11:
Water Fights

Aunt Nell has a pool,
But I can't play there because
Timmy might dunk me.

Roy's room was the first bedroom on the left, a cozy den of golden pine paneling. Nadine's suitcase lay on the bottom bunk, and she was busy pulling hangers out of the closet. Good. I was hoping for the top bunk. I slung my travel bag on its mattress.

Nadine jerked away from the closet and brandished a hanger in my direction. "I'm sleeping up top."

Nice to see you, too. I sent a deliberate stare to her suitcase on the bottom bunk.

She grabbed it and lowered it to the floor. "I didn't know you got here already. Sorry you thought the top bunk was yours."

The sort-of apology didn't make me feel a whole lot better, but I'd play it cool. "It doesn't matter. Either I'll be closer to the roaches on the floor or the palmetto bugs on the ceiling."

Startled, she flung back her head to scan the pine boards above us, as if one might drop on her at any moment. With no obvious insect scuttling into view, she turned back to me. "You just want the top bunk. There aren't any palmetto bugs."

I shrugged. "When we lived in Alabama, they lined the ceilings. *Usually*, they didn't drop on us."

"You're lying."

I smiled, oh so sweetly. "I may want the top bunk, but I'm not lying. Ask Paul and Wade about Alabama." I squinted at the ceiling. "The knots on the pine paneling look kind of like palmetto bugs." I dragged my travel bag off *her* mattress.

She eyed each knot in the wood with suspicion, then shook her head. "I'll keep the top bunk, thank you."

Nuts.

With sleeping arrangements settled, Nadine and I changed into swimsuits and joined the boys at the pool.

Nadine poured baby oil all over herself. By the end of the day, she would be a bronzed goddess. If I did that, I'd be a boiled lobster. I smoothed on my Coppertone lotion and hoped I wouldn't burn too badly.

She handed me the baby oil bottle. "Get my back, would you?" She slid onto the fully reclined chaise lounge and awaited my attention. Next, she'd be commanding me to wave a palm leaf over her. Me: slave. Nadine: Pharaoh's daughter, princess of the Nile.

A splash of cool water sprinkled welcome droplets on my back as I slathered oil on hers.

"Come on in, the water's fine." Timmy grinned at me, brown eyes dancing with anticipation.

What new torments awaited me? "I think I'll get good and hot in the sun before I get wet."

"And no splashing," Nadine said. "The water's cold."

He flicked the surface several times to send a little more spray our way. It felt good to *me*. I lay on my back on the chaise next to Nadine's. Timmy could keep cooling me off if he wanted.

He tired of that game pretty quickly and joined Paul and Wade at the deep end. Fifteen minutes of Florida sun and I was ready to join them. As I slipped over the side, the adults and Krista came through the gate and settled themselves at the corner table under the umbrella. Daddy had covered his nose with zinc oxide. He burned worse than me. At least, I didn't have to wear clown makeup to go swimming.

With my attention still on the adults' table, two hands pressed down on my shoulders. Next thing I knew, I was underwater. So dunking was on Timmy's diabolical mind. I should've known.

It was a good thing the hands released me after a second, because I hadn't inhaled before going under. I popped back to the surface and whipped around to yell at him, but he'd made a quick getaway. *What a jerk.*

Krista did her little tippy toe walk and sat down at the edge, allowing her feet to dip into the water. Without her braces, she looked more petite than ever. I held out my arms, but she shook her head. This pool wouldn't be as fun for her as the one at the officers' club. That one had steps where she could sit and play, but Aunt Nell's pool only had a ladder. If she didn't trust me to hold her, then I'd join Paul and Wade. Which meant I'd have to deal with Timmy.

The boys continued to dunk one another. I avoided them and swam from deep end to shallow end and back again, over and over. Back stroke, breaststroke, side stroke, crawl. I could relax like this for hours.

As I neared the shallow end, I sensed Timmy's presence just before he grabbed my shoulders again and forced me down. There was no sense in trying to dislodge him. He was skinny for a sixteen-year-old, but he was strong. I took time to go limp and position my arms where they might do me some good. He pushed me further down, just for good measure. With my feet flat on the bottom and my knees bent, I used all of my legs' power to push up against Timmy's weight. At the same time, I held up my fist, aiming for where I hoped his chin would be.

As soon as I made contact, I added the force of my forearm into his face.

"Ow!" He let go and massaged his cheekbone. "What did you do that for?"

"You know I hate to be dunked!" If he lunged for me again, I'd scream so loud, the neighboring ranch would hear me. "Leave me alone."

From the adults' corner, Uncle Hank said, "Is there a problem?"

Timmy returned my glare. "No problem." He dove away from me, making sure he kicked a huge amount of water in my face.

Krista had progressed to the ladder. She sat on the top rung. Again, I held out my arms. Again, she shook her head. Krista usually liked it when I carried her around in the shallow end of a pool, but her eyes followed Timmy. If he pushed me under water again while I was holding her… Yeah, I didn't blame her.

The scrape of several chairs against concrete garnered my attention. It looked like the adults planned to head inside.

Mom approached me. "Keep an eye on Krista. We're going to get dinner started, and the dads are ready to grill, so plan to get out of the pool in half an hour or so."

"Okay."

Aunt Vivian joined her. "Nadine, you're in charge. Keep things under control."

Nadine, now lying on her back, eyes shut tight against the sun, offered a limp wave of acknowledgment. *Right.* As if she could control Timmy. Even if she wanted to.

The boys continued thrashing each other in the deep end while I remained close to Krista. I helped her from the ladder down into the water, where she got a grip on the pool's edge. She grinned as cool water reached her sun-warmed shoulders.

The next moment, her eyes widened in alarm. I turned to search for the cause. Too late.

Timmy grabbed my arm and dragged me to deeper water.

"Cut it out! I can't leave Krista."

My last view of her was somewhat reassuring, forearms solidly on the pool deck as her head swiveled to follow my doom. Timmy forced me under and held me there. My desperate kicks and punches failed to get my head above the surface.

I was running out of air. I was going to drown.

Then—abrupt freedom. I broke through to precious

oxygen. Water streamed over my eyes as I searched for my tormenter. Wade gripped Timmy's shoulders, and Paul had Timmy in a headlock. Together, they pressed him under the water. I counted to ten, but they still held him down.

"Let him go." My voice came out as a croak.

I swam toward them and grabbed Paul's arm. "Let him go. We don't have to be like him."

Paul held my gaze, his face grim as he continued to hold Timmy below the water's surface. Then he flipped backward and took powerful, angry strokes toward the oblivious Nadine. Wade followed. They got out of the pool, stood on the side in front of her, then double-cannonballed back in, creating a huge jet of water that rained down on her. That got her attention. She shrieked into an upright position.

I hauled myself out of the water and sat on the pool's edge, letting my legs dangle in the shallow end while I caught my breath. Wade handed me a towel.

Nadine smirked at me. She *did* know what her brother had done.

Krista, who had returned to the ladder, watched me with concern. I smiled reassurance.

She pointed to Timmy who clung to the side of the pool on the deep end as he gulped in air.

"Baa," she said.

I nodded and signed *yes*. Sometimes, Timmy was *bad.*

Chapter 12:
Fire Ants

The big dog scares me.
Bugs scare me, too. Which one's worse?
Little bugs. They bite.

After a late family dinner of perfectly grilled steaks, the adults returned to the pool deck with their coffee. Timmy ran for the boys' tent, probably searching for spiders to put into my brothers' sleeping bags. Nadine wandered to our room declaring her intent to write a letter to her latest love.

As I entered the house in search of my book, Paul and Wade turned the corner swinging Krista between them.

"We're gonna play Hide and Seek in the dark," Wade said. "You wanna play, too?"

"No way. How are you going to know if you're sitting on a fire ant hill or if a snake is hanging from a branch over your head?"

The boys glanced at each other. Even *they* had respect for fire ants. Snakes, maybe not.

Paul shrugged like he had no worries. "Then we'll

just do something in the front yard."

"How about *Mother May I?*" Wade asked. "Krista knows how to play that. And you can be 'Mother' and stay on the porch. That way you don't even have to set foot in the grass." He knew me well.

"Okay. I'll be right back."

After dousing myself with bug repellent—better to stink for the evening than to be polka-dotted with mosquito bites, I returned to the porch with Krista's gleeful squeals in my ears. Paul had started her favorite outdoor activity, "Swing Me Around." They grasped hands, and Paul spun in circles while Krista's feet lifted off the ground. The faster they whirled, the better she liked it.

"Ready?" I asked.

Paul slowed down just as Aunt Nell's collie rounded the corner of the house. He headed straight for the spinning human tops and leaped to join them with a joyful bark. At least, I thought that was his intention. Krista thought otherwise. Her squeals turned into screams of terror.

Paul tried to grab her close to his chest, but he was a bit dizzy and fell down with her in his arms. The dog kept barking and jumping on them, Krista kept screaming, and Wade kept yelling, "Down, boy!" while trying to pull the dog off the other two. He'd succeeded by the time Daddy arrived leading the pack of grown-ups to the rescue.

I remained on the front porch away from the crowd and noticed Timmy standing in shadows just outside the reach of the porch light. *Was he grinning?* Did he send the dog Krista's way? This vacation was not starting off well.

Once the hubbub died down, Mom carried Krista inside to give her a bath and get her ready for bed. She hadn't been hurt, only a minor scratch from the dog's nails. No one was in trouble, not even the dog.

I went inside and wandered to Aunt Nell's music room. After I started piano lessons, she'd given me permission to use her electric organ whenever I visited. I riffled through the music sheets stacked to the side and picked out "Believe Me If All Those Endearing Young Charms," a popular tune when Grandma was young. Aunt Nell didn't seem to own anything more recent than 1945.

I had no problem with the organ's keyboard. Unfortunately, my feet had no sense of the bass pedals, so I had to watch them every measure. It made for slow going. I ran through the song twice, the second time a small improvement over the first. The third time, I sang while I played.

"You've gotten quite good."

I turned to see Aunt Nell leaning against the wall.

"Thanks. I sing better than I play."

"Are you planning a career in music then?"

I shook my head. "I want to teach deaf kids."

A soft smile lit her face. "I understand. But I hope you don't let that voice go to waste."

Wow. Aunt Nell thought I had talent. I hit two keys right next to each other so the sound came out harsh and dissonant. "I thought about going professional after college, but I think I would hate living out of a suitcase almost all the time." My right hand ran up the C scale.

"And my English teacher, who directs our school plays, told me Hollywood would eat me alive."

Aunt Nell waved a hand in dismissal. "Forget Hollywood."

"Anyway, I don't think I have the charisma of Joan Baez or Joni Mitchell."

"What about the Met?"

I snorted. "I hate opera."

She looked disappointed. "I would've loved to try for Juilliard. Opera tests your skills to the limit."

I grinned. "Maybe that's why I don't want it."

She went along. "So… you're a *lazy* singer."

I hung my head in mock shame. "Guilty." Then I got serious. "But I plan to work really hard to become a great teacher."

She motioned for me to slide left and joined me on the bench. "And if that's your heart's desire, I'm sure you'll be a wonderful teacher." She extracted two sheets from the middle of the pile. "Think you can do the bass part of this duet, or should we trade places?"

"I can do it."

When I reached my room, Nadine was already under the covers of the top bunk. Did she think I'd climb up there and refuse to come down?

I heard a sniffle.

"Are you okay?" I peered over the upper mattress.

"I'm fine," came a muffled reply. "I just miss Dickie."

An almost-grown guy still goes by the name of *Dickie?*

I kept those thoughts to myself and worked on my empathy skills. "I miss my boyfriend, too."

She sat up. "You have a boyfriend?"

I leaned against the top frame. "Yeah. He's a sophomore. Plays football and basketball."

"Huh. I forget you're growing up." She looked at me with something that might be called respect. "What's his name?"

"Bill."

"Do you ever worry that Bill might not be your boyfriend by the time you get back to New York?"

I stared at her, shocked into silence. *My beautiful cousin had the same worries?*

She slid back to a prone position and threw the sheet over her head. "Forget I asked." A moment's silence. "It's just that Dickie and I had a big fight the day before we left, and I think he likes someone else. It might be really bad news when I get home."

I finally found my voice. "Are you going steady?"

"We *were*. Who knows if we are now?" Her hand shot out from underneath the covers revealing a class ring I hadn't noticed all afternoon.

"At least, he wanted to give you his ring." I took a deep breath. I'd never confided anything to Nadine before. If she laughed at me, this would be the first and last time I'd trust her.

My fingers found Nora Jean's beads. "Bill hasn't offered to give me his ring when it comes in next month. And even though we've been at dances and parties together all year, he didn't ask me to Winter Prom."

Nadine flipped the sheet off her face. "That is *not* cool."

"Freshmen aren't allowed to go so he took another sophomore." Saying it out loud brought the sting of disappointment back to life like a ghost rising from its grave.

"He should've taken you out to dinner and skipped the prom. Dump him."

I leaned against her bunk in relief but couldn't help asking the obvious. "Like you plan on dumping Dickie?"

She rolled to her side and stared directly into my eyes. "You're right. I don't want to dump him either." She offered a wry grin and repeated, "You really are growing up."

"So can I have the top bunk?"

"Not on your life." She rolled to her other side, turning her back to me. "Turn off the light, will you?"

Our moment of friendship had passed. But one moment was better than none.

I checked the floor for roaches, hit the light switch, and leaped into bed, keeping my head low to avoid smashing it against the top bunk. Shutting my eyes tight, I offered a silent prayer. A reminder of my days in the Mojave Desert. "Matthew, Mark, Luke, and John, bless the bed that I lay on." I added, "Please don't let any fire ants or other bugs crawl on me."

I woke up to shrill cries in dim morning light. *Why was Krista screaming?* Wait. Krista wasn't in this room, so ... *Nadine?*

A pillow sailed over the side from the top bunk. More thumping and squeals emanated from above, and the sheets floated down to the floor as well. I sat up, nearly knocking my head on the slats above.

"What's wrong?" I had to shout over Nadine's shrieks.

"Ants! They're biting me. They're all over the mattress."

I scrambled out from the sheets and squatted at one end of *my* mattress, not daring to set my feet on a fire ant-covered floor. I examined every inch of where I'd been sleeping. Nothing. "Nadine. My bed's okay. Get out of there and come down here."

"I can't. They're climbing up the ladder."

I peeked around the corner where the ladder attached to the foot of the bed. An army of ants climbed the posts, bypassing my bed and marching to the top bunk.

Uncle Hank appeared at our door, his hair sticking up at odd angles, followed by Aunt Vivian who clutched a scanty robe to her chest. While sliding slippers onto his feet, Daddy tripped into the room next, and Mom brought up the rear with a sleepy Krista in her arms.

Uncle Hank lifted his eighteen-year-old daughter directly out of the bunk. Aunt Vivian jammed sneakers on Nadine's feet then brushed her down. Krista blinked in fascination at the circus scene in front of her.

I inspected my mattress again. Not one ant had stopped to visit *me*. Where had they come from? I stood on the lower bunk and peered over the top railing. The line of ants flowed from the upper bunk's footboard, across the middle of the bed, and directly toward some candy wrappers stuffed between the headboard and mattress. I pointed to the source of our troubles. "We can throw out the bedtime snacks, but how do we get rid of the ants?"

"With this." Aunt Nell stood in the doorway, her hair in rag rollers and a can of Raid in her outstretched hand.

Within minutes, the ants were dead, the sheets were in the wash, and Roy's room stank of bug spray. Nadine showed me the welts on her legs and feet.

Krista stared at Nadine's spotted legs and shivered. She checked out my legs. Not one bite. Her eyes questioned why I remained unscathed, and her poor cousin would itch for days.

I winked and interlocked my fingers, mouthing the words, "I prayed."

Chapter 13:
Hours of Torture

Bad girls on the bus.
Mommy thinks I am the one
Who is bad. I cry.

Ever since we'd returned to school after Easter break, Krista didn't want to get on her station wagon-bus. Mom wrestled her into the seat belt while Krista kicked and screamed.

For eight months, she'd ridden back and forth to school, an hour each way, with three other deaf kids. From nine to three, she concentrated on every move of her teacher's lips. Twice a week she endured the speech therapy room where she practiced reading lips and saying sounds she couldn't hear. Over and over again. Add metal braces strapped from mid-thigh to ankles on her skinny legs, and she had to be one weary little kid by the time she arrived home well after four.

But she'd never complained. Until now. What had changed?

Mom had checked with the bus driver who assured her there were no problems on the commute to school and back. Then she'd called the school and asked if her daughter was experiencing any new frustrations in the classroom. Sister Michaelina said Krista appeared perfectly content all day and seemed to love school. So much so that she usually had to be shooed out the door at the end of the day.

Yet, Krista said the children were "baa." Just like she'd said Timmy was bad when he dunked me in the pool.

If nothing terrible happened on the bus and the teachers hadn't noticed any students bothering Krista, who was bad? Mom chalked it up to spring fever. Krista had probably tired of riding a bus for so long every day.

Didn't I tell them way back last summer that the drive was too far? But would anybody listen to me?

On Tuesday afternoon, Krista's bus didn't arrive on time. Mom and I took turns staring out onto the street from the living room's bay window. The tap of a basketball on the driveway indicated Paul and Wade were keeping an eye out as well.

Finally, the station wagon-bus pulled into the driveway. Paul and Wade burst through the front door.

"Krista's here," Paul announced.

Wade added, "And the car looks just fine. No dents."

The three of us watched from the front step as the driver opened Krista's door and helped her out of the seat belt. Before Mom made it halfway down the path, the woman hustled Krista to the flagstones.

"Mrs. Bumpke," Mom called. "What happened?"

Acting as if she didn't hear, Mrs. Bumpke beat a fast waddle to the car and backed out of the driveway without even checking for traffic. Mom tried to wave her down, but the woman only returned the wave and drove off.

Krista limped over to Mom, rubbing the side of her head. Black Jack trailed close behind her. Mom bent down to ask about school, their daily ritual.

She knew Krista couldn't answer, but she asked the same question every day. If it had been a good day, Krista smiled and dug into her school bag to retrieve some trophy from class—a paper with a big red star or a fingerpainted masterpiece. On bad days, she shrugged. They'd give each other lots of hugs no matter what kind of day it had been.

But Krista didn't respond at all to Mom's question. She kept rubbing her head.

Mom lifted Krista's hand away and gasped. "What *happened?*"

The boys and I ran over as she kneeled on the flagstone path and examined Krista's head, which caused my sister to wail.

"What's the matter?"

"What's wrong?'

"What happened?"

Our questions created a panicked three-part harmony.

"Look." The still expression on Mom's face reminded me of the day we found out Daddy's jet had crashed in Thailand. She tilted Krista's head so we could see.

A bald spot the size of a quarter revealed a blotchy, red space on Krista's scalp. *Her hair had been pulled out by the roots.* I used to cry when Mom pulled my hair as she brushed out the tangles. But Mom never left a bald spot.

The slow burn of awakened rage flickered deep inside of me. *Someone* had tortured my sister.

Mom sat on the grass, pulled Krista onto her lap, and planted kisses all over Krista's face while stroking her back and shoulders. "Shhh, baby."

The caresses calmed her down, and she curled her body into Mom's.

Wade's hands balled into fists. "Who did that?" He made sure Krista's puffy eyes were on his lips.

She stared at him, concentrating.

"Who did that?" He touched the side of her head next to the bald spot.

She winced. "Buh."

Mom turned Krista to face her. "On the bus? It happened on the bus?"

Krista nodded. While speechreading lessons always brought on tantrums, her ability to read our lips was helping all of us at the moment. Before she went to school, she could barely read our lips at all.

Mom handed Krista to me, stood, and strode to the front door. "I'm calling Sister Ignatius." As she entered the house, she tossed an order over her shoulder. "Take Krista inside and give her a snack. That will calm her down."

The boys and I escorted Krista to the kitchen. Paul placed her little backpack on the stairs. Wade sat down at the table and pumped Krista with questions, most of which she couldn't understand. I grabbed a box of her favorite crackers, spilled a handful onto a plate, and plunked them on the table.

Mom clenched the phone, voice raised, letting the school know what she thought of a bus driver who delivered a damaged child to her home and didn't explain what happened.

Wade slammed the table with his fist, causing all of us to jump, even Krista, who could feel the vibration through the boards. "I knew it. It was Charlene."

"How do you know?" Trying to eavesdrop on Mom's conversation, I'd missed his interrogation.

"Krista just told me. Weren't you listening?"

I shook my head, pointed to Mom, and cupped a hand around my ear.

"Oh. Yeah. What does the school have to say for itself?" Wade seemed to be vying for man-of-the-house status, even though Daddy came home every weekend.

"Shhh." I held my finger to my lips. "Just listen."

Mom had a pencil poised over a scrap of paper "Yes, I would appreciate the number."

"Bus driver's phone number," I whispered.

Wade's eyes tensed to slits. "Yeah, I'd like to say some things to the bus driver."

"Like Mom would let you," Paul muttered.

"We can figure out what to do later." I leaned over the table toward Wade. "Now, how do you know Charlene did it?"

"I told you." Wade lowered his voice. "I asked Krista. When she said *bus,* I started asking names. She can see the names on our lips. I said, 'Denise?' and she shook her head no. I said, 'Lucy?' and she said no. I said, 'Charlene,' and her eyes got real big, and she nodded yes."

"Ow," Krista said.

We'd been so into our own conversation, we forgot she was right there munching on crackers—and apparently practicing her speechreading.

"So, Charlene pulled your hair out? Was your hair in her hand?" I pretended to yank hair out of my head and then let some of it lie in my hand. I pointed to the hair, then at Krista. "Your hair in Charlene's hand?"

Krista stared at my hand, then raised solemn eyes to my face. She nodded and pointed in the direction of the street.

"Buh. Baa."

"*Bad* girls on the *bus*," Paul said. "Bad Charlene."

Krista signed *yes*. With emphasis.

"Bad Lucy," Paul said.

Krista's eyes widened in surprise.

Paul held his hand above his head and parallel to the floor to indicate *tall*. "Lucy is a big kid." He held up ten fingers, closed his fists, and held up two more fingers. "She's almost twelve." He tapped his index finger against his temple while he nodded his head. "She knew what Charlene was doing and didn't stop it. Did Lucy tell Charlene to stop?"

Krista couldn't follow all those words, so he mimed a scene with "Lucy" holding out an authoritative hand to stop "Charlene."

Krista frowned, thinking through his charade. She shook her head.

Wade cackled to mimic Lucy. "Did Lucy laugh?"

Krista nodded adding another *yes* sign.

"Did Lucy laugh when Charlene had your hair in her hand?" Paul grabbed my hair and yanked. Lucky for me I owned over a foot of it. Otherwise, I would have had a bald spot too. He imitated Wade's Lucy-cackles then pretended to be Charlene holding the hair.

Krista shook her head, then pulled my hair from Paul's hand and tried to hide her hand behind her back.

Except my hair wasn't on par with Rapunzel's so she pulled me along with it, and I wasn't ready.

"Ow!" I leaned toward her to ease the pain, but a few plucked strands remained in her hand when she released me.

She flung the hair to the floor, her eyes filled with tears of remorse for hurting me.

"It's okay. I'm okay." I picked up the three strands, showed them to Krista, then hid them behind my back. "Lucy hid the hair after Charlene pulled it out?" I mimed the hair-pulling again. I played Charlene who pulled the hair, then I handed the hair to Wade, who took on the role of Lucy. He hid it behind his back.

Krista nodded, her eyes gleaming. We got it.

"Two bad girls on the bus." Paul held up two fingers.

Mom hung up the phone and watched our play-acting. "And what did the bus driver do?"

Paul became the driver making an imaginary steering wheel move. Wade played Charlene, and I played Krista. Wade pulled my hair. Paul ignored us and kept driving.

Mom asked another question, this time pointing to Paul. "What did the bus driver do when Charlene hurt you?"

Krista didn't know how to answer.

I added some signs to the charade. I pretended to pull her hair—the poor kid didn't need me to do it for real--then pointed to Paul and signed *do what?*

Krista shook her head. Did that mean she didn't understand, or the driver didn't do anything?

Mom tried a yes-no question. "Did the bus driver make Charlene stop?"

Bus driver Paul turned around and waggled his finger at Wade-Charlene. I added signs. STOP. DRIVER-SAY?

Krista signed *no*.

Mom's lips pressed together so tight they weren't even visible, her anger directed at the bus driver, not because I used sign language. Not today.

I hadn't seen her this angry since Paul took a baseball bat to Wade one time. The *only* time. He found out what it was like to cross a mama bear's path. My gentle mother had run outside, grabbed Paul by the ear, and dragged him back in. Then she sat on him and slapped him, yelling, "How do you like it? How do you like it?"

It's a good thing the driver left before Mama Bear could grab *her* ear.

Mom held up a scrap of paper. "I have the bus driver's phone number. The school doesn't know anything about the incident, but they'll look into it as well." She turned to leave the kitchen. "I think it would be better if I used the phone in my bedroom."

Meaning, she didn't want us to hear what she might say.

As soon as she disappeared into the hall, I lifted the kitchen receiver. "No noise."

My brothers grinned. Wade made a shushing motion to Krista. She put her thumb and index finger together and zipped her lips. Wade must've taught her that.

I heard Mom pick up the extension and dial enough numbers for long distance. After four rings, someone answered.

"I'd like to speak with Jeanette Bumpke please."

"Speaking."

"This is Mrs. Hansen, Krista's mother. You were late in getting her home, and I have some questions."

"Oh, yes. I needed to make an extra stop. I'm sorry for the inconvenience."

"I'm not worried about the *inconvenience*. I'm worried about my daughter's well-being. She has told us a shocking story."

"She has *told* you…?"

So, the woman thought my sister wouldn't be able to explain anything. Not surprising. Krista had feared the bus for weeks, and we hadn't gotten wise.

Mom's cool tone lowered to frigid. "Yes, deaf children *can* communicate. Please tell me what happened on the ride home this afternoon."

The woman inhaled sharply but didn't speak.

Mom added another icicle. "And perhaps you can tell me what's been going on for the last month that's made it necessary for me to force my child into your car."

"Oh… ohh. Nothing terrible's been going on for a *month*." She took another deep breath. "I'd noticed the older girls teasing her a bit lately, and I told them to stop. But ya know, I can't stop the car in the middle of the highway every time there's a little tiff. And they're not going to hear me yell. All I can do is make hand motions while I'm driving."

"Yet you assured me there were no problems on the way to and from school."

Whoa. My mother just called the woman a liar. Silence hung across the phone line like a dead man dangling from a noose.

The bus driver cleared her throat. "I didn't think

things were bad enough to make a complaint to you."

"A *complaint* to me? Was Krista doing something wrong?"

"No, no! I mean, I didn't think it was serious enough to bother you with it."

Mom spoke with slow precision. "Krista came home with her hair pulled out of her head. She has a *bald* spot. Have you any idea how excruciating that must have been for her? Was a child in pain not serious enough?"

"I'm sorry. I didn't see it. I did stop the car when Krista's screams became more than I could bear. That's why we were late." She raced through her words. "I pulled off into a parking lot, made Denise switch places with Krista, and told them all no more screaming. Once Krista moved to where Charlene wasn't next to her, she stopped crying."

Krista's screaming had been unbearable? Tears filled my eyes. I wanted to reach through the phone and rip the bus driver's hair out. Show her what unbearable might *really* feel like.

"I see." Mom continued in a calm voice. "I suggest you move Charlene away from all the other children for the duration of the school year. I will not have Krista sitting next to her."

"Yes, ma'am." The voice on the other end sounded relieved. "That's a good suggestion."

"Good. I'll see you in the morning." Mom hung up without a goodbye. She never hangs up on anybody.

I dropped the kitchen phone into its cradle and hurried to sit at the table. The boys had already scurried over. Again, we put fingers to our lips to remind Krista not to say anything about eavesdropping. Her eyes questioned me, wanting to know what I'd heard on the phone.

"Later," I told her.

She could lipread most of "later." Putting on a disinterested expression, she picked up the last cracker and bit into it.

"So, what're we gonna do about this?" Wade asked.

"Later," I repeated. Footsteps sounded on the wood floor in the front hall. Mom would be back any second.

Grandma walked into the kitchen instead. Her fancy little black hat with its line of tiny, sewn-on rhinestones perched on her head. She always wore it to bridge parties or ladies' teas. She stopped at the sight of all four kids gathered quietly at the table, and it wasn't even time to eat.

"What's going on?" She glanced at the stove. "Hasn't your mother started dinner yet?"

Mom spoke from behind her. "There was a problem." She gathered Krista into her arms and pointed out the bald spot.

Grandma's hand flew to her mouth. She didn't say a word, but her eyes reflected the pain she felt for Krista.

After she heard the story, Grandma drew herself up tall and straight, the little hat looking like a crown, and she spoke in as regal a manner as the queen of England. "The bus driver must be fired."

Chapter 14:
Never Again

I don't ride the bus
Today. Debbie, Wade, and Paul
Are mad at bad girls.

Mom pulled the pork chops and potatoes out of the oven. She hunched her shoulder to hold the phone to her ear as she told Daddy the horrible story. If only he didn't have to work in New Jersey.

Mom finished with, "Anyway, I'll expect a report from Sister Ignatius tomorrow." She listened to Daddy's response and finished the call. "Yes, I'll let you know what I find out, and I *will* make sure Charlene is in the front seat so she can't touch *anybody*." She hung up.

I folded my arms across my chest. "I don't think Krista should ever get on that bus again. Or Charlene and Lucy should get kicked off."

"I didn't say *Krista* would be on the bus. I said I will make sure *Charlene* is in the front seat." Mom transferred the pot of spinach to a strainer and shook the water out of it with the energy I'd use shaking Charlene's brains out.

She dumped the spinach back in the pot. "I can drive Krista back and forth for the next month until school lets out."

Much better option.

"Daddy said to wait and see how the school handles it."

He'd let her back on that bus? Not good enough. It would be up to us kids to do something about two deaf bullies.

As soon as we were excused from our late dinner, I nodded to Paul and Wade. "Come on. We're meeting in the living room."

They started to follow until Mom asked, "A meeting?"

"Yes," I said.

"You and Paul and Wade?"

"Yes. It's a sibling meeting."

"A sibling meeting?"

I drove my point home. "Parents are *not* invited."

She cleared his throat. "I see." And she waved me away.

Was she laughing at me? So, we'd never had a sibling meeting before. It was necessary now.

The boys and I sat cross-legged in a circle on the living room rug. Krista followed us. Well, she was a sibling, too. We widened the circle to make room for her. She pointed to the braces. I unfastened them and pulled them off. She wiggled her toes and massaged her legs. Boy, she must feel so free when released from those contraptions.

"You've got a plan." Paul knew I wouldn't call any

kind of meeting without one.

Wade's eyes gleamed in anticipation. "We pull them out of the car tomorrow and beat them up, right?"

Paul bumped Wade's shoulder, hard. "Get a brain."

Wade ignored the insult. He frowned at me instead. "You're not going to be all nicey-nice and ask Lucy and Charlene to 'please not pull out my sister's hair again.'" He made his voice high and honey-sweet, then dropped to a growl. "Are you?"

"Nope. Nicey-nice won't work for them. At least not for Charlene."

Charlene looked like she could be the star of a girls' football team. She obviously had no conscience about using her brute strength against a girl six years younger. Lucy, on the other hand, had always seemed nice. And she had a crush on Paul. Any time he came out to the bus to get Krista, she batted her eyelashes at him and never stopped smiling.

I planned to use that.

We huddled, heads close together, voices low, motioning to Krista every once in a while. We wanted her to follow the plan, too.

Mom walked in holding Krista's pajamas. "Meeting's over. At least for Krista."

Krista shook her head.

I stood up, pulling her with me. "It's okay. You know what to do." I pointed to her, then tapped my temple.

"And are you going to let me in on this plan?" Mom asked.

"Not exactly." I sneaked a peek her way. "Will you trust us to do it right?"

"We won't beat them up." Wade stood and crossed

his heart. "Promise."

"And we won't yell at the bus driver," I added. "Even though she deserves it."

Mom looked at Paul. "*You* haven't made any promises." Maybe she remembered how his temper almost got him killed last summer.

One corner of his mouth lifted in a smile. He remained on the floor, leaned against one of the chairs, and stretched. "We'll have everything under control."

Silence. Then a squint-glare aimed at each one of us. "You'd better. I'll be watching from the front step."

Okay. Mom was on board.

We convinced Mom to watch the showdown from the living room window. The morning sun provided pleasant warmth, and the ocean breeze carried the soothing aroma of salt air, making it difficult to believe the world could ever be cruel.

Paul, Wade, and I escorted Krista to the station wagon-bus. The boys stood near the passenger side of the car, faces grim, totally silent. Krista and I stood by the rear door on the opposite side since she usually sat directly behind the driver.

I touched the beads of my necklace, then opened the door. Little Denise sat in Krista's usual spot instead of next to Lucy, who now had the third row's rear bench to herself. But Charlene remained in her old seat, which placed her beside Denise instead of Krista. The bus driver had lied. Charlene was *not* separated from the other kids.

I circled the bus to join the boys while Krista

remained where she was. Paul opened the door next to Charlene. I nodded to my brothers. They positioned themselves so Charlene and Lucy could see them through the open door. In unison, each boy began a rhythm of one fist pounding into the palm of the other hand. Their grim expressions never changed. Paul's glare bored into Lucy, his brown eyes dark and cold. And with steely blue eyes, Wade stared straight into Charlene's.

The driver raised an eyebrow but remained silent. Maybe she thought the boys and I could help her improve the little monsters' behavior.

I waved to get both girls' attention. "We are *mad.*"

We might be staging this performance to make a point, but our rage was no act. Just the thought of Krista's bald spot boiled my blood.

I pointed to the girls. "And you are *bad.*" I signed *bad.* Oh, yeah, they knew a little sign language. Their shock that *I* knew signs gave me tremendous satisfaction.

The boys continued the drum roll of fists smacking into palms.

Charlene had the nerve to crack a smile and mimic their actions, but Lucy's lips trembled.

I leaned into the car and grabbed Charlene's chin. "You think we are funny?"

Seeing my lips form "think" and "funny," she knew what I said. Her eyes darted between me and Wade. The beginnings of fear changed her expression. *Would I sic Wade on her?* While Paul showed cold disdain, Wade looked ready to pounce with the ferocity of a wildcat.

"Do you think *this* is funny?" I let go of her chin

and pointed at Krista.

Seeing her cue, Krista turned and tilted her head so Charlene could have the best view of her bald spot.

Poor little Denise gasped. Only a year older than Krista, she knew she'd be the next target of the bus bully. A little squeak came out of Lucy. Maybe she hadn't realized the full extent of yesterday's damage. Charlene turned sullen.

I looked each girl in the eye. "*Never again. No more.*" I locked in on Lucy and pointed to Paul. "Paul thought you were nice." She could easily read those words.

Lucy looked back to Paul, who without changing expression, turned his back and walked toward the garage.

Her eyes filled with tears.

I *almost* felt sorry for her. "You think about this." I waved my hand around, my finger pointing to Krista, to Charlene, to every corner of the car. "Never again."

Now sobbing, Lucy nodded.

Charlene glowered, as grim as my brothers.

"You understand me?" I asked her.

She lifted her chin, gray eyes dark like an overcast sky in winter.

"You." I jerked my thumb in a motion to "get moving," unlatched her seat belt, and opened the front passenger door.

Mrs. Bumpke protested. "Hey…"

I ignored her as Charlene plopped herself into the front seat. Passing within two feet of Wade's fist maybe shook her up a little. Or maybe not. She glared and snatched the seat belt strap from my hands.

Once she buckled herself in, Wade joined Paul in

front of the garage door. Their fists still smacked into palms in a slow, funeral-dirge tempo.

I made sure Charlene could see my lips, and I pointed in Krista's direction. "If you ever do this to my sister again, we will pull *your* hair out." I signed *IF, AGAIN*, and gave a little tug on her hair. She jerked away from me.

That last line wasn't in our script, but I could see Charlene remained as hard and cold as an iceberg. My words spurred the bus driver to heave herself out of the car.

Her nostrils flared as she huffed the fire of authority across the car's roof. "You can't threaten these girls."

"Lucy is sorry, but Charlene isn't." I glared at the woman. "And they both need to know there are consequences for their actions." I sounded like my teachers at school.

"You have no right to come out here and—"

"*Ms.* Bumpke." I used her preferred title of respect. "If you had done your job, I wouldn't *have* to be out here."

I marched away from the car and up the flagstones toward the front step. The boys followed, hands at their sides. Their job was done. Krista took their place near the garage.

"Get back here, or I'll—I'll..." Ms. Bumpke's spluttering dissolved into mutters.

I turned around. "If you would like to complain to my mother, she'll be happy to come out and speak to you herself."

The woman ducked into the car and slammed the door. At least she had enough self-control not to peel out of the driveway. With a big smile, Krista waved goodbye to them until her bus drove out of sight.

Chapter 15:
First Date/Beach Bonfires

Debbie was happy
Last night. But she is sad this
Morning. What happened?

On Thursday, I had news to share at the lunch table. "The school fired the bus driver."

"Good," Ronni said, her mouth full of macaroni and cheese.

Bill laughed as he grabbed a French fry off my plate. "You really took it to that bus driver. I like a girl with sass. Standing up for justice."

"Yes, she should stand up for justice more often." Ronni held her smile, but it didn't reach her eyes as she stared at Bill from across the table.

She still didn't like him, and for all of second semester while we shared a lunch table with Bill and his friends, she made sure I knew it.

I returned to the subject at hand. "My mom showed the principal Krista's bald spot when she drove her to school, and by noon, Sister Ignatius called her and let her know a substitute would drive the kids for the rest of the year." I took a sip of my orange soda. "Oh, and she called Charlene's and Lucy's parents to let them know what happened."

"I bet those girls are really unhappy now." Ronni scooped the last piece of pasta off her plate.

"If Charlene's parents are anything like Charlene, she won't be able to sit down for a week." A sudden thought struck my conscience. "Or—do you think they would beat her?" What if Charlene bullied little kids because her family bullied *her*?

Nobody had an answer.

"Hey, you did the right thing, Debbie. Don't sweat it." Bill pushed his chair back and picked up his tray. "I'll see you after last period."

When I got to my locker at the end of the day, he leaned against it, waiting for me, already dressed for baseball practice. I couldn't help but notice the bulging muscles in his arms, the same arms that wrapped around me on most Saturday nights. Come September, I'd be allowed an extra half hour before curfew. So those arms would be around me that much longer. I smiled in anticipation of life as a sophomore.

Bill returned it with one of his own. "What's got my serious girl so happy?"

His girl. I liked that. "Just thinking about my future."

"Future is looking that good, huh? What do you see in your crystal ball?"

My finger drew a line down his forearm. "I see…college, maybe a solo in the school musical next year, and…you."

I glanced up to gauge his reaction. He kissed me right there in the school hallway. He must've liked my answer.

When his lips released mine, he asked, "Are you planning to go to the Bonfires at the end of the month?"

"Definitely."

The Bonfires on the Beach were as big of a deal in the spring as Homecoming was in the fall. I'd been waiting to be able to participate since sixth grade.

"Why don't I pick you up for that on Saturday night?"

Had he just asked me out on a real date?

As I struggled to catch my breath from the shock, he frowned at my lack of response. "Or do your parents still have the no-teen-driver rule?"

I shook my head as if that would unscramble my brain and restore my ability to speak. "I think they'll be okay with you driving. They know you." I remembered to smile. "Yes. I would love to go with you."

"Great." He kissed me again, light and quick. "I gotta get to practice. See you tomorrow."

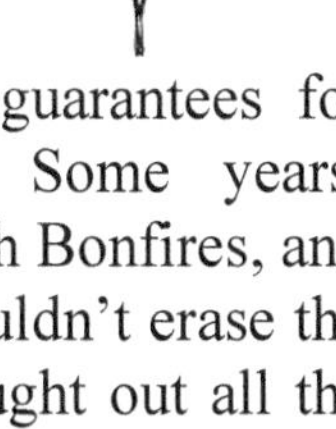

Memorial Day weekend held no guarantees for summer temperatures and sunshine. Some years, everybody wore winter coats to the Beach Bonfires, and even flames blazing twenty feet high couldn't erase the shivers. Other years, torrential rain brought out all the jokes about needing an ark. All the high school kids swarmed to the beach anyway, and the winning bonfire was the one that burned at all. As soon as a flicker of flame was recorded, they hightailed it to the school gym to finish out the festivities.

Nothing stopped the Bonfires. It marked the last

stretch of the school year and the beginning of the summer tourist season.

On Saturday, the weather was perfect. Warm and sunny with no rain in the forecast. Ronni and I tried on a dozen outfits apiece all afternoon. First, we went through her closet until we found the perfect combination of hot pink cut-off shorts matched with a pale pink tee shirt. Then we ran over to my house and decided my peach tank top with the lace around its V-neck was the best choice to go with my newest denim shorts. Neither of us had any kind of a tan yet, but who'd notice in the dark?

Before Ronni left, I promised that Bill and I would meet up with her. String Bean—I mean, Roger Bechelman—was supposed to meet her there. He'd better not disappoint her.

My stomach was so knotted I could barely eat supper. My first Beach Bonfires, and Bill would actually take me. Our first. *Real.* Date. I was ready by eight-thirty.

"You should take along a sweater," Grandma said as I preened in front of the upstairs hall mirror. "It gets chilly on the beach at night."

I considered telling her that Bill could keep me warm, but I didn't think she'd appreciate that. "I'll be fine. Remember, there'll be a big bonfire."

We went down the stairs together.

"You could at least take one along. Just in case."

Grandmas.

Mom and Daddy were dressed for an evening out. They'd been invited to the country club or something.

"The outfit's adorable," Mom said.

"Thank you."

"Won't you need a sweater?"

I ignored her question.

Daddy gave me an appraising glance. He wasn't smiling. "A sweater would cover you up a little more."

The V-neck didn't plunge deep enough to reveal a hint of cleavage, and if Daddy thought I would wear shorts down to my knees, it wasn't going to happen. Good thing I didn't choose the halter top and hot pants. He would've ordered me back upstairs.

I looked to Mom for support.

"Now, Grant. This is quite modest for today's standards. Do you want her to look frumpy in Bermuda shorts and a baggy tee-shirt?"

"Yes." He grabbed me in a quick hug. "I guess I don't want my little girl to grow up."

I kissed his cheek. "I already did."

"And it's killing me."

Grandma patted his shoulder. "I remember when you took Dorothy to her first prom. Her father cried after you left the house."

"You never told me that before," Mom said. She patted Daddy's other shoulder. "It must be a fatherhood rite of passage."

"You can cry over me next year when I go to Junior Prom," I said. "*If* someone asks me."

Bill and I had been together for the whole school year, sort of. Most couples didn't last that long. Would we still be together by next year's prom?

"Maybe no one will ask you, and I can avoid the pain for a little while longer." If Daddy was back to joking around, then he'd accepted the fact that I had a first date. He opened the door for Mom. "Ready?"

Mom gave him her special smile. "Thank you, sir,"

she said as she stepped outside, brushing his cheek with her fingertips.

The grandfather clock chimed nine o'clock. Then the single tone of nine-fifteen. Well, Bill did say *around* nine. Since he'd never picked me up before, how far past the hour did he consider "around?"

Grandma was upstairs watching television. My brothers each planned to spend the night at a friend's house. I grabbed my book and settled down to read for a few minutes until Bill arrived.

The half hour sounded on the clock, startling me. This was no longer *around* nine. By now, the bonfires would be lit, Ronni would be wondering at my absence, and the first of the competitions getting started.

But what if something had happened? What if he'd been in an accident on his way to pick me up? No, everyone at the bonfires would hear about it, and Ronni would find a way to call me.

Which meant… *Bill stood me up?* Not possible. He wouldn't be *that* rude, would he?

Grandma peeked into the living room. "Oh. I assumed you left without telling me. He's late."

Like I don't know that. And the disapproval in her voice only annoyed me further.

I fingered Nora Jean's beads. "He said he'd pick me up, so I guess I keep waiting."

"Do you want me to drive you down?"

Tempting. But if we left, and Bill arrived, then what? Besides, I'd feel like a fool showing up alone at this point. "No. Either he shows up, or I don't go." And if I missed the Bonfires, I'd never forgive him.

I should've known. Ronni had always thought Bill was a jerk, and since she had pegged Melissa as a liar as soon as she'd met her in seventh grade, I knew my best friend was a good judge of character. My mother's words backed her up. Mom constantly reminded me about all the wonderful things Daddy used to do for her back in high school. I'd just figured my dad was extra special, and I couldn't expect somebody *that* good. But I sure expected something better than missing the Bonfires.

"Make sure to tell me you're leaving once he gets here." Grandma went back upstairs, and I went back to my book. Bill wouldn't be at my door, and I didn't want to think about it. It was time to escape from reality.

At ten-thirty, I stopped reading, sent Black Jack outside for his evening business, and tucked him into his bed upon his return. I left one lamp lit in the living room and headed up the stairs before my parents returned. I didn't want to face them.

Grandma's door was blessedly closed. Krista had been sound asleep since eight. A hot bath didn't thaw the icy rage inside of me. I didn't even cry. The best, most anticipated night of my life had turned into a disaster. Like Scarlett O'Hara in *Gone With the Wind*, I pulled the covers to my chin and consoled myself that tomorrow would be another day.

Only I woke up with no plan. Just more misery.

Dishes clinked in the kitchen. The aroma of

pancakes spiraled its way through my open bedroom door. Not hungry.

Krista's rumpled sheets thrown to the foot of the bed greeted me as I opened my eyes. The clock radio read 8:11. Too late to go to early church which meant I had to act sociable at the late service. How had I slept so long?

Any moment, Daddy would be calling me down to Sunday breakfast. With Paul and Wade gone, why were we even having a huge breakfast?

And by now, my parents would know all about last night's fiasco. Grandma would've told them, and she'd cluck all over the place like a sympathetic chicken once I got downstairs. Mom was going to ask a hundred questions that I didn't want to answer. Daddy would...I didn't know what Daddy would do. He wasn't the type to march over to Bill's house with a shotgun in hand, but if he hated to see his little girl grow up, he'd hate to see her hurting even more.

Krista toe-skipped into the room. Without braces, her heels didn't touch the floor. She tugged my hand to pull me out of bed. Managing a small smile, I let her drag me out from under the covers.

I pointed to the closet. "Let me get dressed and I'll be right down."

She got the idea and skipped back out of the room.

I slipped on a pair of old jeans and my favorite T-shirt. The previous night's outfit mocked me as it hung over the desk chair. Carefully, I folded the shorts and lay them in the bureau drawer. The beautiful tank top joined its sisters in the closet. I'd never wear those two pieces together again.

I stood in front of the mirror before going

downstairs. *Did I look as tragic as I felt?* A serious girl returned my gaze, but she often looked like that.

    I squared my shoulders. Time to face the music.

Chapter 16:
Secret Place

Mommy and Daddy
Were mad. Debbie stayed home from
Church. I don't know why.

Awkward silence greeted my entrance.

Krista, oblivious, chowed down on two pancakes loaded with syrup. Daddy kept his back to me as he concentrated on the griddle. Mom offered a smile overflowing with pity. And Grandma made her exit from the kitchen by kissing my cheek. Better than getting fussed over.

I slid into my place at the table. "Is it okay if I skip church today?" I might as well enter the imminent battle with guns blazing.

Mom returned fire. "I'm sorry to hear about last night, Debbie, but that doesn't give you an excuse to sulk. You're going to church."

"I could just use some time alone. Figure things out. I can't do that at church when everybody expects a smile and asks if I enjoyed the Bonfires, and blah, blah, blah."

Mom didn't care. She had other things on her mind. "I hope you're finally willing to consider all our warnings about this boy."

I really didn't need that slap in the face.

"Dorothy."

We both heard the rebuke in Daddy's voice, and Mom got all defensive. "Well, we *have* warned her. Bill's only been to the house, what? Once or twice the whole year? You almost *lived* at my house at that age."

Daddy ignored her. Sliding the pancakes off the griddle and onto the serving plate, he carried them to the table and squeezed my shoulder.

"Why don't you take a walk on the beach and sort it all out?"

He really understood me.

I almost cried. "Thanks."

"You're spoiling her, Grant."

Daddy ignored that, too.

As a peace offering, I volunteered to clean up all the breakfast mess, and once finished, I rolled my bike out of the garage. Then I rolled it back in.

If I headed for the ocean, I'd park at the Village Beach and see the remnants of last night's celebrations. Not helpful.

Right now, I needed my secret place. Only a block away from home. Clumps of bushes dotted the hill sloping up from an inlet of the bay. Four of those bushes had grown into a circle leaving an empty center—a perfect hideout—my secret place. I could belly-crawl through a low opening and reach that empty space. If anyone passed by, they couldn't see me.

With Black Jack at my heels, I walked the short distance to the meadow and slid under branches through the passage. A doggy nuzzle was just what I needed, but Black Jack's nose snuffled the ground, hot on a rabbit trail or something. Which offered no comfort to *me*.

The morning held a chill. Hugging my knees to my chest, I waited. Nora Jean's necklace, anchored at the back of my neck, draped over my knees, and lay across my shins. One finger caressed the beads. Sometimes, God's peace surrounded me like a warm blanket, but even if it didn't, just being alone and breathing in the salt air helped me to rebalance.

I whispered, "So it's over. Bill is no longer my boyfriend. Maybe he never really was."

God seemed to agree.

"So many people think Bill is cool, and all I ever wanted was for people to think I was cool, too. Is that so bad?"

By His silence, did God mean that wanting popularity *was* bad?

I ran down a mental list of popular girls in my class. Thea, Andrea, Liz, Leigh, Melissa, Monica, Linda, Suzanne. I didn't get along with Leigh and Melissa, but I admired the rest of them. They weren't bad. Were they?

Do they want people to like them?

Was that God's thought or mine? Sometimes, it was hard to tell. I waited.

The voice in my head repeated. *Do they want people to like them?*

Whether it was my subconscious or God asking the

question, the answer seemed obvious.

"Of course, doesn't everybody?"

Compare Thea and Leigh.

Okay… The God-and-me conversation continued in my head. "Thea and I have the exact same class schedule. I see her all the time. She's nice to everybody. She laughs a lot. She's pretty, but her teeth are crooked.

"I try to be nice to everybody, too, but I'm much more serious. And I'm not as pretty, but—"

Compare Thea and Leigh. Not Thea and you.

Oh. I reset my inner monolog back to the starting line. "Thea is nice, and Leigh is only nice to certain people. Popular people. They both laugh a lot, but Thea laughs when she's happy or has heard something funny. Leigh laughs at other kids, especially when she thinks she's better than they are. Thea is pretty and doesn't even wear lipstick. Leigh looks like a model out of *Vogue.*"

A hint of approval fringed my thoughts, and I continued my comparisons.

"Thea seems to be true to herself. Like when we tried out for cheerleading, she knew she probably wouldn't make it, but she didn't seem to mind. She always shows interest in what people are doing, really cares for them. Leigh only cares about herself. She tried out for cheerleading just so people would see her status. She doesn't know squat about football and basketball. With all that make-up, she's striking to look at—and people remember her. She figures out exactly the right things to say so her audience is entertained. So, I think *Leigh* wants to be popular, but Thea doesn't think about popularity."

Which way for you? Thea or Leigh?

"I want to be like Thea. Or Ronni. Ronni might not be as popular, but she's happy with herself. At least, happier than I am with *my*self."

But.

"What? I know I'm not as good as Thea or Ronni. But I'm not as bad as Leigh."

Silence.

I sulked.

Why did you want to be a cheerleader? Why do you want popularity?

Now we were back to square one. "Because if people like me, I will be happier. Is that so bad?"

YOU will be happier?

My words boomeranged back to selfish me.

A little poke from God felt like a heavyweight boxer's punch to the gut. I was far more like Leigh than Thea. Even worse, I didn't know how to stop being like her.

Black Jack wiggled into the hollow, licked my face, then lay down with his head on my lap as I massaged behind his ears.

How could I stop caring about what others thought of me? How could I be happy with just plain old me? How could I start to care about other people more than I cared about myself?

Let Me help you.

Chapter 17:
Pushing Back Misery

The whole family
Will go to the beach. I love
Water on my toes!

Black Jack and I slipped in through the front door. Good thing Grandma left it unlocked since I walked out without a key. She must think crooks take Sundays off. The kitchen clock read eleven-twenty. Everybody would be back by noon. I wandered outside to the deck and settled into the chaise lounge while Black Jack collapsed at my feet for a midday nap.

Was I happy yet? No. But I wasn't the mess from three hours ago. Impressions from time in my secret place rippled through me.

What to do about Bill ended up pretty simple. Hard. But simple. Forget about him. When—*if*—he showed up at my locker next week, I'd let him know I wouldn't be playing his games anymore. I'd resigned from the position of doormat.

How could I love people the way Thea and Ronni

seemed to? Maybe I could start with my family and Ronni. Too often, things had been all about me. Ronni, especially, deserved better. And I'd be babysitting five brothers and sisters this summer, ages eleven down to three. I could think of ways to love those kids while I was taking care of them. It must be hard to have both parents gone from breakfast until dinner.

Everyone arrived home at once, as if cued by a stage director's call for action. Paul appeared from the woods. Wade thumped through the kitchen yelling, "Anybody home?" The station wagon rumbled into the driveway, and the phone rang.

Paul hopped up the three steps to the deck. "I didn't see you at the Bonfires. Where were you?"

My little brother got to go, but not me? Misery returned in a hurry.

"You were supposed to be at Craig's house."

"We were. And we walked down to the beach to check it all out."

Why didn't Ronni and I do that last year? Because girls aren't supposed to wander around by themselves after dark. Add a little more self-pity to the mix.

"So where were you two?" That protective, big-brother glint appeared in his eyes.

Bill never showed up? *Should I be worried instead of angry?* No, if something awful had happened the whole town would know by now.

Wade shouted through the kitchen window. "Debbie, phone for you."

"Be right there," I shouted back. "And it's not what you're thinking," I said to Paul as I stepped inside.

Wade handed me the phone. "It's Ronni."

Good. No matter what happened, I wasn't ready to

talk to Bill. Mom, Dad, and Krista bustled in as I said hello into the phone.

Ronni peppered me with questions. "What happened? Where were you? How could you skip the Bonfires? The freshmen might have won the song contest if you'd been there."

I edged into the den for a little distance from the noise of an entire family gathering items for lunch. "I can't talk right now. Can I come over in about an hour? And believe me, what happened last night was not my idea."

"Okay. If Vickie is here, we'll just take a walk." Ronni's little sister, only a year younger than us, always wanted to stick her nose into our business.

"Right."

Ronni giggled. "I think last night was the best night of my life."

Somebody was happy. That made one of us.

Nobody brought up the subject of Bill at lunch. Paul glanced my way every few minutes, but kept his mouth shut.

Once everyone finished, Mom stood and gathered plates from around the table. "As soon as we're cleaned up, gather your stuff for the beach."

Uh-oh. Mom had a big Memorial Day planned for the whole family on the beach, right down to a refrigerator filled with picnic food for dinner. Even Grandma was going. I'd forgotten all about it.

"And Debbie, while I pack the dinner cooler, you fill the drinks cooler."

"But I told Ronni I'd come over after lunch."

The fire in her eyes should have turned me into instant ashes. "You've known about today for over a week. And how come you weren't feeling social enough to go to church, but you have no trouble being social with Ronni?"

"You didn't go to church?" Wade might as well have said, "You robbed a bank?"

"Daddy let me have some time alone. To think."

"You must have gotten in a lot of trouble if you had a two-hour time-out." Now Paul was probing for answers.

I sighed. "I was upset. Bill stood me up."

How humiliating to have to admit it. If I weren't so depressed, I would've laughed at the shock and anger on my brothers' faces. Their desire to protect their sister reminded me of what they did for Krista last month. Somehow, knowing that eased my pain. Just a little. But this time, no sibling meeting was needed. No action would be taken, not by them. They couldn't protect me from the hurt that had happened, and I already knew how to protect myself from future incidents.

"Just let it go, okay?" I eyed both brothers. "And if you ever think I'm getting all ga-ga over the wrong guy, tell me." Their stone faces didn't clue me in as to whether they were with me. I turned to Mom. "The time I spent alone this morning really helped." I doubted she'd understand if I said God was talking to me. "And I owe Ronni an explanation of why I didn't show up last night."

"You can get together with Ronni a little later." Mom was adamant.

"And I don't want Ronni to wait." Sometimes, Mom was only interested in what *Mom* wanted.

The thought stopped me cold. If I argued with Mom, I was only looking for what *I* wanted.

"How about this? I go over to Ronni's for an hour, then I ride my bike to the beach and join you."

Mom contemplated the offer, her face grim. "You be there before three."

Ronni and I sat cross-legged facing each other on her bed. She slowly shook her head. "I always knew Bill wasn't good enough for you, but I never thought he would do something like this."

"I should've listened to you back in September."

"Now I feel guilty." She pounded a steady beat on the footboard with her fist. "I was so ticked off with you, at first. Roger was waiting for me, and I thought the four of us could have a great time together."

"So Bill ruined your night, too."

"Only for the first fifteen minutes." The drumbeat stopped as she halted an involuntary giggle. "That's why I feel so guilty. First, I was mad, then I was having such a good time, I forgot to even worry about where you were." Her eyes widened. "What if you'd been in an accident? And if I'd known you were sitting in your house waiting and waiting…"

"You would have stayed with Roger because you've been waiting and waiting for two *years* for the guy."

She hung her head. "I know. Now I feel even more guilty."

"Don't be." I slid off the bed. "Nothing would have helped me last night. Not even you. Besides, you were stuck there until your dad came back to pick you up."

Silence. Apparently, I hadn't convinced her.

"I have to get back home and head for the beach like I promised. Walk me back and tell me all about the best night of your life."

Ronni's normal exuberance returned. "It was like a fairy tale. He was waiting for me at the top of the dune like Prince Charming standing at the top of the palace steps…"

She told me the whole wonderful story, the story I wished were mine. I really was happy for her, but it was over for me and Bill.

No boyfriend.

No group to belong to.

Two years ago, I found myself in the same boat. I was back to square one.

At least this time I had Ronni.

Chapter 18:
Surfer Beach

Everybody went
To the beach except Debbie.
She had her own beach.

As I straddled my bike on Monday morning, I slung the small duffel bag over the handlebars. It held a beach towel, tanning lotion, a watch, and enough money to buy lunch at the concession stand. After doing the Memorial Day Weekend thing with my family at the Air Force beach on Sunday, I hadn't planned to go back to the Village Beach on Monday, but Ronni begged. *Why?* She'd spend all of her time with Roger. I told her I'd think about it. What I didn't want to think about was how to handle things once Bill got there.

He hadn't called, so whenever I saw him again, was he going to act like nothing had happened? Or would he ignore me? His way of letting me know we broke up? Wow. *That* took courage.

But how could I *not* go to the beach? Sunshine and

salt breeze called to me like the sirens luring Odysseus to his doom. Besides, Memorial Day was the official opening of the summer season, even though we still had almost a month of school left.

Just as my foot pushed on the pedal to roll out, Paul swung open the screen door and bellowed, "Mom says to come back inside for a minute."

I'd made my bed, brushed my teeth, rinsed out my orange juice glass, and put it in the dishwasher. There were no chores on a holiday. What had I missed?

I toed the kickstand in place and turned back toward the house.

Grandma and Krista sat at the kitchen table playing Go Fish while Mom wiped down the counters. Krista grinned and pointed to her thick pile of cards. She was winning. I gave her a thumbs-up.

Mom glanced at me, then returned to a stubborn sticky spot. "Debbie, will you be home by five?"

"Probably."

She turned at my glum tone and offered a half smile of pity but said nothing further on the sore subject of the weekend. "Grandma plans to go out to dinner with friends. Daddy and I are going out, too, since he doesn't have to return to Jersey until tomorrow night. I'll leave a salad in the fridge. Can you boil some hot dogs and open a bag of chips for all you kids?"

Gee, even Wade could do that much. "Sure."

"Then have Paul and Wade clean up."

That sounded better. Cooking was more fun than cleaning. "Okay."

"Good." She tossed the dish cloth in the sink, then gave me a quick hug. "Have a good time today. There are plenty of other fish in the sea."

I groaned. What a worn-out phrase.

She didn't back down. "The words may be trite, but they're true."

"So how come you only ever wanted one fish?"

She smirked. "Actually, there were two, but I chose the right one early on."

"And Bill's not the right one, huh?"

"Not by a long shot."

She had me there.

As I crossed the bay bridge over to Dune Road, a car slowed beside me. *Not Bill. Please, not Bill.* A surfboard was strapped to the roof of a sleek Dodge Charger. Good. Not Bill.

A girl's voice called from the passenger side. "Hey, Debbie, you heading for the Village Beach?"

I'd hardly seen Mary since she invited me to her party last fall. I still felt guilty about that. "Yeah," I answered.

"Meet you over there."

Weird. She always went to Quogue's beach a few miles east.

I crossed Dune Road straight into the parking lot and stopped at the bike racks.

Mary stood by the car, a wide smile on her face. "You want to come with us to Quogue instead?"

Had she heard about my humiliation already? And who was "us?" But if I stayed here, I'd have to explain to ten other girls why Bill wasn't lying next to me on a beach towel.

"I guess I could bike over."

A deep voice rumbled from the driver's side of the car. "Leave the bike here and hop in the back."

I peeked in the window. Al Stephenson? He was a junior with a bad boy reputation. I hadn't known Mary was his girlfriend.

Arguments raced through my mind. The only reason to go to the Village Beach instead of Quogue's was Ronni. Although she certainly didn't need me. Once everyone knew she was Roger's girlfriend, they would suddenly adore her.

I pictured a feline Melissa meowing her way to Ronni's side and rubbing against her ankles. *Please be my friend,* says the nice kitty. Ronni had better be on her guard when the claws came out.

So, why *not* go with Mary? She'd always been kind to me. Maybe her friends were much nicer than I ever gave them credit for. Maybe they'd be smarter and figure out I was shy, not stuck-up.

It could be my own secret experiment. Would this new group accept me, try to get to know me? If I had a good time today, I'd know that at least some people found me likeable. If I didn't have a good time, I could blame it on myself. Just not all that likeable.

But what if I didn't get a ride back? Would my parents care that I wasn't where I said I'd be? There weren't any phone booths at the beach so I could call.

The answers galloped past at the same speed. I could walk back to my bike if I had to. Most of the kids at the Village Beach pretty much ignored me anyway. As long as I got home by dinner, my parents didn't need to know.

I jumped as a car horn blared.

"It's not a life or death decision." Al leaned out the open window. "You comin' or not?"

I locked my front wheel into the rack and hopped in the car.

We drove past the entrance to Quogue's public beach. My head swiveled to stare out the rear window as the entry gate receded from my view. When I turned forward again, Mary greeted me with a smug grin.

"I never said we were going to *that* beach." She dipped her chin like she was drawing me into a conspiracy. "Al doesn't have a season pass, so we always go to Surfer Beach."

I'd heard of that but didn't know where it was. The surfer crowd didn't advertise its whereabouts. Why pack "their" beach with a bunch of jocks, or worse, summer tourists?

Mary waited, seeming to expect a reaction.

I couldn't think of anything intelligent to say so just stumbled with, "I've never been there."

Al snorted. "Of course not."

I guessed that meant he figured me for being too goody-goody to hang out with surfers. Which made me more nervous than ever because, basically, he was right. Every surfer I knew at school was a pot-smoker, skipped classes a lot, and didn't seem interested in college. As a singer, I would never smoke anything whether it was legal or not, I loved school, and I worked for good grades so I could get into the college I wanted.

What was I doing in a strange car heading to a

strange beach with no way to contact my parents if I needed help?

Storm clouds of doom hovered in my future. People would be smoking weed in broad daylight, and if the police wanted to, they could raid the place. I could end up in jail. *Then* I'd have a phone available to call home.

Meanwhile, we traveled farther and farther from my bike.

Al turned into a narrow parking lot of packed-down sand filled with a dozen cars and trucks. A rickety set of wooden stairs was built over the dune. No clubhouse, no concessions, and…no restrooms? Better not drink anything offered to me. *If* anything was offered to me.

While Al retrieved his board, Mary and I climbed the steps over the dune. For a moment, it didn't matter that I barely knew a soul as a panorama of sea, sand, and a colorful array of surfboards spread out before us. We headed down the steps on the ocean side of the dune, and Al raced ahead to join a stocky guy on the beach. Their conversation seemed pretty lively, and Al pointed in our direction.

I yanked on Mary's arm once we stepped on the sand. "Is something going on that I don't know about?"

Her smile faltered. "What do you mean?"

It was bad enough that I never tried to be a friend after going to her party. Even worse, all I could think of was how to stay in the good graces of Bill's group where Mary wasn't included. *How could I put this without insulting her?*

"I'm…I'm not sure why you asked me here."

She frowned. "I figured you were alone."

So, she knew about the Bonfires. Word travels fast.

I stared at my feet, toes digging into the sand. "I didn't realize the whole school already knew Bill and I broke up."

"You and Bill broke up?" The surprise in her voice wasn't faked.

"You mean, you didn't know?" *Debbie, you are such an idiot.*

"No! When did that happen?"

I heaved a sigh. "Saturday night, I guess. But he didn't have the guts to tell me."

"That's terrible." She squeezed my arm. "True confession time, huh?" She offered an embarrassed smile. "Al saw you on your bike, said you had a cute figure, and maybe Rocky would enjoy your company." Before I could respond, she rushed on. "But I wanted your company, too. I just don't fit in with Al's friends."

Somehow, her words gave me a little more confidence. I grinned. "That makes two of us." I inclined my head toward Al and the other guy. Rocky? Was that his name? "So why Al?"

She blushed, and the ocean breeze whipped her curls to a frothy tangle. "He's gorgeous. And he likes me. I don't know why."

I'd said the same about Bill. Until Saturday night.

We joined the guys. I'd seen Rocky at school, but juniors and freshmen didn't have a lot in common. He eyed me up and down like a fisherman admiring his latest catch.

"Hey, Debbie." The dark wavy hair and a smile to rival Burt Reynolds' set my pulse racing.

"Hi." Should I add a comment about surfing? No. I didn't know the right jargon. Better to keep my mouth shut.

"Let me introduce you around." He grabbed my hand and almost dragged me to the group of kids lounging in between surfboards.

A limp hand raised in greeting, a silent nod, and they went back to lying in the sun or puffing on bongs. At least, that's what I thought they were. I wasn't about to ask.

I settled on my towel and gazed at the ocean. Al dropped his yellow board and an Army camo knapsack next to Mary, and Rocky dragged his dark blue surfboard close to my other side. With its gray stripe down the center, it looked classy, but it must've been invisible in the water.

Al cozied up on Mary's oversized towel, placing an arm around her shoulder. Rocky sat in the sand next to me. What should I say? What would Ronni say? What would I like to know about him?

"How long have you been surfing?"

"Since I was twelve." He stroked the board but didn't add anything else.

Now what?

"Tell her your Hawaii story."

I turned toward Al's voice in time to see him wink at Rocky.

"Sure," Rocky said. "Best shark story ever."

For the next twenty minutes, maybe more, he told me a fantastical tale of traveling to Hawaii on vacation, renting a surfboard for the first time, every possible detail on how he learned to surf, and he finished off with a final run side by side with a great white. Less than halfway through the saga, I glanced at Mary. She grinned and shook her head, adding a dramatic eye roll.

I lay back on the towel, soaking in the sun and listening to Rocky drone on. No need for me to add comments. Rocky was doing great all by himself. If the story ever finished, I could ask for another. He was probably full of them, and I wouldn't have to talk at all.

Al's bellow thundered through the breeze. "Tide's coming in."

No "Surf's up!" like in Frankie Avalon movies.

Guys and girls alike scrambled to their feet, grabbed their boards, and plunged into the sea. It didn't look like Rocky would offer to teach me how to surf. Should I be insulted or relieved?

Mary hadn't budged from her towel.

"You don't surf?" I asked her.

She opened one eye. "I tried it. Once. Decided I'd look better in a dry bikini than snorting water out of my nose after a wipe-out."

Good. I wasn't the only one worried about stuff like that. And as long as the tide was rising, I could work on my tan and not worry about what to say to people I barely knew.

Chapter 19:
No Excuses

Daddy is angry
With Debbie. What did she do?
I want to hug her.

I pulled the wristwatch from my duffle bag. Three-thirty. After watching the surfers for hours, "disappointment" was the only word that came to mind. The Atlantic Ocean's waves were tame ripples compared to what I'd seen in Gidget movies, yet even the best surfers in this group fell off their boards a lot.

Mary and I had walked along the shore for a mile or so to the Quogue beach, used their restroom, grabbed a hot dog and a soda, and walked back. Splashing in knee-deep water had cooled us off. You can't swim at a surfer beach without spending all your energy avoiding out-of-control surfboards. I didn't try. For the last hour or so, we were back to roasting ourselves to a golden tan, front and back, as if we were marshmallows.

I tapped Mary's arm already tawny from half a day in the sun.

She shaded her eyes to look at me. "Mmmm?"

"Is Al going to be able to take me back to my bike in an hour?"

She frowned and sat up. "He'll stay till the tide's almost out. That'll be a while."

"Then I'd better get going. It'll take over an hour to walk." I pulled up my towel and walked away from her to shake the sand out of it.

Mary followed me. "Before you walk all that way, let me ask him." She trapped her lower lip between her front teeth.

Why would asking him for a favor make her nervous?

She trotted to the water's edge and intercepted the yellow surfboard as soon as it reached the sand. Al stood in the shallows, an expression of impatience on his face while Mary spoke with her hands as much as with her mouth. He gave a short nod and headed back into the waves.

"You're good," she announced upon return to her towel. "He said to just call him out of the water at four-thirty."

"Great. Another hour of beach time." I added a dot of Coppertone to my nose. It always burned first.

"Better get your shoulders, too." She pressed a finger to my skin, and white contrasted with a medium pink.

I slathered the lotion over every part of my body exposed to the sun.

At four-thirty we both stood and waved to Al.

He ignored us, but Rocky glided in. "Whaddya need?"

"Al said he'd give me a ride back now."

Rocky stared at me in amazement. "Now? We've

got a good two hours of great waves."

I shrugged. "That's what he said."

He shrugged back. "I'll go get him."

He paddled to the group sitting beyond the breakers and leaned over to say something to Al, who looked back at me and Mary. He made no move in our direction.

Instead, Rocky rode a couple of small waves to get back to us. "He says you'll have to wait."

Panic and anger whirled into an inferno of temper. "That's just great. I would've started out an hour ago if he hadn't said he'd take me." I spun away from him. "Is this my weekend for super-jerks, or what."

I shook out the towel, and a shower of sand sprayed all over Rocky. "Sorry. None of this is your fault."

He gave me an easy smile, despite the sand thrown in his face. "So, you've endured a weekend of super-jerks?"

I said that out loud? I silently added *and a weekend of humiliation* to that last statement.

"Sorry," I repeated. "*You* weren't one of them." I pulled shorts and shirt out of the duffle bag, then stuffed my towel into it.

"What are you going to do?" he asked.

"I'll walk to the Village Beach."

"But that'll take almost as long as if you wait for Al."

"As long as I'm going to be late, I'd rather walk than wait for *that* super-jerk."

"If you hitch a ride, you won't be late."

I jammed the suntan lotion into the bag. "With my luck this weekend, some pervert would pick me up. Or my next-door neighbor would come along and tell my parents I was hitchhiking. Doomed or busted either way."

"Wait five minutes, and I'll take you." Rocky ran back to the shore and retrieved his board.

My anger evaporated like dew in the desert. *He'd do that for me?* Definitely *not* a super-jerk. I slipped my shirt over my head, then almost landed on my behind when sand shifted under one foot while the other struggled to slide through the leg of my shorts. *No more humiliation, please.* I zipped up and looked around for Mary. Where did she go? Her towel lay empty and rumpled on the sand.

I turned to the water. Al was back beyond the breakers. No Mary. I scanned the whole beach. There she was, her neon orange bikini easily visible as she headed toward the jetty. I ran to catch up.

"Rocky's going to give me a ride. Sorry I have to leave in such a hurry, but I'm still going to be late getting home, even with his help."

Mary's shoulders slumped. "I shouldn't have asked you to come along. I got you in trouble."

"I'll be fine. Maybe we can do this again. Plan for it."

She shook her head. "Not at Surfer Beach. I think I'm done with Al. How rude can you get?"

"So, we're now officially The Sisterhood of Girls Who Swore Off Super-Jerk Boyfriends." I grinned at the name. For the first time since the Bonfires, my mood lightened. I'll see you at school, and we can figure out when we can meet for another day of fun in the sun."

A smile lit Mary's face. "Deal."

Rocky got me to the Village Beach at 4:50, and I pedaled home at breakneck speed.

Brandishing a small paring knife, Mom greeted me at the door. Loudly. "Where have you been?"

And why are they home? "I'm less than five minutes late."

She whipped around and stalked into the kitchen. No question about whether I should follow. "Daddy drove over to the beach to let you know you didn't have to worry about dinner and could stay an extra hour if you wanted. We decided not to go out after all." She sliced the cucumber with vicious strokes. "And lo and behold, he couldn't find you. Your bike was there, but no one had seen you, not even Ronni."

My entire insides froze. Mom's voice faded. *My father went out on the beach and questioned the whole group?* Any hopes for my social life were over.

Mom hadn't stopped talking, and her next words snapped me back to attention, pulverizing those hopes once and for all. "…call the police."

"You called the *police*?"

She dropped the knife into the sink, giving it a look of disdain I was sure was meant for me. "I said— apparently you weren't listening—I said I *wanted* to call the police." Her volume had dropped, but her words hissed with venom. "Your father wouldn't let me."

I remembered to breathe again.

"He told me to wait. If you didn't come home when you were expected, *then* we would call the police."

And thank you, Rocky, for the lift. If I'd had to walk to my bike, the police would've been searching for me right now.

She stood, fists on hips, as her eyes bored into mine. I gazed at the floor to avoid her accusations. Who knew a simple change of plans would cause this much trouble?

"So where were you? You have nothing to say for yourself?" The volume dial soared.

"I was with Mary Franketti at a different beach. There wasn't a phone."

She waved away my explanation. "Go talk to your father. I'm too upset to deal with you right now."

"Where is he?" My voice sounded like I was six years old.

"On the deck."

Daddy, with Krista on his lap, sat in the rocker. Black Jack leaned up against it while Dad gave him a neck massage. Mom the Tornado had dropped me into the calm and beautiful Land of Oz.

If Daddy was just as angry with me, though, I wouldn't be able to hold back a hurricane of tears.

"Mom told me to talk to you."

He nodded. "I heard."

Of course, he could hear the whole conversation through the open window. "So, you know what happened."

He pointed to the second rocker while still scratching Black Jack behind the ears. "No. Other than the word 'Mary,' I couldn't hear *your* answers very well."

I sat, took a deep breath, and started to recount

how my plans changed.

Krista's eyes darted back and forth between my face and Daddy's. She knew something serious had happened.

What went on in her mind as she tried to guess what people said? And if no one took her aside to explain, did she feel sad and left out, or did she drop it and move on? Maybe I'd remember to act it all out for her later.

When I finished my tale, Daddy summarized things for me. "Okay. No harm intended, and no harm came to anyone."

"Right."

His reaction sounded promising.

"And let me recap events. You arrived at the Village Beach, talked with Mary, locked up your bike. Then you got into her boyfriend's car, someone you barely knew, and drove to a place that your mother and I know nothing about."

"Yes."

Not so promising anymore.

"The boyfriend refused to take you back to the bike when you asked him to. And you were stranded."

"If he hadn't told me to wait the extra hour, I would've walked back to my bike. It's not that far."

He stopped me with a look. My throat closed as tears gathered.

"Instead of walking back, you accepted a ride from another stranger."

I remained silent. Rocky wasn't exactly a stranger, but it wouldn't be wise to point that out.

"You retrieved your bike, rode home, and arrived at the agreed-upon time."

I nodded.

He regarded me for a moment, disappointment in his eyes. My tears spilled over.

Krista looked like she wanted to cry, too. She'd seen that expression from Daddy when he disciplined *her*. She knew I was in trouble.

Daddy turned his gaze to Black Jack, who was blissfully unaware of any tension thanks to the amazing back rub. Daddy lifted his hand from the dog and pointed at me. "I understand why you felt free to change your plans. But here's where you made your mistake. The Village Beach does have a phone."

"But—"

He held up his hand to stop any excuses. "No phone booth, but there's an office behind the concession area. You should have asked to use it."

And I'd have been a total dork telling Mary, *let me see if I can use the phone in the office to call my parents.* Al probably would've taken off without me.

"If your new friend didn't want to wait for you to communicate with home, then I'm not impressed with your choice of friends."

My lips trembled. I wasn't impressed with my choice of friends either. Not Al, not the surfers, not Bill, not my old group.

Most of all, I wasn't impressed with me.

I was an awful person. I had jumped into a beautiful pool to join Bill and the popular people swimming in it, and I'd discovered it was a sewer. To get away from the stink of it, I had tried out a new pool, which wasn't any better.

"I have one question for you," Daddy continued. "And I want you to think carefully before you answer.

If Mom hadn't confronted you as soon as you walked in the door, would you have told us where you were today?"

My first thought? *No.*

I wouldn't have wanted to face an interrogation. But maybe I *would* have been honest once I had a little time to think it over.

If I answered with an automatic "yes," I'd still be in trouble. For lying. Mom says whatever I'm thinking shows on my face. I couldn't tell a convincing lie to save my life.

After way too long of a silence, I settled for the most honest answer. "I don't know."

Chapter 20:
Fishing

Debbie doesn't smile.
Won-ni doesn't visit me
Anymore. Why not?

Ronni joined me like usual on our walk to school on Tuesday. "Where were you? You keep disappearing on me. First the Bonfires, then your dad comes looking for you on the beach." She stopped midstride on the sidewalk. "Are you mad at me?"

"Why would I be mad at *you?* You should be mad at *me.*"

As we passed a lilac bush with a few flowers still on it, I paused and twisted off a sprig of blossoms. They'd be shriveled by the end of the day. Like my life. "The whole thing with Bill and the Bonfires has just messed me up."

She nodded, but she wasn't about to let me off the hook completely. "So where were you yesterday? Once your dad showed up, everybody got curious."

I groaned. "How about when we get to school, you

go inside, and I'll keep walking. Right out of town."

She laughed. "It's not that bad."

Her easygoing smile and the twinkle in her eyes reminded me of when we met on the first day of school in eighth grade. Instant friendship then. Solid friendship now.

I told her every detail about the day before—from not wanting to face the people we usually hang out with, to the surfer beach, to getting busted as soon as I got home. "So, until next Monday, I'm grounded. No phone calls, no beach, no going anywhere except to and from school."

"No phone. And here I thought you just didn't want to talk to me."

The corner of my mouth barely lifted. "We'll have to do all of our talking at school for the next week. And we've only been talking about me. Was Roger at the beach with you?"

Her face clouded. "His lifeguard job at the Sunfish Club started on Saturday. Once school's out, Wednesdays will be his only days off."

So, she didn't have Roger *or* me with her yesterday. I'd really let her down. I was a worse coward than Bill.

Ronni patted my shoulder. "Don't feel bad. I understand why you didn't want to be there. I had a nice time once Thea and I started talking."

I had no right to a twinge of jealousy. If I'd spent the day with Mary, why shouldn't she enjoy being with Thea?

As Ronni dragged me through the school doors and we headed to our lockers, I watched to see if anyone noticed me. They did. Some grinned, some gave a thumbs-up. Not what I was expecting.

One guy whispered, "Mystery hideaway?" and winked at me.

I leaned closer to Ronni. "Why did John say that?"

She blushed. "After your dad left, everybody started wondering where you and Bill were. Both of you don't go to the Bonfires, neither of you show up at the beach, then your dad is searching for his missing daughter. You know what they're all thinking." She raised one eyebrow in a leer. Except Ronni's open, honest face wasn't capable of anything with a hint of nasty.

Nobody knew I'd been stood up except Ronni! And Mary. Which meant Daddy's appearance at the beach made it look like Bill and I were a modern version of Romeo and Juliet. Thanks to people jumping to the wrong conclusions, I was a celebrity. For five minutes anyway. My life was only *half* shredded.

Maybe when everybody found out Bill and I hadn't been together at all, they could jump to the next wrong conclusion that Rocky and I were a new item. Let them. I wouldn't mind. His kindness in leaving the waves to try to keep me out of trouble made him a hero in my book, and he was even better looking than Bill. But I had the feeling we had nothing in common. It would never work.

I skipped lunch to avoid running into my *former* boyfriend, but at the end of the day as I worked the combination lock, a familiar shoulder leaned against the locker next to mine.

Bill.

I waited for an apology, an explanation. I wanted to see him down on his knees begging forgiveness. Everyone hurrying for the buses could assume he was proposing.

"Hi, gorgeous. Sorry I missed the Bonfires, but me and Dave had a great weekend fishing. We took his dad's boat all the way to Montauk Point, spent two nights camping out on a beach and frying up what we caught."

While he droned on and on about bait, how to start a campfire, and who knows what else, I stopped listening and fiddled with the contents of my locker. His interests were no longer mine. As soon as I collected what I needed for homework, I would walk away, preferably with him in mid-sentence.

"So. How did the Bonfires go?" he asked.

Oh. He'd like to know about *my* weekend? The weekend that might've been okay if he'd made one little phone call to say his plans had changed. Just *one* teeny-weeny phone call, and I would've seen the Bonfires, would've danced around the freshman fire, would've added my voice to our cheer, would've sung with my class—and maybe we would've *won*. One itsy-bitsy phone call, and I would've met Ronni at the Village Beach, and I wouldn't be *grounded*.

In an effort to keep my face expressionless, I gently shut my locker before facing him. "How did the Bonfires go? I don't know. I wasn't there."

A startled blink from his adorable puppy dog eyes. No. *Manipulative* puppy dog eyes.

He removed his weight from the locker and stepped back. "You're pretty mad, huh?"

So much for keeping emotions off my face. "Yeah." If I said one more word, anyone left in the building would hear me clear to the science labs in the opposite wing upstairs.

Bill took another step backwards, his hands up in a calming motion like I was a lion ready to attack. "I'll give you time to cool off, and we can get together later."

I lifted one shoulder in reply.

He spun and walked away in his nonchalant amble, but it sped up to a power walk by the time he turned the corner of the gym hallway.

Like my mom told me, it was time to go fishing.

Chapter 21:
Fat With a T

Ow-ee, Ow-ee, Ow!
The doctor hurts my legs. Ow!
And braces stink, too.

Other fish in the sea? Apparently, I needed a different ocean. Not one fish thought I was worthy of interest for the entire last month of school. Once everyone found out I broke up with Bill—the football player breaks up with the girl, not the other way around—his buddies wouldn't even talk to me. Leigh and Melissa made sure the girls knew I'd been an idiot.

Rocky smiled at me if we passed in the hall, but that was it. I hadn't seen Mary since I'd left Surfer Beach. The only class we'd ever shared had been P.E. last fall. I switched to music theory in the spring while she moved on to a cooking class in home economics.

I could forget about ever having a boyfriend until I went to college. I could forget about a new group of friends, too. My social skills ranked as #1 klutz.

And I couldn't depend on Ronni alone. She had a

life. She had Roger.

Ronni and I still walked to school together, still ate lunch together—not at Bill's table anymore, but *Roger* walked her home. Ambling alongside them was just too weird, so I made excuses to stay longer after school. Ronni didn't object.

Since my babysitting job wouldn't start for another week, I spent the first day of summer vacation with Mom and Krista. At the orthopedic doctor's office.

He watched Krista walk, took the braces off, and observed as she tippy toed without them. So far, she hadn't smiled once. She'd learned a long time ago that doctors made her life painful, but she never threw a tantrum in front of them. Maybe she'd learned screaming at a doctor was a waste of energy. She always lost the battle.

He had her lie on her back on the examining table. Then he lifted one of her legs and pushed it toward her head causing the muscles on the backs of her thighs to stretch. When he forced her foot to flex, Krista winced.

Mom lifted one of the braces from the floor. "It's been awful trying to get her to wear these. Is there any end in sight?"

He checked his chart. "She's not quite four? We really want to keep stretching those muscles and tendons for at least three more years."

Three years might as well be forever for a little kid. Krista fought Mom while putting the braces on in the mornings, then she slipped them off when Mom wasn't looking, which only brought another fight as

Mom wrestled them back on.

Mom sighed. "Between the deafness and these braces, this poor child endures one frustration after another. Plus, we're looking to get new hearing aids for her next year. Who knows what kind of behaviors those will cause? Is there *anything* you can suggest?"

The desperate look on Mom's face could've melted a heart of ice. The man glanced from Krista's legs to his chart and back to her legs. "The main weakness is from heel to knee. How about a compromise? In three months, when Krista turns four, we'll put her in below-the-knee braces. They're not as heavy, and she'll have a little more mobility."

Sunshine radiated from Mom's face.

He returned the smile. "It can be her birthday present from me."

Getting back to the car, we dropped lipreading for the moment.

"When you are four." I held up four fingers as I pointed to her.

"On your birthday," Mom added.

"New braces." I pointed to the braces and signed *new*.

Krista rolled her eyes.

"No! No! They will be different!" I touched her leg below the knee. "New braces."

"No more old braces." Mom touched high up on Krista's thigh and placed her other hand on her knee. "No more." She pretended to throw away the top portion of the brace.

Krista looked down at her legs with interest. "Smah?"

"Yes!" I clapped my hands. "They will be small

braces."

We enjoyed a happy ride home until the car started to bounce. *Thump-a-lumpa, thump-a-lumpa.*

"What is that?" I asked.

Mom grimaced. "Flat tire."

One good thing about the Long Island Expressway, there were lots of exits with lots of service stations. Within a minute of our bad luck, we bump-a-lumped into the first available gas station.

The man in charge sported greasy coveralls and a stout physique. Maybe he received most of his nutrition from the line of candy machines planted next to the cash register.

"Easy fix," he said. "You folks can sit in the waiting area." He pointed to three rickety chairs sitting against the wall across from the candy.

"Thank you," Mom dazzled him with her smile. "Do you mind if I use your phone to contact my husband? I think it's a local call."

"No problem." He helped himself to our car keys and drove our wounded vehicle into a service bay.

I caught a scurrying motion out of the corner of my eye. A long, skinny tail disappeared under the far-right vending machine. Mouse? Rat? I glanced at Mom. Her back was turned as she dialed the phone.

Had Krista seen it?

Yup. She slid off her chair and kneeled on the grimy floor before I could stop her. At which point, Mom turned back to face us and almost dropped the phone.

"Debbie! Get her off the floor." She snapped open her purse and pulled out a lemon-scented towelette. "Wipe her hands. And her knees." She gave a little shiver. "Hello, Grant? I've had some trouble…"

As I wiped Krista's hands, I screwed my face into an expression of disgust. "Dirty. Don't put your hands on the floor. Yuck."

She got the message but wasn't deterred from her quest to find the mysterious critter. She pointed to the machine. "Mouse." The word came out as clear and loud as the whistle ending Fred Flintstone's workday.

Mom heard it and immediately ignored whatever Daddy was saying on the other end of the line. "Where's a mouse?" Her attention returned to the phone. "A mouse in the tire? Of course not!" Back to me. "There's a mouse?"

I shrugged an "I don't know."

Back to Dad. "I don't know. Krista thought she saw a mouse." She glanced around the gas station's "office." "Which may be entirely possible."

The service guy came through the door wiping his hands on a dirty towel. "You're ready to go."

Mom's voice brightened. "We'll be home within the hour, dear." She hung up and smiled at the man. "Thank you very much. What do I owe you?"

"Two bucks should do it, ma'am." He lumbered around the end of the counter to reach the cash register while Mom dug in her purse for her wallet.

Through this short exchange of words, Krista had been staring at the man. She turned to me, pointed to the man with her lemon-clean finger, and for the first time in her life pronounced the final T of a word. Perfectly.

"Fat," she declared.

Mom turned an unlovely shade of red and batted down Krista's accusing finger. She handed me the keys.

"Take your sister to the car."

She gave the man *three* dollars as I skedaddled out of there dragging Krista at a pace that forced her to run in those heavy braces.

When Mom dropped into the seat behind the steering wheel, I asked, "Did you explain about Krista?"

Mom lay her forehead on the steering wheel. "Sometimes the less said, the better." She peeked back at Krista. "Of all the times…"

As she pulled onto the road, I told Krista, "Never call people fat."

She could read most of those words, but she looked puzzled.

I persisted. "It's mean." I drew my brows together in a mean look. "It's bad." I signed BAD. "Don't point and say *fat*." I aimed my finger at her belly.

She gazed down at her skinny self. "No faa!" Her little face was indignant.

"Not you. The man." I pointed toward the gas station, now some distance behind us. "You pointed to the man and said he was fat. When I said 'fat' and pointed at *you*, you were mad." I signed what words I knew in those sentences.

She continued to frown at me with a question in her eyes. She knew the difference between truth and lying. It was a lie to call her fat. But she had told the truth. Why would pointing out the truth be bad?

I tried to drive the point home. "It hurts people's feelings."

What a useless thing to say. She couldn't read all those words. And I didn't think she'd understand the word *feelings* anyway.

Sometimes, you just have to let it go. Wait for another day. I shrugged and sat back in my seat. Krista stared at me for a moment, imitated my shrug, then turned to watch the passing cars out the window.

Chapter 22:
The Smythe-Halseys

Debbie has a job.
Works for five days, home for two.
She says, "Play Sundays."

Mrs. Smythe-Halsey (Smythe with a long i) opened the front door of her modest, cedar-shingled home at my knock. "Welcome, Debbie. I'm so glad you'll be with us for the summer."

The lady looked like a petite version of Marilyn Monroe. Same platinum-blond pageboy hairstyle and pouty red, red lips, but her stick-figure couldn't fill out the movie star's curves. How did she have five kids and stay that skinny? My mom always bemoaned the fact that she gained five pounds after every pregnancy.

I stepped into a house that would make *Better Homes and Gardens* drool. This place was much bigger than it appeared from the street. A staircase curved on my left, and polished wood floors stretched toward the back wall. The huge living room started with formal furniture and progressed to casual as we advanced toward the French doors which opened to the back yard.

An afghan draped one corner of the plush sofa facing a large television console. Knickknacks graced every table as well as the mantel above the stone fireplace. If my family lived in this museum, Paul and Wade would have to be hog-tied and caged to prevent them from breaking anything.

Mrs. Smythe-Halsey turned left where the side wall ended, and lo and behold, my mom's fantasy kitchen slid into view. The countertops gleamed, uncluttered and spotless, while a long row of cupboards had the capacity to hold every small appliance known to modern America. And probably Europe, too.

The opposite wall contained the stove, refrigerator, dishwasher, and sink with a few narrow drawers and cupboards between them. A wood table formally set for eight spanned the center of the room. The little Smythe-Halseys must be angels of tidiness. Not one breakfast dish had been left in the sink. I'd have to brush up on housekeeping skills if I was expected to keep the kitchen this immaculate.

Mrs. S-H swept a hand in the direction of the refrigerator. "Deli meats and fruit are in here for lunches. Whole wheat in the bread drawer." She pointed to the overlarge drawer opposite the fridge. "Milk only, please, for drinks. Feed the whole gang at eleven. They only get a small breakfast before the doctor leaves for his office at seven. Millicent and Minerva can help you clean up, and while you're doing that, Montgomery and Maddock can keep an eye on Maximilian."

"Okay." Three-year-old Max couldn't be left unattended for ten minutes of clean-up? When I'd seen them at church, the kids sat dutifully in the pew, a descending line of five white-blond, look-alikes.

"I'll return between twelve and one to take all of you to the beach." She led me through the door at one end of the kitchen, and we were in a three-bay garage. Pails, shovels, tub toys, and Styrofoam noodles filled the shelves. "Let the children choose which beach toys they want and have them piled in the driveway as soon as lunch is finished."

"Do you have a limit of how many they can choose?"

"No more than two apiece." A smile flashed across her face and disappeared. Her hands fluttered in no particular direction like two butterflies hovering over a flower garden. "Any other questions?"

"Ummm…where are the children?"

Her hands darted upwards. "Of course, the children! They're watching television in the basement. This way."

We returned to the living area where she opened another door leading downstairs. "And please always keep this closed. Maximilian has no sense of danger. He'll tumble right down."

I always thought Max was able to walk just fine at church. Couldn't he handle stairs?

Turning left at the bottom step revealed another sprawling room which must have paralleled the living room above us. The two girls reclined on couches set perpendicular to one another while the older boys lounged on giant floor pillows. All four dedicated their attention to a giant console television where the Three Stooges were poking each other's eyes out.

"Where's Maximilian?" Mrs. Smythe-Halsey's already high voice rose another half step.

The children, apparently hypnotized by the program, didn't reply.

"Millicent. Millicent!"

With a bored expression, the oldest girl turned toward the strident sound.

"Where's Maximilian?"

Millicent pointed toward the far end of the room and returned her attention to Moe, Larry, and Curly. I scanned the length of the room but didn't see any little kid. A ping pong table and a foosball table sat side by side adjacent to the television area. Beyond them, a pool table was centered with a rack of cue sticks attached to the closest wall. Beyond that seemed to be a wet bar. The perfect party room. A tiny dart of jealousy jabbed me. My brothers and I would love a basement like this.

Mrs. S-H trotted toward the far wall and turned left. I followed her. Ah, just like the kitchen. No wonder I hadn't seen Max. Sure enough, a little boy sat on the floor, with a tumble of toys surrounding him. The kiddy-height shelves against each wall stood empty.

He greeted us with a grin. "Hi, Mommy."

"Maximilian Alexander Smythe-Halsey, you pick up this mess right now. Play with only one toy at a time."

A scowl replaced his happy face.

I felt sorry for him. "I can help you, if you want."

The scowl intensified. "Don't want."

His mother sighed. "I need to get going." She checked her watch. "I'll be back in about three hours."

She almost ran up the stairs. She never even introduced me, didn't give me any emergency contact number, and left me with five little strangers.

This was weird.

Max, or should I say Maximilian, remained sitting in his glorious mess of toys. I figured we could clean it up together before noon, so I returned to the TV area to get to know the other kids.

While Dr. Halsey and his family had always attended our church, I really didn't know any of them. The kids never went to Sunday school. The oldest girl was in Wade's class, fresh out of sixth grade, which made babysitting someone that close to me in age a little tricky. Why did Mrs. Smythe-Halsey ask me to babysit this summer? You'd think she'd want somebody older.

I waited for an ad to come on the TV before speaking to the group. "Hi, I'm Debbie. I live on the other side of the park."

They acted as if I hadn't spoken. All eyes were on the ad.

"Your mom says she's taking us to the beach after lunch. Which beach do you usually go to?" I hoped it wasn't the Village, although I'd never seen them there.

The youngest boy—Maddock?—answered. "Rotunda."

I blinked. *The* Rotunda? The swankiest beach club in Hampton Shores? Movie stars showed up there. I needed a new bathing suit.

But back to the information I needed now. "So, at the Rotunda, do you usually swim in the pool, or do you go to the beach? And who already knows how to swim?"

How come their mother didn't tell me any of this stuff?

No one answered. Their program was back on. Should I assert my authority or let them run this show? I stepped in front of the television.

"Hey." Montgomery reared up from his floor pillow.

I stared at him with what I hoped was a cool expression on my face. "How old are you, and are you allowed in the deep end of the pool?"

His eyes narrowed as he sized me up. "I'm eight, and I know how to swim. All of us know how except Maximilian."

I nodded a thank you. "So, when we're at the club, I can trust you guys not to drown, but should keep my attention on Max."

"Maximilian." Minerva corrected me.

"Really?" I focused on the younger girl. "A three-year-old boy with a fifty-year-old's name?"

Maddock sniggered, but Montgomery, Minerva, and Millicent remained serious.

Millicent set me straight. "Our parents named us with purpose."

I could already hear her mother's voice in the words, "with purpose."

"They *are* unique names," I allowed, "but wouldn't *you* prefer to have a nickname?"

Uneasy silence followed as the four traded glances all around.

"Calling all five of you is a mouthful." I bellowed a farmer's call to pigs. "Millic*ent*! Minerrrrva! Montgommmmmmery! Maaaddock! Maximillllian!"

"What?" Max called from the back of the room.

The others cracked up.

Minerva sobered first and raised an eyebrow in my

direction. "So what would you rather call us?"

I exaggerated a deep breath and bellowed once again. "Millie, Minnie, Monty, Maddy, Maxie! Get over here!"

Except for Millicent, they all cracked up again. "Mother won't like it if you call us that."

"I certainly want to do what pleases her," I responded. "But I also want to do what pleases you." I made sure to look each of them in the eye. "What do *you* like to be called?"

Maddock answered first. "I'd rather be Maddock than Maddy."

I nodded in agreement. "Maddock is just as short of a name anyway."

"I kind of like Monty." Montgomery grinned. "It sounds like jaunty." And he gave me a jaunty smile. For eight years old, he had a great vocabulary.

"I like my name," Minerva said. "Don't call me Minnie."

I couldn't resist a little tease. "You don't want to be a cartoon mouse?"

A quirk of her lips indicated she wanted to smile. "No."

I focused on Millicent.

She jutted her chin in defiance. "I don't need a babysitter."

"You're right."

Her attitude deflated like a tire leaking air, and I followed up with some reinforcing sealant. "I was babysitting my sister when I was your age, but there are four kids younger than you who do need a babysitter." Come to think of it, I was looking after Paul and Wade, too, when I was twelve. I looked her straight in the eyes. "Are you willing to be my assistant?"

She frowned as she thought about it. "They won't listen to me."

And that's why I'd been hired. "Then you help me with Maximilian and prove I can trust you, okay?"

She hesitated and glanced at her brothers. Some kind of signal passed between them.

"Okay." She smiled a little too sweetly.

Uh-oh. I tucked away my doubts for later.

"And I kind of like Millie."

Point taken. "So now, when I call you at the end of the beach day, it sounds like: Millie, Minerva, Monty, Maddock, Maxie!"

Maximilian ambled into the group. "No. I want Max."

I held out my hand. "Max it is." And we shook on it.

Chapter 23:
Initiation

Debbie doesn't play.
Now Wam-ma is my best friend.
Maybe tomorrow.

The children's private domain more than made up for the "public" rooms waiting for a photoshoot. The closet in the girls' room overflowed with a trail of shorts, tops, dresses, underwear, and bathing suits, which then spread out to a field of clothing— clean AND dirty—across the entire bedroom floor. The beds hadn't been made, and the adjoining bathroom shared with the boys was knee deep in towels.

Monty's and Maddock's room was no better, except instead of clothing, a wall-to-wall carpet of toys filled the space. Little toys, the kind that kill bare feet. Matchbox cars, Legos, miniature toy soldiers, marbles. Neatly pressed items filled the dresser drawers, and the laundry hamper contained nothing. Either the day before had been laundry day, or the boys had worn the same outfits for—weeks?

Max had his own room—with a bolt on the outside. Odd. All his toys must have been relegated to the basement because his room only held a few stuffed animals. The bed was stripped of sheets, and a suspicious gray stain shaped like a child's drawing of sunshine decorated the center of the mattress.

Was I supposed to pick up these rooms or make the kids do it? Or leave them as they were?

Lunch hour was designed to rid the children of any babysitter, which explained why a fifteen-year-old got the job. The four older kids had polished their arguments to an art form.

"Millicent has salami with mustard."

"No, Minerva likes mustard, and I get mayonnaise."

"You're both wrong. Give Millicent ham and mustard, Minerva gets salami and mayonnaise, Maddock gets ham and mustard, I get plain ham, and Maximilian only eats ketchup sandwiches."

"He eats more than that, Montgomery. Stop being stupid." Millie gave him a *look.*

And so on and so on. I didn't make the girls clean the kitchen. With their squabbles about who should put away the condiments and who should put away the bread, I could do it faster by myself. Which had probably been their plan.

Gathering beach toys was another exercise in driving the babysitter insane.

"I want the blue noodle."

"You had the blue one last time. Mother said it's my turn."

"She did not."

"Did too."

"Did not."

"If you're going to fight over the blue noodle, nobody gets it." That was me.

It took twenty minutes to get an agreed-upon pile of toys on the driveway by noon.

Max headed for a bathroom every few minutes. Play with a toy. Go. Take a bite of his sandwich. Go. Pick out a sand shovel. Go. Was something wrong with his bladder? Millie informed me he just liked to splash his hands under the faucet. Some kind of fetish.

Better than splashing his hands in the toilet.

At least Mrs. Smythe-Halsey would be helping out at the beach. How could I take a kid to the restroom six times an hour and still watch four other kids? She returned at 12:52 p.m. I knew the time to the minute because I'd been counting one hundred eighty of them.

As soon as their mother pulled in the driveway, the kids piled into the station wagon. No one helped me stuff the toys in the cargo area behind the third seat.

"Where are the beach bags with towels and sunscreen?" Mrs. S-H asked.

"I'll get them," I said. "Where do you keep them?"

"Millicent was supposed to have all of it ready." She stared at her oldest daughter riding shotgun.

Millie offered an elegant shrug, with eyes wide and innocent.

"Go get them." Mrs. S-H stared her down, and with a huff, Millie slithered out of the car and made her way into the house. A tortoise could have brought back the gear in less time.

Once we parked at the Rotunda, the boys raced ahead. Each girl carried one beach bag, and I unloaded the pile of toys.

Mrs. S-H gathered half of them. "You'd better chase down Maximilian. He has a habit of disappearing on us." She signaled to Minerva. "Give Millicent your bag and carry this for Debbie." She turned back to me as I collected the rest of the toys. "Put everything in the reception area until you catch up with Maximilian. Then find a spot by the pool. You'll be able to leave all of our things there for the afternoon. Safer than on the beach. *Any*body can pass by and help themselves out there."

She dumped the toys in Minerva's arms, slipped back into the car…

And took off.

What?

Minerva looked at me with pity. "C'mon. I'll show you where everything is. And Maximilian will be at the aquarium."

Overburdened, we stumbled our way up the steps to the boardwalk. Minerva wiggled a door open with one free finger, and I followed her into the "reception" room where a pony-tailed lady in a black polo shirt sat at a rattan table. The shirt displayed the club's insignia on the breast pocket, and her name was embroidered above it. *Sylvia.*

Gold thread. Swanky.

As for the Rotunda itself, I had pictured "chic" and "ultra-modern" and "beach elegance." After all, this was *The* Rotunda. Instead, I got "tacky." The musty, mildewed scent of old wood by the sea permeated the room. A weathered counter stood behind the table. I guess it was supposed to look "beachy" like driftwood. Instead, it looked more like ocean waves had battered it full of splinters. Dozens of hooks were screwed into the counter's front wall, about half of them holding keys.

Minerva dropped her armful in front of the rickety table to the tune of thuds and clatters. "Mother says we're to leave these here until we find Maximilian and get into our bathing suits."

That's not quite how I remembered it, but okay. Sylvia glanced at me and raised her eyebrows. She lifted two keys from the board and handed them to me. "Good luck."

"Thanks."

"You'll need it."

By four o'clock, I'd chased Max out of the restaurant with its fascinating aquarium three times, he'd fallen into the pool's deep end twice, and he'd run away down the beach, requiring me to chase him and leave the other four on their own.

Millie and Minerva fought over who got which bathing suit, who called dibs on the purple noodle—*didn't we do that already?*—and whether they should buy ice cream sandwiches or Good Humor Toasted Almond Bars for their snack.

That last argument came to an abrupt halt when I ordered three of each and promptly helped myself to one of the almond bars.

"You can't choose for us!" Millie informed me.

"I just did." I allowed my tastebuds a moment of sheer ecstasy before handing out the rest of the ice cream.

Minerva snatched up an ice cream sandwich, Millie grabbed a second one, and the boys didn't care what they received as long as it was sweet.

After snack, Millie, Minerva, and Max wanted the pool. Monty and Maddock wanted the beach. It went without saying that Max remained in my sight at all times. Since the boys had stayed out of trouble, I allowed them to be on their own on the beach. I could peek over the dune every few minutes to make sure they hadn't disappeared. With lifeguards on duty, how much trouble could they get into?

Plenty.

I was teaching Max the "Motorboat" song when one of the beach lifeguards escorted two blond boys into the pool area.

I climbed out of the water and waited. Yes, they headed directly for me.

The guy pushed the pair toward me. "These two tried pulling a drowning act on me. No beach privileges for the rest of the day." He spun both boys to face him. "If I see you out there, you can forget about going into the ocean for a week."

His threats didn't exactly faze them. Within minutes, Monty tried the same stunt in the pool. I jumped in ahead of the lifeguard, collared him in the crook of my arm, and "rescued" him. By the time we reached shallow water, he was a bit oxygen-deprived for real.

"You almost choked me to death!"

His sputtering brought out my first satisfied smile of the day. "Show a little gratitude. I saved your life."

"I was fine until you almost killed me."

"I've got two brothers of my own, mister, and I'd know if I almost killed you. Do we understand each other?"

He blinked first. "Yeah."
"Pass the message to Maddock, too."

194

Chapter 24:
On the Fringe

Doctors, doctors, speech!
Debbie doesn't want to play.
I want school again!

The summer couldn't end soon enough. Arguments and hissy fits on Tuesdays through Saturdays. Boredom and church on Sundays. Mondays should have been the best day of the week. No little monsters in sight. Just blessed hours on the beach with Ronni and any others who had the day off from summer jobs. Except it didn't happen that way.

By noon we'd all arrive, lolling side by side on our towels like a pod of elephant seals staking out a stretch of shore. Roger, soon-to-be captain of the JV basketball team, was the alpha male this year, which made Ronni a member of the inner circle. A dozen towels surrounded hers. Not mine. My towel lay on the fringe of the group. Without Bill, I didn't rank anywhere close to the center.

I couldn't even have fun at the beach. It wasn't Ronni's fault. If I were in her place, I would've reserved the spot next to my popular boyfriend, too.

She tried to make sure we connected at some point during the day, either in the water, or a short walk on the beach, but it wasn't the same. She didn't want to ignore Roger for too long, just like I had worked so hard to hold Bill's attention. Why do girls *do* this?

I could tell myself it was stupid to depend on a guy, but if Bill had ever apologized to me, I would have wiggled my way right back to the center of the pod, confident I had a place. Since he didn't, I didn't even try to inch past the outer edge. I had *some* pride left.

Every workday, or more like every work sunset, I dragged home, my mind as frazzled as my windblown hair. All I wanted was to go to my room and read.

I was enjoying a great mystery novel when Krista climbed the stairs for the third time in a week, a pack of cards in her hands. Holding out the deck, she made her appeal. "Pway?"

I'd only been home for an hour. I'd lost Max twice at the beach club, and neither parent arrived home before the prescribed supper hour. Which meant I got to be the cook, too. According to the motley crew, the hamburgers were burned, and they weren't well done enough. Maddock wanted the flavored potato chips, not the plain ones, and they all agreed no one eats vegetables with a burger meal, not even canned corn. It took me over half an hour to scrub the fry pan so it looked like it did when I placed it on the burner. Max squirted ketchup on the floor, then stepped in it. Millie took him upstairs and locked him in his room, a practice that horrified me when I first arrived, but at the end of a terrible day, I welcomed such a move. We let him out as soon as the kitchen was in order.

"Pway?" Krista repeated.

Krista's summer hadn't been fun either. Speechreading therapy, physical therapy, and trips to the doctor for checks on her ears, eyes, heart, and legs. But the only thing I wanted was my book. A place to run away from my life.

I shook my head. She didn't beg, just turned away and trudged out of the room. The disappointment in her eyes only added to my shame. I couldn't do anything right. Not babysitting. Not loving my own family.

What happened to the girl who couldn't wait to have a forever friend in a sister?

On my days off, Krista and I still practiced speech and speechreading. The effort gave me headaches, and if Krista's reactions were any indication, she suffered headaches, too. We had spent three years building our imperfect communication system based on a little sign language, charades, and facial expressions. Teachers and doctors told us to force her to read our lips, an exercise guaranteed to bring on a tantrum.

Typical scene at home.

Mom: Krista, what do you want for lunch?

(Krista squints at Mom and looks puzzled.)

Mom (making sure of eye contact and enunciating clearly): What do you want for lunch?

(Krista shakes her head no.)

Mom: No lunch?

Krista: Eeeeeeeee!

Mom: Yes lunch? (Nods her head then stops. She's not supposed to give body language cues).

(Krista nods yes.)

Mom: Say "yes."

(Krista folds her arms across her chest and glowers.)

Mom (points to cupboards. Oops, puts her hand down.): What do you want for lunch?

(Krista opens the fridge and pulls out a jar of strawberry jam.)

Mom: you want peanut butter and jelly?

(Krista nods yes.)

Mom: Say peanut butter and jelly.

(Krista scowls and slams the jar on the table.)

Mom (frowning): Say "jam."

Krista: Yam.

Mom (smiling): Good. Say peanut butter.

Krista: Pee nuh buh.

Mom: Almost. Pea-nut but-*ter*. (Gets in Krista's face and shows how the tongue presses against the top teeth for the "ter."

Krista (throws herself on the kitchen floor, kicks, and rolls in one direction, then another): Ah-eeeeeeeeeeee!

At which point, Mom either spanks her or gives up and makes the stupid sandwich.

Daddy could joke with her and prevent a tantrum. Sometimes, I could do that too. Like one Sunday we were playing Concentration with a deck of cards. Krista had figured out I was more likely to say yes to her "pway" request after church. Maybe an hour concentrating on God had a good effect on me.

Concentration was our favorite card game. Krista often beat me—and I didn't just let her win—as she easily found pairs of numbers, remembering where she had seen the match from a previous turn. We added a rule: for every card we turned over, we had to say the number on the card. Sometimes, Krista was fine with that. Sometimes not.

"What number do you have?" I asked her.

"Fife." (five).

"What's the other number?"

Krista frowned in concentration. "Ih." (six).

I waited until she looked up. "Six. Look at my tongue. Ssssss. Six." I pointed to my throat for the "x."

"Ssssssssih." Krista made a slashing motion across her throat.

I'd been warned. I picked up two cards. "Four and…ten."

They went back to their positions face down.

Krista picked up a five and a ten.

"What number?" I asked.

"Fife."

"Fi-vuh." Adding the "uh" helped to show the slight difference between F and V.

With eyes hooded, Krista responded. "Fi-vuh."

"Yay! Say ten." I smiled, hoping to head her off from a tantrum.

"Deh."

"No. Tennnnn."

"No-oooooooo!" She slammed the ten card back in its place.

"Are you mad?" I twisted my lips and brows into an exaggerated frowny face.

She nodded.

I threw my arms wide. "Say "I'm mad!"" And I howled at the ceiling. "I'm maaaaaaad!"

Krista cracked a smile. "I maaaaaaaa!"

"I'm maaaaaaa-*duh*!" I got in her face and blinked

ten times.

She giggled. "I maaaaaaa-duh!"

Krista deserved a reward for the effort. I signed, "YOU-RIGHT-YOU-MAD." I went back to speech. "Because I know where both tens are!"

I snatched them up, and Krista laughed.

She was always a good sport about stuff like that.

Chapter 25:
Angel on the Beach

We went to the beach.
We saw a nice church lady.
Deh-bee played with me.

On a Monday afternoon in August, I gave myself a break from the pod of elephant seals (AKA, the Hampton Shores cool kids) and rode to the Air Force Beach with Mom and Krista. The day promised rain, so the beach was relatively empty.

It was kind of relaxing. I felt like a little kid again. Mom worked on her tan while Krista and I stood at the water's edge and let the gentle ocean roll over our toes. Shifting sand buried our feet. Who would be first to free herself?

We carried pails to the wavelets and collected enough water to start a sandcastle. Back and forth, back and forth, until we had dozens of wet sand-bucket towers to create a wall for our castle. Once our creation was complete, Krista produced some of my brothers' toy soldiers to man the walls. I left her to her imagination and entered my own book world of

Upstairs, Downstairs.

A stranger's voice pulled me away from Lady Marjorie and her husband.

"—your little girl?"

"Yes," Mom replied. "She'll be four next month."

"She's adorable."

"Thank you. We think so, too."

I glanced up from my book. An older lady stood in front of Mom, a bit dumpy and wearing one of those old-fashioned, black bathing suits that almost looked like a mini skirt. Still seated in her beach chair, Mom looked up at the woman, shielding her eyes to avoid the sun's glare.

Krista paraded her soldiers on top of the fragile, crumbling wall. The first ripple of incoming tide lapped at its base. Krista rushed her army toward the damage and helped them shore up the wall with new, wet sand.

The lady watched the action with interest, fingering a medallion hanging from a long chain around her neck. Her gray hair glowed silver in the sunlight.

"Her name is Krista," Mom volunteered. "She's deaf."

The woman turned back to Mom, regarded her solemnly, then smiled. "You don't need to worry about Krista. She will be an excellent model for others to follow. And a blessing in your old age."

What an odd person! Nobody normal says such a thing when they don't know you. Not even when they *do* know you. I tensed, in case this lady started acting crazier. For all her nice words, did she plan to grab Krista and run for it? Did she have a knife hidden under that bathing suit skirt?

Mom hadn't moved, didn't respond to the

woman's statement.

The woman lifted the necklace over her head. "Here. A remembrance. Be confident the Lord is watching over her."

She held it out. Mom opened her hand as if it were the most natural thing in the world to accept a gift from a stranger. The lady dropped the necklace into her palm, then folded Mom's fingers over it.

Mom said nothing. Not "thank you," not "who are you?" Nothing.

The lady squatted next to Krista. I scrambled to my feet and joined them.

She smiled at my sister, then pointed to the castle. "Beautiful," she said.

Krista smiled back and offered one of the toy soldiers, an invitation to play.

So, Mom seemed mesmerized by this person, and Krista liked her. I was the only one prepared to defend my baby sister to the death.

The woman spent a couple of minutes moving the toy soldier next to Krista's. They added more thickness to the walls where the sea kept crashing closer and closer. Then she stood and waved goodbye to Krista, who waved back.

She started to walk toward the nearest jetty, then turned to face me. "Don't worry so much, dear. Your heart's desire is closer than you think."

It was my turn to lose the power of speech while she continued on her way. How did she know I was miserable? My heart's desire? I didn't even know what that was.

I looked back at Mom, who examined the necklace.

"What is it?" I asked.

"It seems to be a medallion. It's got Saint Jude printed on it."

We weren't Catholic. Why would anyone give us a saint's medallion? Maybe I should run after the lady and ask her to explain. I scanned the shoreline. No older lady in a black, skirted bathing suit was visible. *Did she sit down somewhere?* A slim lady sat under her umbrella. Three young families were the only other groups on the beach.

I scanned the opposite direction. Two little boys played catch with a beach ball. Their mother, in a bikini, lay on her back soaking up rays.

Did the woman go for a swim? Small children played in the shallows. A young couple, wrapped in each other's arms, bobbed in the waves beyond the breakers.

This was a wide stretch of beach. There was no way she had time to walk out of our sight, not even if she were to cross the dunes to the parking lot.

"Mom!"

She looked up from the necklace. "What?"

"Where did she go?"

"Krista's right here."

"No! The lady who gave you the necklace. Where did she go?"

Mom looked around. Her expression changed as she realized the meaning behind my question. Our gazes met, and we both looked at the medallion.

Had we just spoken to an angel?

Chapter 26: Not Exactly Maria

Debbie works a lot.
I don't like that. She comes home
So tired and angry.

You'd think after an encounter with an angel, life would get better. I *tried* to spend more time with Krista, but all week, the Monsters, I mean the Smythe-Halseys, invented new forms of torture for me. I would never win them over like Maria did in *The Sound of Music.*

On Thursday, Max was safely locked in his room for "nap" time. I always allowed him to take a toy with him. He could sleep or play, his choice. I had the feeling he appreciated the peace and quiet away from his siblings. Maybe he even liked me for giving him a toy. He knew I didn't lock him in for punishment.

The girls had been especially helpful as we cleaned up after lunch, asking me about high school and did I have a boyfriend and what subjects I liked best in school. They eagerly answered my questions about what they liked at *their* school. It was probably the most enjoyable half hour I'd experienced all summer.

I should've known something was up.

A shout, a thump, then the thunder of running feet over our heads, down the stairs, and clattering toward us on the hardwood floors. Maddock raced across my vision, shoved open one of the French doors, and Monty flew by holding a trash can spewing flames.

I fired the wet dish rag into the sink and followed hot on their trail.

Maddock jumped up and down in the grass, screaming, while Monty had the presence of mind to set the blazing trash can on the brick patio away from flammable objects. I grabbed the garden hose coiled on the bricks, turned on the spigot, and aimed the spray at the mini inferno. Within seconds, the fire was out, and I aimed my weapon at Maddock. Cold water caught him full in the face. The shock brought abrupt silence.

Like a camera in the key scene of a movie, my eyes panned the set, recording every nuance. Millie stood just inside the open door, arms crossed, a smirk on her face. Minerva was a step ahead on the patio, her mouth hanging open. Monty stood next to the wet trash can, peering down at what was left of its contents. Maddock, too shocked to complain about his wet face and soaked shirt, stared at me. Flowers bloomed behind him along the edge of the patio. A contrast of utter tranquility. The hose continued to dribble water from the now-deactivated nozzle, which created a small river flowing into the grass.

I stepped back to the faucet, turned it off, then lifted tongs hanging from the barbecue grill to stir the rubble in the trash can. The tongs closed on what was left of a pack of cigarettes and pulled them up like one of those claw machines at the county fair.

Quite a prize.

"Care to explain?" While I took in Maddock's guilty expression and Monty's eyes gazing anywhere but in my direction, the question was posed to Millie.

Oh-so-innocent eyebrows rose in contrast to her chin jutting forward. "What? *I* didn't do anything."

I lasered in on Minerva. Her lips quivered.

Millie wrapped an arm around her shoulder. "You didn't do anything either."

Minerva shook her off. "They weren't supposed to start a fire!"

"We didn't do that on purpose!" Monty snatched the offending cigarette pack from the tongs. "We tried one of these. Just one. We didn't like it, so I threw the whole pack in the trash. Then Maddock threw the pack of matches in the trash, and *then* he threw the cigarette in the trash." He glared at his brother. "Stupidhead."

I finished the story for him, not bothering to scold his language. "And the cigarette was still burning, which lit the matches, which set fire to all the trash."

Monty hung his head. "Yeah."

Where did an eight-year-old even get cigarettes? Never mind. His parents could figure that one out.

A sudden thought clobbered me. *What if something in their bedroom had caught fire?* Max would be trapped!

"Don't move. Any of you." And I ran back in the house and up the stairs. A faint scent of smoke emanated from the boys' room, but all else was peaceful.

I unbolted the door and peeked into Max's room.

He lay on his mattress, arms wrapped around his

teddy bear. "Why was Maddock screaming?"

"He was scared of a fire."

Max sat up and sniffed. "Something stinks."

"Leftover smoke." I held out my hand. "Do you want to stay here or come outside and see the burned-up trash can?"

He pulled himself to standing. "I want to see."

When we got back outside, all four kids were exactly where I had left them. They really did scare themselves.

With alternate sounds of disgust and awe, Max examined the blackened trash can with its wet, mushy insides.

I motioned to the rest of them to circle the trash can. "Come here."

They *obeyed*.

"Think about this." I made eye contact with all four of them. "What if the curtains caught fire as you ran out with the trash can? You two saved yourselves." I pointed to the older boys. "And the rest of us followed you to safety outside." I indicated the girls and me. "But where was Max?"

No one answered. It wasn't a rhetorical question. "*Where* was Max?"

"In his room." Monty and Minerva answered as one.

"And if the curtains caught fire which means the upstairs caught fire, what would have happened to Max?"

A sob exploded from Minerva. Monty stared at the ground. Millie's eyes slid toward her baby brother, then slid away. Maddock kneeled and hugged Max, who looked completely confused by the unexpected affection.

"So are you gonna tell on us?" Monty's bravado didn't hide his fear.

"I don't have a choice."

I'd rarely complained to Mrs. S-H about the kids' shenanigans. If I couldn't handle them, it was my own lack of ability. This was different.

"The upstairs smells like smoke, the trash can is a disaster, and this is a lot more serious than your constant, stupid fights." There. I'd used the dreaded word "stupid" in their presence.

Unlike her brothers and sister, Millie wasn't shocked. "You tell Mother what happened, and she'll fire you."

What a happy thought. I smiled. "She might. Maybe she should. The four of you planned this for after lunch, and I didn't catch on. I should've."

"No!" Minerva wrapped her arms around my waist. "How were you supposed to know?"

Maddock finally found his voice. "You're the best babysitter we ever had."

Was this another con job?

Monty met my eyes. "And you're the only one that's been fair. The others either quit or tattled to Mom about everything, or told us stuff like, 'Do what you want. Just don't burn the house down.'"

I busted out laughing.

After a moment, he got the joke. "And we almost did!"

Millie's snigger was contagious. Minerva and Maddock joined her in hysterical relief while Max just watched us. "What's so funny?"

Chapter 27:
Krista Knows

Debbie stays home now.
She plays with me. I like that.
And we build sand forts.

I got fired. Sort of.

Mrs. Smythe-Halsey asked me to stay on for a couple of days while she rearranged her schedule before taking care of the children herself for the last two weeks of summer. She still trusted me enough for that amount of time. The kids were angels for those two days. Their farewell gift.

My guess? Doctor Halsey, who was hardly ever around, had decided I should have been able to sniff out any plot hatched by his amazing spawn. Mrs. S-H knew better. Poor woman.

But yay for me! I could hit the beach every day. Maybe improve my standing within the elephant seal pod as they sprawled on the sand. Maybe find a new boyfriend. And definitely spend time with my sister.

With Paul and Wade at summer camp, I drank in the peace and quiet. Every morning, I taught Krista how to say the letter sounds in the alphabet. She really liked the game we played on the back deck.

On our first day, I took chalk and drew the letter A. Giant-sized. Big enough to walk on. Next, I plugged in my clock radio and turned on a rock music station. Full blast. Hopefully, the neighbors wouldn't mind.

Krista jumped at the sound and stared at her feet.

I tapped her shoulder, so she'd look at me. "Can you hear the music?" I tapped my ear.

She shook her head and pointed to her feet, followed by little hip wiggles that matched the drumbeat.

She couldn't hear the music, but she could feel it. *Perfect!*

I clapped my hands to the same rhythm. She copied me. We grinned at each other.

I stepped over to one leg of the A and danced my way to the top, pivoted, and danced down the other leg. Then I jumped to the middle and danced across the A's horizontal line.

Krista followed me. She kept the beat the whole way—except when she stumbled at the jumping part. With short legs and braces, she couldn't make the leap and keep her balance.

I stepped off the A. She stepped off, too.

I turned down the music and pointed to the chalk letter. "Say 'aa.'" I made the *short a* sound.

"Aa," she said.

"Say 'uh,' like your name. Krist-*uh*." I signed, NAME-YOU.

"Uh," she said. "Wih-uh."

Hmmm. She could usually say the S in her name. Good thing school started soon. She needed more practice. I decided not to try long A. She always had trouble with the "eh-ee" blend.

DANCE-MORE? I signed.

Her face and hands responded with a vigorous *yes*.

"But first." I held up my pointer finger. "We say, 'aa-uh' while we dance."

No answer other than a puzzled frown.

"Watch." Without turning up the music, I danced around the A and made sure she could see me talking. "Aa-uh, Aa-uh." I kept my hands in the fingerspelling A position and moved them side to side with the rhythm, two beats on "aa," two beats on "uh."

The frown disappeared once Krista caught on.

I signed, READY? She nodded, and I turned the radio back to full volume.

The new song had a slightly faster tempo, but Krista's little wiggle started, and up the leg we went. "Aa-uh, aa-uh, aa-uh," with our A fists swinging side to side.

We danced to "eh-ee" on a giant chalk E. I drew a giant I and we danced to "ih/ah-ee, ih/ah-ee," and we started our "ah-oh" on a giant O, but Mom called through the kitchen window.

"Enough!"

I turned off the radio.

Krista stared at the deck, then at me. The boards had stopped vibrating.

"Mom's ears hurt," I said. I signed MOM, pointed to my ear, and shook my fingers in an "ow" motion.

Krista laughed.

In the afternoons, I biked to the Village Beach. Nothing had changed. I still lay on my towel on the fringe of the group, kind of accepted but not really. It didn't help that Ronni was on vacation at one of the Finger Lakes with her family.

On Monday, Melissa and Leigh ignored me. No surprise there. But on Tuesday, an upper classman settled his towel next to mine. *Oh, be still, my heart!* I got so tongue-tied; it was like I had no idea how to start a conversation. I guess he had the same problem since he didn't think of anything to say either. He didn't rejoin me on Wednesday.

On Thursday, Krista was delighted to have my company at the Air Force Beach. I planned to be with her the rest of the week to make up for being such a horrible big sister all summer. Mom and I kept an eye out for the angel lady.

The wind was strong, and I ate my sandwich, constantly brushing sand off of it. While I chowed down on extra-gritty peanut butter, I kept puzzling on the phrase, "my heart's desire."

What did the angel lady mean? I had lots of desires. I wanted to be close friends with Ronni again. I wanted to be accepted by that group. I wanted a boyfriend. I wanted to keep getting good grades. I wanted to be a teacher. I wanted to teach Krista to talk.

A *heart's* desire must be a really strong one. But they were all strong. I missed being with Ronni, lucky to spend an afternoon with her when it rained. If I were in the cool group, I'd get to spend time with Ronni and a whole bunch of others. If I didn't like a few of them, so what? I'd *belong*. I hadn't been welcomed to a group since the first semester of seventh grade. It got lonely.

And maybe having a boyfriend wasn't all that important with my whole life ahead of me, but how would I ever get married if I never had a boyfriend again?

Getting good grades and wanting to be a teacher. Were those strong enough desires? I should toss those off the list. I'd earned good grades since kindergarten. I kind of expected to keep doing that. And I'd already been a teacher, too. I'd taught little preschoolers in my own summer nursery school after sixth grade, and I'd been teaching my sister all kinds of things since she was born.

But she couldn't even say her own name yet.

Krista tapped my shoulder, jolting me back to sun and sandcastles. The day's wall was half-built before we had stopped for lunch from the cooler. She must be ready to finish the job. I stood and picked up one pail, but she tugged it out of my hand.

"HOME," she signed.

We hadn't even been here for two hours. And she never left a sandcastle unfinished. "Not time for home." I spoke and signed.

She frowned. "HOME-FATHER." The thumb of her open hand jammed against the right side of her forehead, an intense way to sign FATHER.

I shook my head. "Father home tomorrow."

She shook her head right back at me and grabbed my hand, marching us over to Mom leafing through her newest *Ladies Home Journal*. "'Ome. Nnnnow." Krista was good at m's and n's.

Mom's eyebrows rose in question. "Home? Now?"

Krista nodded vigorously. "Fah-thuh. 'Ome."

"No. Father is *not* home. He comes tomorrow. At night. Not Thursday in the day."

Krista peered at Mom's lips trying to follow all those words. She got the gist of it. Her scowl returned. "Nnnnow," she repeated. She signed NO and TOMORROW. She couldn't *say* "tomorrow." Not even with the m in the middle of the word.

Mom looked at me like I could settle the argument. I shrugged. There was no arguing with Krista.

Krista returned to the sandcastle, filled both pails with her soldiers, gathered the two shovels, and dumped it all by Mom's beach chair. She stared down at Mom. "'Ome." With arms crossed against her chest, she waited for Mom to obey.

If Mom said "no," she'd be dealing with a temper tantrum on the beach. If we went home, Krista would think she was the boss.

Mom pulled her wristwatch out of the beach bag. "It is one o'clock." She held up one finger. We can go home at two." Two fingers up.

No tantrum.

Krista rolled her eyes in disgust, limped to the water's edge and sat down, her back to us. I followed. Her hands repeated the same signs over and over, mumbling to herself in sign language. It was kind of cute. Tap fingertips on her forehead, tap thumb with hand wide open nearer the temple, then an *A* fist from chin to cheekbone. "KNOW-FATHER-HOME."

I sat down beside her. She glared, daring me to challenge her. I shrugged again. Not my fight. She scooted away from me. If I wouldn't agree with her, she'd rather be alone. I obliged and found my latest library book.

Not ten pages later, a deep voice interrupted. "Are the lovely Hansen ladies willing to invite a gentleman to sit under their umbrella?"

I jerked out of my story world of Medieval Europe and glanced up. *Daddy?*

"Grant! What are you doing here?" Mom made room under the umbrella. Daddy would be a bright pink in no time if he didn't get some shade.

"What kind of greeting is that for the man of your dreams?" He crawled onto the blanket and kissed Mom, leaving a smear of zinc oxide on her cheek.

She giggled. "People are staring."

"Let them."

I got up and walked toward Krista. People could stare at them without *me* being associated with the crazy man in trousers, white paste all over his nose, and getting fresh with a lady under her umbrella.

Krista still sat where I left her, shoulders hunched and facing the sea.

I blocked her view of it and signed, "YOU-RIGHT."

She tilted her head to question what I meant, and I pointed behind her.

She turned, saw Daddy, and smiled. Then she stared at me. "I told you so" was written all over her face. With that, she ran on tippy toes toward the umbrella.

How had she known?

Chapter 28:
Betrayal

Time for school again!
Now I know school starts with S.
Saying "sss" is hard.

Ronni and I sat at adjoining desks in our homeroom, a.k.a. the biology room, on the first day of school.

"I can't believe the only class we have together is history." I slumped in my chair. "We don't even have the same lunch!" *Who was I going to sit with?*

She looked almost as glum as I felt. "That's a bummer."

The buzzer sounded, signaling announcements, and there was nothing more to say. After spending the next half hour on first-day paperwork, the buzzer sounded again, and we were off: me to English 10, Ronni to Geometry.

We walked out the door and parted at room 208. She beamed me a smile, what I used to call her *Cousin It* smile until she cut her bangs and I could see her whole face.

"See you in History," she said.

That wasn't until sixth period.

I trudged further down the hall to room 203. Last year, I'd walked these halls with either Ronni or Bill at my side. I had wished I could share *one* class with him, an elective, like choir or something. Bill would've endured three hundred push-ups, every *day*, rather than join the choir. This year? I was glad he'd never be in any of my classes.

Mr. Crane's back was turned while he wrote on the blackboard. The half-filled room contained familiar faces. Thea, Melissa, Leigh, Chip, and Roger. Chip hadn't spoken to me since the day I moved to California, and Roger never started a conversation with anyone. Having Ronni for a girlfriend must have relieved any pressure for him to talk.

I chose a seat in between Thea and Libby. I could count on their kindness.

Turning to Libby first, I took a stab at conversation. "I haven't seen you all summer. Did you have a job?"

She ducked her head, rare for her to ever look a person in the eye. "I worked at the stables."

"You got to work with horses every day?" That had to be better than where I'd worked. Horses didn't talk back or try to make your life miserable.

She nodded her head. "It was great. Except for shoveling manure."

Maybe working with mostly clean children had some advantages.

Since I couldn't think of any other topic of conversation, our silence grew uncomfortable, at least for me. I sure hoped Krista's first day was going better than mine.

I looked over to Thea's desk. Was she done talking to Leigh? No, and I wasn't going to interrupt that conversation and get some kind of MYOB look from Leigh.

She moved down the aisle toward her seat, and Thea glanced my way and smiled. "Ready?"

"I hope so."

"Oh, you're always fine. This year will be easy for you." She was talking grades, not social life. Thea probably didn't worry about her social life. Like Ronni, she was easy to like.

I stuck with her topic. "Geometry and biology? We'll see."

"I can't wait until we dissect stuff."

Libby made a strangled sound, and Thea leaned forward to see past me. "Libby, it'll be cool."

Libby shook her head. "I'll probably faint. Or get sick."

"If we're in the same class, we can be partners when we start that stuff. You won't get sick, I promise."

Libby kept shaking her head.

"No, really," Thea persisted. "When is your biology class?"

Libby consulted her schedule which lay on top of her books. "Fifth period."

"Oh." Thea sighed. "I have it next period." She brightened. "But just get a guy to do all the guts and glory work, and you'll be fine."

Like Libby would have the guts to ask any guy to be her partner. But Thea and I had the same biology class. Maybe *we* could be lab partners.

It turned out Thea and I shared most of our morning classes and Spanish at the end of the day. And Mary and I shared gym again. We could take our time combing the snarls out of our hair and then go to the latest lunch section. My days wouldn't be so bad after all.

Ronni and I walked home together. I hadn't been sure that would happen, but she explained Roger was at an organizational meeting for the tennis team. He figured he could get into shape for basketball by running back and forth on a tennis court.

Which reminded me. "Are we still going to practice together for cheerleading try-outs next week?"

"Sure," she said. "I promised we would." She grinned at me. "And I still believe what I said last year. You have a good chance of making the squad."

"I hope so." I'd practiced what little I knew off and on through the summer in my backyard.

We headed straight for the refrigerator once we got to her house and helped ourselves to a couple of bottles of root beer, then had an impromptu cheerleading practice in *her* backyard. Kind of hard to do in bell-bottoms. They drag you down.

The first two days of school were great. For both Krista and me. Krista liked her new teacher, Sister Evangeline, and her best friend, Christie, was in her class again. *My* best friend and I spent both days after school practicing cheers. *And* Mary invited me to her

First Weekend Since School Started Party, just like she did last year. This year, I planned to go. If people were smoking pot, it didn't mean I had to. And maybe Ronni and Roger would come, too. I could always dream.

On Thursday, as I headed for the gym doors, so not eager for another hour of field hockey, I saw the sign-up list. *The cheerleading try-outs.* This year, I would be confident. I didn't need Ronni to take the pencil out of my shaking hand and sign up for me. She and I would nail whatever cheers they told us to perform. I would be perky. Exuberant. It would be like I was on stage playing the big role of: CHEERLEADER.

I marched up to the form, already half-filled with scrawls of other people's names in the two columns. Melissa and Leigh were at the top of the list. Partners in crime and try-outs. Some freshmen pairs of names followed as well as single names without a partner attached. Then Thea and—Ronni.

My pencil dropped. I read the list again. No mistake. Thea and Ronni had signed up as partners.

224

Chapter 29:
Two Become Four

Last year I practiced
Cheers with Debbie and Ronni.
It's that time again.

I backed away from the gymnasium, wanting so badly to tear down the hall, slam into the crash bars of the exit doors, and never stop running until I reached the ocean and screamed into the breaking waves.

My best friend had ditched me.

But no. I was Debbie Hansen. Steady. Smart. A soldier. Her father's daughter.

I pivoted away from others waiting to sign up and opened the door to the locker room to get ready for gym. On the field, Mrs. Anniston complimented my precise and aggressive moves with the hockey stick. I thanked her, a fake smile pasted to my face, and proceeded to smash the ball into the net. My first-ever goal. *Whoopee.*

After class, Mary and I stood side by side at the mirrors, once again working on our hair. She couldn't stop talking about her party. The party where I would now go alone. Without Ronni.

"This year, I made my parents keep the Japanese lanterns hanging from our trees since the Fourth of July. I promised I'd take them down myself if they'd hold off. It's gonna look so cool back there." She caught my eye in the mirror, and her expression turned to one of horror. "You're ripping your hair out by the roots. Let me tease out that knot with a comb."

I had welcomed the pain, but I allowed her to work on me. I couldn't hide in the girls' locker room forever. "Who all is coming to the party?"

Would I know anyone?

"Sheila and Diane and Sally Griffin and Damon and Jim Rhodes and Mark and…" She glanced my way via the mirror and offered a coy smile. "Rocky will be there, too."

I ignored the hint. If Rocky paid attention to me, it would help my ego, but I doubted he was interested. "What about Al?"

She rolled her eyes. "He was such a jerk. Not only to you that day at the beach. I broke up with him, just like I said I would." She teased out another knot. "It's kind of a relief."

Kind of the way I felt about Bill.

She added, "He is definitely *not* invited." Did she mean Bill or Al? My mind had wandered for a moment.

"And you'll definitely come this year? No babysitting?"

Did she know I had lied last year? If so, she didn't hold it against me.

"If my parents want a babysitter Friday night, they can hire my brother instead. Paul is fourteen now. He's more than capable." At twelve, Wade was fully capable, too, come to think of it.

"There." The comb glided through eighteen inches of hair without a hitch.

"Thanks." Not just for getting the knots out. The gentle tugging on my scalp had calmed the storm of the last hour. Somewhere during Mary's chatter and my hair falling in silky waves down my back, tangled thoughts had smoothed out as well. I would go through with the try-outs, and I would do my best, and I might make the cheerleading squad without Ronni's help.

What about Mary? She hadn't tried out last year, but you never know. Maybe she'd been too scared to try.

When I asked, her laugh ricocheted off the lockers in the empty room. "Me? All that rah-rah stuff when I don't even care about sports? I don't think so."

As we made our way to the cafeteria for what was left of our lunch period, I wondered why I couldn't see things as clearly as Mary. I didn't care about sports either. So, *why* did I want to be a cheerleader?

As soon as I left the cafeteria, I returned to the bulletin board by the gym doors, new pencil in hand, and looked for a spot to write my name. If no partner was listed, I assumed the person needed one. There. Wendy Kavanaugh. She was a freshman, quiet, and close to my size, which meant bigger than the average cheerleader on the squad. If nothing else, we'd look well-matched when we tried out. I hoped she wouldn't mind. Maybe I'd see her in the hall and ask her.

On to history. Did I even *want* to see Ronni today? Here I'd been whining that we only had one class together. And now? Awkward didn't begin to describe what I was feeling.

Mr. Nation (what an ironic name for a world history teacher) had allowed us to sit wherever we wanted and then assigned us those seats, so of course, I was sitting right next to Ronni for the whole semester. She waved to me as soon as I entered the room. Not a hint of guilt showed on her face.

Okay. I'd play it cool. For now.

"Hey, did Mr. Crane really give a pop quiz on the third day of school?" Her worry created a V just above her nose.

"Yeah. I think he wanted to see if we read last night's short story."

Ronni groaned and rested her forehead on her desk. "I spent two hours on math and figured I could catch up on English later." She raised her head. "Was it bad?"

"No."

"You never think anything is hard. Will *I* think it's hard?"

As mad as I was, I still had to grin at the question. "Not if you read it."

"Well, now I don't have time!"

"Maybe you can read it now, and I'll take notes for you."

Maybe Mr. Nation wouldn't notice that Ronni's pencil wasn't moving.

And why was I helping her anyway?

Like usual, Ronni and I walked home together. She never said a word about the try-outs list all the way to her driveway.

I couldn't stand it any longer. "So, when were you planning to tell me?"

"About what?" Her face expressed *innocence.* And *bewilderment.* She'd become a good actress.

"About try-outs." I ground out the words like a cigar-chomping mafia boss.

Her expression shifted slightly into *confused.* "Why would I tell you about try-outs? You already knew about them." Her frowny eyebrows rose to accent wide, innocent eyes. "You did sign up, didn't you?"

"Yeah, I did. And so did Thea."

"Oh…Thea." The not-so-innocent eyes slid away from my gaze. "She asked me in gym class if I'd sign up with her. I didn't think you'd mind."

My silence told her different.

She held up her hands, palms up. "If Melissa had asked me that, I would've said no."

That was her defense?

"It would've been nice if you'd asked me first. I'd already assumed we were partners. Guess I assumed too much."

The whole summer should've warned me this would happen. I stepped toward the road.

Ronni reached out a hand as if to stop me. "Look. I'm sorry I didn't think about how you might feel about this. But you don't need me as a partner. You're good enough on your own." Her finger poked my shoulder. "You're much better than you think."

Was she right? I had confidence in some things like English and history and music. But athletics? Cheerleading? People smarts? Ronni was the people person. She didn't understand why I got tongue-tied in large groups. Probably like my inability to understand why some people can't spell.

Ronni sighed. "So, who did you sign up with?"

"Wendy Kavanaugh. And I couldn't even find her all day to ask if she'd mind."

Ronni brightened. "She's really sweet. Not sure her voice is loud enough, though."

"I'll teach her breath support."

"That could work." She laughed. "So, we're good? Stay and practice with me?"

"Okay." Yeah, we were good. What a relief.

Her smile widened again, and her eyes danced in anticipation. "And tomorrow, we can add Thea and Wendy, and we'll all practice here together."

Wendy had readily agreed to our partnership and our afternoon practice, so the four us walked to Ronni's together. On the way, Ronni led us in short sideline chants, and I demonstrated the basics of breath support with some "yo-ho-hos." Thea and Wendy doubled their volume, and we sounded like pirates after a few rounds at a tavern. Any neighbors who were outside shook their heads and grinned at us. One old man sitting on his front porch joined us with a booming bass voice, which cracked us up, and we couldn't "ho-ho" properly anymore.

Practicing all the moves was much easier this year. Maybe I did have a good chance. Wendy learned quickly, too. She might be shy, but she possessed more ability than I'd had at my first try-out. But Thea? So smart, so kind. Another people person. But the more we practiced, the worse her rhythm got. She couldn't even clap with the rest of us much less add a jump or a twist.

After half an hour she flopped onto the grass, flat on her back, and giggled. "I'm hopeless, aren't I?"

"No, no, no," Ronni assured her. "Not everybody gets it right away."

"And I'm one of them." Thea groaned and pulled herself into a V-sit. Lack of strength was not a part of her problem.

Ronni pulled Thea to her feet. "Let's do it again."

We kept going for another hour. Ronni, of course, was the best. Wendy was so good she might take the spot I hoped for. Her cheerleader voice boomed across the yard. All the "yo-ho-ho" practice had worked.

Thea hadn't improved by much. She never looked frustrated either. Why couldn't I have been that kind of a good sport last year?

As we gathered our stuff to head home, Thea shook her head. "Maybe tomorrow when we're with a larger group, I'll be able to sense how the whole thing works."

A larger group? Weren't we meeting at Ronni's tomorrow morning?

Ronni said, "You could be right. It's a little different when eight girls are coordinating at different angles and different heights." She turned to Wendy. "A bunch of sophomores are getting together at Melissa's house, and since you and Debbie are partners, I'm sure you can go with us."

How come I hadn't heard about a sophomore practice? I had my suspicions.

Wendy's smile wavered. Anyone as reserved as she was would probably be nervous joining a bunch of upperclassmen. I would've been, and I'm not *that* quiet.

"Why don't we all meet here and walk to Melissa's together?" I asked.

Melissa lived down the street from me, even closer than the five blocks to Ronni, but I sure didn't want to walk over to Melissa's by myself. Especially since she didn't want me there.

"Good idea," Thea said. "We can meet here fifteen minutes ahead of time."

Wendy's voice lowered to almost a whisper. "What time do we have to be there?"

And thank you for asking. I needed the same information.

"Ten." Ronni and Thea spoke together.

"Okay." Wendy started to leave, then turned back to me. "Thanks for signing up as my partner. Today's been a lot of fun. Even if I don't make it."

I followed Ronni into her house once the other two left. "Got any idea as to why you and Thea knew about the sophomore practice, and I didn't?"

Her head whipped around in surprise. "Melissa didn't tell you about it?"

"Did you really think she would?"

Ronni rolled her eyes. At *me.* "You're always so critical of Leigh and Melissa. They're not as bad as you think."

She *knew* our history with those two. How could she brush off my concerns like that?

"And she was *so nice* she invited all of the sophomores on the try-out list to her place, but she didn't ask *me.*" If I were a cartoon figure, Ronni could've seen the red rage rising through my body until it blew off the top of my head.

Ronni bit her lip. "Maybe she forgot."

"Do you remember the first day of eighth grade and what you said to me about those two?"

She didn't answer. Had she forgotten?

"You remember how they talked bad about me after I left for California in seventh grade, and once *you* talked to me that first day of school the next year, you realized they'd told a lot of lies?"

She nodded. "But that was two years ago. I got to know them over the summer. They were good friends."

"That's because you're Roger's girlfriend. He's popular so they're nice to you."

Her face wanted to argue, but she kept her mouth shut.

I relented. Just a little. "Maybe they like you for more than that. You're a very likeable person, but I learned the hard way how they really felt about me."

"Remind me."

She sounded angry. *Didn't she believe me?* She used to.

"In seventh grade, I thought they were my best friends. And I had Chip, the popular boyfriend. When I left for California, they hung all over me and cried. They were going to miss me so much. Four months later? No more boyfriend, and they wouldn't acknowledge my existence. And *you* noticed."

Ronni's expression hadn't changed. "That was junior high. I think we've all grown up since then." She raised one eyebrow, maybe asking if *I* had grown up since then.

I sighed. "I hope you're right. All I ever wanted was for things to be the same as when I left. It's been two years, and I'm still waiting."

"But you'll be nice to them tomorrow?"

"When have I ever *not* been nice to them?"

She cracked a grin, and I made a hasty correction.

"When have I ever been the one to *start* a not-nice scene with them? I just try to stay out of their way."

"I guess." She walked to the end of the driveway with me. "But I think things have changed with them. See if being nice makes a difference."

"Okay. I'll be nice. We'll see if you're right."

But I'd bet all my babysitting money that she was wrong.

Chapter 30:
Mary's Party

Ronni is not here.
But Debbie is going out
By herself. Where? Why?

Mom dropped me off at the party and waited for Mary's door to open before driving away. Music blasted onto the front step.

"You came," Mary shrieked. She yanked me inside.

About a dozen kids gyrated to a beat from Sly & The Family Stone on the stereo in the small living room. I knew most people's names but had classes with none of them.

Mary led me into the kitchen where bowls of chips and boxes of pizza were spread out across the counter. "Sodas are in the fridge, and a few people are outside on the back porch." She nudged me. "Including Rocky."

I took the hint and slipped out the kitchen door leading to a screened-in porch. Nice. Minimal mosquito bites that way. And with distance, my ears didn't hurt from the music.

Rocky lounged on a double-wide swing, one of those rattan kinds suspended from the ceiling. He offered a lazy grin and made room for me. I perched on the edge of the swing, not certain if his welcome was meant for the moment or for the next hour. Not counting Mary, he was the only person at the party who had ever spoken to me. And I never knew what to say at *any* party.

Why couldn't I connect easily with people like Ronni always could?

I had good qualities. I was smart. But no one seemed interested in the things I liked to talk about. Anyone over fifty told me I sang like an angel. But kids my age preferred Carole King to my operatic tones. While I wasn't glamorous, I wasn't ugly either. And why did I worry about this stuff? Would I ever burst through the walls of my own fears about what people think and soar with self-confidence?

I felt like a butterfly stuck inside the cocoon. No longer a blob of a caterpillar, but my iridescent wings couldn't be seen. Yet.

Damon, the Greek god with the raven curls, relaxed on a cane rocking chair across from Rocky and me. One foot anchored him as he gently swayed back and forth, while the other ankle rested on the opposite knee. I could barely breathe, much less speak.

Shelley Dorsey saved the awkward moment only to create another. She wriggled her skinny little self between me and Rocky and pinned me with her eyes in that universal expression of "He's mine."

No problem. But. Would I be able to fit in with this group? Probably not, if Shelley had anything to do with it.

Damon winked at me. Had he figured out Shelley's body language? "Didn't you get yourself a drink before you came out here?" He lifted his can of orange soda. "I'm going for a refill. What can I get for you?"

"A Coke will be fine," I said.

"Not Tab?"

"Can't stand the stuff. It tastes terrible."

Did he think I needed a zero-calorie drink? I might be curvier than Shelley and Ronni, but in the past year, most of my baby fat had disappeared.

Damon chuckled. "You're the first girl I've ever met who admitted that."

Was that a good thing or a bad thing?

In Damon's absence, Rocky said, "You never came back to Surfer Beach. You got home in time, right?"

Another dirty look from Shelley as she tucked herself under Rocky's shoulder.

"I have you to thank for that." Good. My voice sounded solid, not as shaky as I felt. I smiled at him with all the warmth I could muster in a crowd of almost-strangers—a deliberate poke at Shelley's possessive attitude. "But I still got grounded. My parents were already home."

"Bummer."

"Yeah." I sighed. "So, a week stuck at home, then I started a summer job, and I don't have my driver's license yet…"

And Rocky was the only person I had felt halfway comfortable with—all reasons *not* to go back to Surfer Beach.

"I get it. I ended up mowing lawns all summer, so I

didn't get to hit the waves much either."

Jobs! An opening for conversation! I told him my terrible tales of babysitting the Little Monsters. By the time Damon returned to his seat with the sodas, I had Rocky howling over the trash can fire. Shelley was jiggling her foot so hard, I expected her to kick me— accidentally on purpose.

After accepting the cola, I dared to lean back against the swing and let Rocky take over with some of his giant wave stories. The four of us stayed put for a while, as the porch filled up with more and more partygoers.

When Mary came by, her eyes darted from me to Rocky to Shelley and back to me with a silent question. Her matchmaking attempts had ricocheted in the wrong direction. I grinned at her.

"Are you guys hungry yet?" she asked. "Still plenty of pizza and stuff in the kitchen."

I was getting a little hungry now that I'd loosened up some. "I could go for a slice of pizza. Have *you* eaten yet?"

"Nope. I guess I've been the door-greeter all this time, but I think everybody's here by now." She looked around at the crowded porch with people spilling into the backyard. It wasn't quite dark yet, but she had lit the Japanese lanterns already.

Mary and I returned to the kitchen and helped ourselves to pizza with extra cheese. Damon followed us and grabbed a slice of pepperoni and sausage. Mary's eyebrows rose in question. I shrugged and grinned, then took another bite of pizza.

As I wiped sauce from my fingers, Damon asked, "You wanna dance?"

"Sure."

He grabbed my hand, and we headed for the living room. Mary grabbed my arm and pulled in the opposite direction.

"Before you do that, can I borrow Debbie for a minute? I need her help with something."

Damon's grin could only be called "sardonic." Just like I'd read about in books. Which made me nervous again.

"I'll wait," he said.

Mary and I walked down a hall to what had to be her bedroom. "You be careful around him," her voice low and intense.

"We'll just be dancing in your living room." I hadn't expected a friend to sound like my mother.

"He won't want to stay in the living room."

"But your parents are here, aren't they?"

"Yeah, they're downstairs in the family room, and once it gets dark, they'll be cruising the house and stepping outside now and then."

"So, nobody's going to be drinking or doing drugs or any other funny business, right?"

She stared at me, incredulous. "After going with Bill for as long as you did, I can't believe you're so clueless."

"What?"

"Guys came here with their *cars*. My backyard ends up in the *woods*. Lots of places to get yourself in trouble."

"Oh." I felt stupid that she had to explain things. But then again, I knew how to say *no*. "Thanks for looking out for me." I tugged on one of her wild curls that flowed down her back. "And you look fabulous tonight."

"Thanks." She ducked her head as if unused to compliments. When she looked back at me again, her mom-attitude had returned. "And Damon has noticed that cute little halter top you're wearing."

Yeah, Mom hadn't been too pleased about that. And Daddy wasn't home yet this weekend to see it.

Mary and I returned to the kitchen. Damon flashed another movie star smile and took my hand as we headed toward the music. My ears would be ringing into tomorrow, but at least the volume prevented conversation. Damon was a good dancer—far better than Bill ever was—and every once in a while, he'd do some kind of old-fashioned jitterbug step and twirl me around. He made it so easy, I didn't even trip.

Finally, "Crimson and Clover" came on, nice and slow, and he pulled me close. Me. Dancing with the most handsome guy in our class. I was Cinderella at the ball, and Prince Charming only had eyes for me.

The song ended, and he led me off the dance floor back to the kitchen. After retrieving two more cans of soda from the refrigerator, we strolled through the back porch—no seating available—and out the door. The Japanese lanterns strung across the yard created a wonderland of lights as they swung in the light breeze. So romantic.

But like Cinderella, I could only enjoy it until midnight. Eleven-thirty, actually. But my coach wouldn't turn into a pumpkin for another hour.

Damon wrapped an arm around my bare shoulders. "Cold?"

"It feels good after that hot living room."

"I'm glad you came to the party." His arm

tightened around me. "You were the last person I expected to see here."

"Why? Mary and I are friends."

"You never came before."

"Things are different for me this year."

"As in you and Bill are no longer a thing?"

He knew about that. I guess the whole school knew about it. I shrugged, not knowing how to answer. It wasn't his business anyway. Not anybody's business but mine.

Damon guided me toward the far end of the yard away from the lanterns. The music from the house faded. Shrouded in shadows, we reached a gate at the back fence, and he unlatched it.

Alarm bells sounded in my head along with Mary's warning. "Where are we going?"

"I know this cool spot. The trees grow in a circle and if you lie down, you can see the stars right in the middle of the woods." He opened the gate and motioned for me to go through.

And just how was he so familiar with this circle of trees?

I shut the gate.

"What are you doing?" he asked.

I nodded toward the woods outside the fence. "If we're lying down looking at the stars, what else are we doing?"

He flipped on that heart-stopping smile in answer, pulled me close again, and kissed me.

With his reputation, I kind of knew he'd expect me to make out with him, but I wasn't leaving Mary's yard.

He stepped away from the embrace and opened the gate.

I shut it.

The glorious smile disappeared. "Look. Either we take off into the woods for a little bit, or you're on your own for the rest of the night." He opened the gate and walked through, so sure I'd follow, he didn't look back.

Easy decision. Too bad, because he kissed even better than he danced. I shut the gate. The metal latch clanged in the silence, and he turned around in surprise.

"I'd rather be on my own." I pivoted toward the house and didn't look back.

I had just turned down the guy who, hands down, would be voted the Best Looking of the Class of 72. Not exactly the fairy tale ending I'd hoped for, but the tiniest matchstick flame of rebellion warmed something inside me. Maybe I'd be welcomed in this group about as much as I'd been welcomed in Bill's, but for the first time, I didn't care. I had stood up for *me*.

Chapter 31:
Four Become Two

*Debbie has a new
Friend. They let me jump with them.
But where is Ronni?*

As the four of us approached Melissa's place, we heard scattered cheers and chants from behind the house. She even had a sign posted with an arrow toward the fenced backyard. Ronni pushed open the gate, and we strolled in, single file.

"Hi, Ronni!" Melissa handed her a pair of green and white pompoms. "Hi, Thea. Find an open spot in the grass."

Another pair of pompoms went to Thea, and the partners bounded over to some green space.

Then Melissa saw *me*. The Miss America smile disappeared. She stared past my shoulder where Wendy stood. "Umm. This was supposed to be just for sophomores. I can't fit forty-five people in my yard."

I hoped my "bless-you-my-child" smile looked as sweet as Sister Michaelina's. "Wendy will probably be the only freshman here. She has a sophomore partner."

"Everyone else managed to find a partner in their own class."

Yes, I know…

Melissa looked down her nose at me, easy to do since she was four inches taller. Still no offer of green and white pompoms. She wasn't going to back off.

Well, this girl wouldn't either. Gone were the days when I rode my bike home, blinded by tears. I stood and waited. And I looked at her.

Poor Wendy hadn't said a word. Maybe she'd fled. I refused to break off the stare-down to check behind me.

Melissa leaned forward and hissed into my ear. "There are others waiting to get in."

I stepped through the gateway and to my left to make space. Melissa put her smile back on and let six more sophomores through. I peeked back. Wendy stood outside the fence, unmoving, like a deer trying to decide if she should cross the busy highway or bolt back to the woods.

With no more newcomers in sight, Melissa turned her back on the group in the yard and focused her contempt on me. Amazing how she knew all the right stage moves, so no one else could see her face. She opened her mouth to say something, but Ronni came up behind her.

"Hey. Why is Wendy standing out there? Is she afraid to join all of us?"

"Yes—" Melissa started.

"No." I interrupted. "Wendy has not been allowed in." I motioned for Wendy to join us.

Ronni frowned at Melissa. "Why not?"

Melissa swept one arm in a half circle outward.

"There are twenty here already."

Her face pleaded for sympathy, but her pathetic expression didn't move Ronni.

"There's room for one more."

I wasn't sure Ronni's logic would prevail. No one bested the Wicked Witch of the East in her own castle. If I'd had a pair of ruby slippers to transport me and Ronni and Wendy to the safety of my own home, I would've invoked their magic.

Melissa fulfilled my fears. "I'm sorry. I'm just not willing to add one more. My mom was kind of upset that I invited as many as I did."

Ronni turned cold, reminding me of how she used to treat Bill. "You're saying Debbie and Wendy can't join us?"

Melissa's half smile held no warmth. "Well, *Debbie* can, if she wants." Her eyes challenged me.

I spoke up for my partner who had reached my side. "I don't take a step further unless Wendy stays, too."

Thea had watched us from afar and took a step forward, but Ronni held up a hand telling her to wait. She glared at Melissa. "Either Debbie and Wendy come in, or Thea and I leave with them."

Melissa smirked. "Don't you think last year's cheerleaders ought to be here? What's everybody going to think if you don't stay? You and Leigh and Amy are supposed to be our teachers."

Ronni held onto her glare for another couple of seconds, then sagged. Her eyes met mine, begging me to understand.

That was the trouble. I *did* understand. I understood she had chosen cheerleading and the group's admiration over her best friend.

I'd told myself all summer she wasn't really rejecting me, that she only wanted to be with her boyfriend, and boyfriends ranked at the top of priorities. But she had grown to enjoy the popularity, and she wanted to keep her queen bee position. Even if it meant stepping aside while her best friend was demolished in front of a crowd.

The showdown was over. Ronni and I had both lost in more ways than one.

Mom was surprised to see us back home so soon. She didn't comment on my explanation, but maybe she realized, at last, that Melissa hated my guts.

We practiced in *my* back yard, close enough to hear distant cheers down the block at Melissa's. I really wanted to quit the whole idea of cheerleading, but I wouldn't desert Wendy unlike another person who had just hung *me* out to dry.

Later that afternoon after Wendy had gone, Mom called up the stairs. "Debbie, you have mail from California."

Nora Jean had only written one time right after I moved back to New York two years ago. Although she hated anything to do with pencil and paper, she'd wanted to let me know her life in foster care was over.

I thought she'd never go through with her plan. Yeah, the Loughmillers were strict—and weird—but leave a safe place to go live with her brother? I'd seen the filthy shack he and a friend lived in. But she kept her promise to herself. She ran away on her sixteenth birthday, quit school, moved in with Kase, and got a job as a waitress.

I'd written a couple of letters after that, asking how things were going, not expecting an answer, and I was right.

Why now?

I fingered the beads of Nora Jean's necklace as I hurried downstairs. Mom handed me a package. Return address: Mr. and Mrs. Stanley Loughmiller. *Why would her ex-foster parents send me anything? Especially after all this time?*

Mom's face mirrored my own feelings. Puzzled. A little worried.

I needed scissors to cut away all the tape on the small, lumpy box, which required a trip to a kitchen drawer. The lumps proved to be seashells decorating the box. *My* seashell box, the one I gave to Nora Jean when we said goodbye.

I removed the lid. A folded piece of paper covered the contents. I lifted that, and underneath lay two rocks. One smooth, one jagged. The rocks I had given her. The rocks proving to her that she'd been a great teacher to Krista. But they also held a secret meaning for me. The jagged granite represented the hard life Nora Jean suffered. The smooth quartz symbolized the dreams for a better life that I hoped for her.

Had Nora Jean messed up living on her own and returned to the Loughmillers? Had they made her return my gift as punishment? She would never let them go on her own.

Mom peered over my shoulder. "What on earth? The Loughmillers sent you *rocks?*"

Slowly, I unfolded the paper. This couldn't be

good news. "They're *my* rocks. I gave them to Nora Jean. Remember?"

Mom stepped back and allowed me some space.

Exquisite handwriting, almost as perfect as if it had been machine-generated, filled the page of fancy stationery.

> *Dear Debbie,*
>
> *I'm so sorry to have to write this letter. As you know, Nora Jean had been living with her brother, who is not a savory character. Apparently, there was a fight at his house. Nora Jean stepped in front of Kase as the other man's gun went off. She was in the hospital for a couple of days and sent word to us.*
>
> *Of course, we rushed to the hospital. She told us where to find the rocks you had given her, and she wanted to send them back to you if she didn't make it.*
>
> *As you can see, I have returned the rocks. Nora Jean passed on September 4th. For all her faults, she was a good girl. Her action to save her brother proves that. And you were a good friend to her. Thank you.*
>
> *Again, I am sorry to be the bearer of such sad news.*
>
> *Yours truly,*
> *Louise Loughmiller*

I handed the note to Mom.

The polished quartz never stood a chance.

While I tried to finish my homework that night, Mom walked into the bedroom with Krista fresh from the bath. "How much longer do you need?" She combed through Krista's damp hair.

"Maybe half an hour."

"If it takes any longer, bring your work downstairs. I'm going to tuck her in now."

"Okay." I returned to scanning my overview notes on Shakespeare's *Julius Caesar*, vaguely aware of the baby prayers behind me. "God bless Mommy and Daddy and…"

Once blessings were granted to the whole family, Mom turned out the bedside lamp and left the room.

Krista hopped out of bed and leaned against my shoulder, her arms wrapped around the old giraffe she'd slept with since she was an infant. I glanced at her. She grinned. A little imp who knew I'd let her get away with it.

I pointed to her bed and signed SLEEP.

She grinned again and shook her head no.

I kissed her cheek, then pointed again.

With a mock pout she returned to bed, and I returned to the Ides of March summary.

Yeah, Caesar's best friend betrayed him, too. All the negative thoughts, the anger, and the hurt feelings spilled out—tears dropping on my spiral notebook. How was I going to endure three years of high school without my best friend? The girl who *wasn't* my best friend anymore.

And while I'd never expected to see Nora Jean

again since we lived on opposite sides of the country, I *had* expected her to be alive for years and years and years.

I wiped the wet page with my shirt sleeve and shoved the notebook aside. Then I just sat there, staring at my desk, propped on my elbows, as I let tears slide down my face.

A gentle tap on my shoulder. Krista out of bed again. She must have realized I was crying and wanted to know why. The idea of explaining broken friendships and dead friends… I couldn't do it. I ignored her and leaned my forehead into the palms of my hands.

Another tap.

I shook my head no.

Something soft and furry wiggled between my arm and the desk. The nose of Krista's giraffe inched into view. My eyes slid toward where she concentrated on nudging her precious companion upward until it offered a kiss on my cheek.

I straightened and turned to her. Krista's eyes whispered, "I love you," into my gaze. She knew I was hurting. She didn't need to know why.

THANK YOU, I signed, accepting her gift with my other hand.

She wrapped her arms around my waist while I held the giraffe, and we stayed like that until Mom returned to remind me to go downstairs.

Wendy, Krista, and I practiced again after church on Sunday. We were ready. I was so much more coordinated than last year, and quiet Wendy had surprising talent—a voice that could belt out a chant with the best, a great sense of rhythm. I told her to put on her cheesiest smile, which turned her into a beauty. Then she giggled when I told her so, and her natural smile was even better.

After school on Monday, we joined the crowd in the gym. Thirty-six girls with as much nervous energy as the last time I tried out.

I waved to Thea—*she* wasn't responsible for Ronni rejecting me—and I chose a spot as far away from Ronni as I could find.

"Are you nervous?" I asked Wendy.

"Not exactly."

"I was terrified last year. It probably showed."

Wendy smiled. "I think we work really well together. If we don't make it, or if one of us doesn't— well, it was the best we could do."

And here I thought she was a scared mouse like Libby Wojcieski. No, Wendy was just quiet. She had plenty of confidence. The right kind of confidence. Not conceit. I wanted to be like her.

My fingers automatically searched for Nora Jean's beads, but those were in my locker. You can't have any kind of chain flopping around your neck while you dance and jump all over the place.

What would Nora Jean think about cheerleading try-outs? I grinned inside. Nora Jean would have had plenty to say about the "Barbie Dolls," using language that would have sent me to my room if *I'd* said those words.

I watched Ronni on the other side of the gym. She bubbled laughter at something Leigh said. When she looked my way, our eyes connected. Her smile froze, then faded.

Memories flipped through my mind like an Olympic gymnast performing her floor routine. Ronni and me gabbing in our favorite tree. Ronni and me designing our bridesmaids' dresses. Ronni helping me serve lunches at the church bazaar. Ronni and me standing on the bridge and waving to cute guys in their boats. Ronni peeking around the corner of the den with Krista just before the glass door broke.

Put on your armor, Debbie. Pick up your sword and move on.

I grabbed both pompoms and literally shook off the melancholy. Turning to Wendy, I smiled. "Let's do it!"

Mrs. Anniston ran the try-outs the same way as last year. The whole group moved together with a couple of cheers. No problems for Wendy and Debbie. Each pair then performed a cheer of their choice and then a cheer of the judges' choice.

Ronni and Thea got an easy cheer. Thea still got the rhythm wrong. Melissa's and Leigh's assigned cheer proved a little harder than their first choice. Unfortunately, Melissa had also improved over the year. Wouldn't you know Wendy and I were given the same difficult "Who's Got Spirit" cheer as I had my first time around with Ronni?

I inhaled, let my rib cage expand, then whooshed out the air. "Ready?"

Wendy grinned. "We did it perfectly three times yesterday. No worries."

I sent up one more prayer for extra help, and we did it perfectly. Like Wendy said, it was the best we knew how to do.

And we both made the squad!

With Wendy taking gym early in the day, she found out first, and when we passed in the hall before third period, she hugged me. Quiet, calm Wendy *hugged* me!

"Meet me at the gym doors before lunch," I said. "I want you with me when I see our names on the list for myself."

At the appointed time, I read the results. Too quiet to scream for joy, Wendy and I settled for smiles that wouldn't stop.

I'd done it. I was on the squad. Without Ronni's help, too. Maybe now I'd be accepted back into The Group.

Wendy and I studied the list. Ronni was on it, of course. She'd probably be captain. And Leigh and Amy again. Wendy and two other freshmen. And…Melissa.

Chapter 32:
The Rose

I can spell two words!
And I know what's in the box.
I know lots of things.

As usual, we lost the football game. We were only in week three of the season, but we'd started out the same way we ended last year. The team would be lucky if they managed four wins.

As usual, the JV squad gathered at Melissa's for after-game snacks, and as usual, Wendy and I hung around for about twenty minutes.

Our hostess barely tolerated me in her home, and neither Wendy nor I felt comfortable in the crowd of giggling girls. They constantly gossiped about the latest class romances or boasted over every fashion purchase they'd made that week.

Ronni used to be like Wendy and me.

As usual, Wendy and I walked back to my house where she could call her mom to pick her up. After mixing with crowds all afternoon, it seemed like both of us preferred the peace and quiet of our own homes.

Although mine wasn't exactly quiet.

Wade and Paul ran around the yard playing *Keep Away* with Black Jack. Kind of like *Monkey in the Middle*. They tossed a dog biscuit to each other while Black Jack raced from one boy to the other, only to see the treat sail away in the opposite direction. After several laps, the poor dog stood midway between the two and barked in frustration.

I could relate.

Wade leaned down to pet him. "Paul will let you have it next time." He stood. "Go on and toss it to him."

Paul held out the biscuit. "C'mon, boy. You want it?"

Black Jack leaped up, but Paul tossed it toward Wade. Before he could catch it, I batted it to the ground. Black Jack dove for the prize.

"What did you do that for?" Paul scowled. "We were all having fun."

"It didn't look like Black Jack was."

Wade sulked. "I would've given it to him once I caught it."

"He got it faster my way." I led Wendy into the house. "They tease *me*. They tease each *other*. They tease *everybody*. I get sick of it."

She shrugged. "My brothers do the same kinds of things."

"Well, I won't let them tease the dog."

As Wendy dialed the phone, Krista ran into the kitchen holding a small, gilt-wrapped box. With her free hand, she touched all four fingertips to her nose. "Fwow-uh."

"Flower? I don't think so." I pointed to the box. "Too small. Maybe jewelry?" It was about the length of something that might hold a necklace but not as flat. "I made the sign for *necklace.*

She shook her head. "Fwow-uh." She was certain.

"Who is it for?" I asked.

She cocked her head, not understanding my question.

"*Your* box?" I pointed to the box, then to her.

A shake of the head. "Mom."

Mom walked in. "Mystery gift. It came in the mail. The outer packaging had Tiffany's logo on it, but no tag on the wrapped gift."

"*The* Tiffany's?" The New York City store sold the best jewelry and china in the world. "Open it!"

"I'll wait for your father to come home from the hardware store. If he sent it, then I want him to be here when I open it."

"Why would he *send* you a present? He lives here. Besides, it's not your birthday or anniversary."

A little smirk reflected her amusement. "I certainly hope you have a husband who will give you a surprise present every once in a while."

I hoped so, too, but that was so far into my future it wasn't worth spending time thinking about. So back to what *was* important. "Krista says there's a flower inside."

Mom patted her on the head. "Yes, she insists. I keep telling her a flower needs a bigger box."

Krista scratched at a seam in the wrapping paper. Mom lifted the box from her hands. "Oh, no, you don't," she said with a smile. "Mommy's box."

Krista folded her arms and pouted, but not really. The corners of her lips kept trying to turn up.

We waited for Daddy to get home, which didn't

take long. I said goodbye to Wendy as she walked to her mom's car idling at the side of the road. At the same time, Daddy pulled in the driveway.

Krista met him at the door, the box back in her hands.

"For me?" Daddy reached for the box.

He must not have sent it.

Krista hugged it to her chest. "Mom."

"Okay, then. Give it to Mom."

Whether she read his lips or not, it was the natural thing to do. She skipped back to Mom and handed her the box.

"You're not the one who shipped this from Tiffany's?" she asked.

"Not on my salary." He lifted an eyebrow. "Do you have a wealthy admirer?"

Mom sent him a flirtatious glance. "If I do, this is his first overture."

She tore the gold paper off the box. What a shame. I would've smoothed out the gorgeous wrapping and kept it.

A small, handwritten notecard was taped to the box. She read it out loud. "When I saw this, I had to get it for you—our rose in a family of thorns. Love, Vivian."

For all of Aunt Vivian's craziness, sometimes she blessed the world with beautiful generosity. Mom opened the box. A single rose—blossom, stem, and leaflets all gold—nestled under a thin layer of tissue.

Krista peeked into the box then looked at Mom with a smug expression. "Fwow-uh."

Mom and I stared at each other, both of us thinking the same thing.

How did Krista know?

While Krista mystified us with her "sixth sense," she still couldn't understand English very well. None of the kids in her class could either. The deaf school decided fingerspelling might be helpful when a word was not understood through speechreading. Helpful for older deaf kids, maybe, but what three-year-old in the whole country knew how to read? And if a kid couldn't read, what good was fingerspelling?

Krista had known her ABCs for a while, but other than her name, she'd never put the letters together to make words. I decided to teach her.

We would start with consonant sounds she could see, like B and F and M, and put them with vowels. She could see all the vowels, too.

Along with Krista's picture dictionary, I gathered drawing paper, crayons, and letter flashcards and spread them out on the kitchen table one Saturday morning. I had several hours before I needed to meet the bus for our away game, and it wasn't like I had anything else to do. I only saw Ronni in class and at cheerleading.

I pointed to all the school stuff. "Home school."

"'Ool? 'Ome?" Krista's puzzled face made me laugh.

I signed YES and picked up the B card and held it up? WHAT? I signed.

She held up four fingers, her thumb close to her palm.

I put my finger to my lips and brought the finger forward. "Say B."

She frowned.

I shrugged, like it was no big deal. "You know how to say B." EASY. I flicked my third finger off the back of my hand.

"B," she said.

I nodded and showed her the picture of a bee in her dictionary. "Same thing." I signed SAME. "Bee sounds like B." I pointed to the picture, pointed to my ear, and held up my hand with the B sign.

"And look at the letters. B-E-E." I pointed to the letters under the picture and fingerspelled each of them.

Krista automatically copied my actions.

I applauded. "You just spelled a word!" I fingerspelled B-E-E again.

Krista allowed herself a cautious smile.

"Say 'bee.' Just like B." I pointed to the picture, pointed to my lips, said "bee," pointed to the B card, and said "B." Whew. One letter, one word, totally complicated.

"Bee," she said clearly as she pointed to the picture.

I hugged her. "You can do this!"

I pointed to the picture in the book, then fingerspelled B-E-E, then said the word. "Now you do it." I signed YOU-DO.

She grinned and followed my directions. More hugs.

"Now let's do *me*." I pointed to myself for *me* and then to the cards. "Find M," and I fingerspelled the letter.

Krista stared at the cards and found the correct one. YES.

I found the E card and put both letters together. M-

E, I fingerspelled. "Me."

Krista did the same. M-E. "Mmee," she said and pointed to herself.

"Now, you can spell two words," I told her.

She beamed back at me. No tantrums today.

Chapter 33:
The Great Race

I have new braces.
I will run as fast as Wade.
I like to run fast.

I arrived home from school, and Krista greeted me at the door showing off shiny, new, below-the-knee braces. The doctor kept his promise just two days before her fourth birthday.

"Wun," she called out, then turned and ran down the hall. She wobbled a bit but not with the clunky gait from the old, heavy braces.

We celebrated with her favorite dinner. Thrilled with the extra pounds removed from her limbs, Krista swung her legs as she slurped her spaghetti at the dining room table. She must've felt almost weightless.

Mom tapped Krista's shoulder to get her attention. "On Monday, I will come with birthday cupcakes for school."

Krista peered at Mom's lips, then grinned. "Paw-wee."

"Yes. A class birthday party." Mom tapped her legs. "And you will show your new braces."

Krista nodded enthusiastically. "Wun."

"Run in school?" Mom raised an eyebrow in surprise.

Krista's grin remained in place, and she wrinkled her nose, looking like a mischievous pixie. "Wun."

"Sister Evangeline will say, 'No run.'" Mom scowled, but even Krista could see she was teasing.

She lifted her chin in mock defiance. "Wun."

Wade pounded the table, and Krista looked for the source of the vibration. "You want to run after dinner?"

Grandma answered for her. "No. Running is an outdoor activity."

"Then we'll run outside."

"It's too chilly for a little child to run outside at this time of year."

Too late. Krista read, *"out,"* on Wade's lips, slid off her chair, and wobble-ran toward the front door.

Mom hurried after her. "Wait. Get your coat." She opened the closet door and yanked Krista's coat off its hanger.

Wade and Paul left the table, too.

"I can beat both of them," Paul said.

"We know." I jumped out of my chair and grabbed his elbow. "But this is between Wade and Krista, so butt out."

Daddy, who'd commuted home early for a long weekend, cleared his throat. "Did anyone ask to be excused from the table?"

Paul, Wade, and I spun around. We chorused in unison. "May I be excused?"

Daddy inclined his head, giving permission.

Grandma objected. "But we haven't finished dinner."

"After the Great Race," Daddy replied.

Mom zipped Krista's coat and squashed a wool hat over her head. The evening was cool for September, but Krista really didn't need *that* much covering. Besides, it would slow her down.

On their way out the door, Paul instructed Wade. "You guys start at the street end of the driveway and run toward the house. Whoever touches the garage door first is the winner."

"Okay."

"And give Krista a head start, just a step or two."

"Okay." Wade hurried toward the road.

"Hey, Wade." Paul raced after him, Black Jack at his heels.

"Yeah?"

"Don't ever quite catch up to her, okay? At least not until the last step."

Wade peered at him with suspicion. "Is that what you do when *we* race?"

Paul laughed. "The only way you'll ever beat me in a race is if both my legs are broken."

Wade's appraising gaze lasted a moment longer, then he lifted his chin. "It's gonna happen someday."

"Yeah, right. I'll always be taller, and I'll always be stronger."

"Says *you*." Wade marched to the street, Krista and Black Jack following.

Paul moved to the garage door while Krista and Wade positioned themselves where the driveway met the road. A car approached from the highway.

"Move off the road until the car passes," Daddy

called from behind me.

Wade pulled Krista and the dog forward, then pointed toward the lights so she'd understand. I hopped up and down in the cold. No coat.

The car passed, and Wade and Krista repositioned themselves. Paul raised his arm. "Ready, set…go!" His arm slashed down.

Krista lunged forward, and after a moment's hesitation, Wade followed. He didn't run according to Paul's directions though. Instead, he immediately passed her, then kept his pace a step or two ahead of Krista's. As they approached the garage door, he slowed a little more. Krista poured on the speed and touched the door a fingertip ahead of him. In glee, she ran in little circles.

Wade fell to his knees and beat the ground with his fists. "Oh, man! I can't believe you won." Black Jack, who'd made it to the garage door and back to the racers twice before any human reached the finish line, snuggled under his boy and tried to lick his face.

Krista ran circles around Wade, tapping his head as if she were playing Duck, Duck, Goose. Her victory dance.

Mom joined me and Daddy on the steps. "Back to the dinner table."

Paul and Black Jack immediately responded to the word *dinner* and hightailed it to the front door. Wade stood and offered to shake hands with Krista. "Good race." He saluted her.

With a grin, she returned the salute, then slipped her hand into his as they walked back to the house.

Chapter 34:
Swimming Against the Tide

Debbie has been sad
For a long time. What can I
Do to make her smile?

Anybody watching me from a distance would think I was having a great time in tenth grade. I kept my grades up. Yay! I earned a solo for the Christmas program. Yay! I was a cheerleader. Yay! I went to all the "right" parties. Yay. A couple of guys had wanted to meet me at the Saturday night dances. Yay…

Mom mentioned more than once how relieved she was to see me so busy both in and out of school. Daddy didn't pay attention to my social life unless my skirt was too short. And with the school's dress code thrown out the window, my skirts were always too short. But he was in New Jersey during the school week, and Mom didn't need to know I rolled the waistbands to lift the hem by a good three inches once I arrived at school.

Maybe Grandma sensed I wasn't happy. She watched me carefully as if she were trying to figure out a puzzle. And Krista knew. Some evenings when I did my homework after dinner in our room, she'd walk to my desk and wait for me to notice her. Then she'd cup my face in her hands and stare into my eyes. After a few seconds, she would pat my shoulder as if to say, "It will be okay."

Ronni probably knew even though we barely spoke to each other. Just like I sneaked quick peeks at her and could see how Leigh's and Melissa's attitudes made her mad, I'd catch her doing the same thing watching me. But neither of us said anything. Not to each other, not to the evil duo. It was like there was some rule that no one could disagree with those two. If you tried, you'd be banished to a dungeon in some dark, hideous castle, never to see sunshine until you escaped to college.

And Wendy wasn't terrifically happy either. After that disastrous Saturday practice before try-outs, her pipe dream of the perfect high school career for a shy girl who succeeds at cheerleading went up in the same puff of smoke mine had. We loved game days. We loved performing what we'd rehearsed during the week, but the practice hours were the pits.

"Debbie!" I twisted to look down the line for wherever Leigh was standing.

Her jaw had clenched so tight, I was surprised she could spit out words. "It's hands up--stomp, arms out--stomp, clap twice, *then* jump. You've messed it up three times in a row."

I was still a slow learner when it came to cheer patterns, and Leigh didn't have the patience my former best friend had. But Leigh was our captain. Back in September, I had voted for Amy and assumed everyone but me and Melissa would vote for Ronni. I was wrong.

"Sorry." I tightened my lips to prevent even one more syllable to escape that might make me more sorry, especially with Melissa's arrogant smirk focused on me.

"Let's do it *again*." Leigh spun back to her place in the line.

I recited the moves in my head while Ronni called out the words that accompanied this new cheer. When practice ended, she paused beside me where I sat on the first row of bleachers and retied my tennis shoes.

"You'll get it."

I looked up at her. "Get what?"

"That new cheer."

"I know." I plucked at the laces of my second shoe. "I'll practice more at home."

When she didn't move, I looked up again. She opened her mouth like she planned to say something more, then shut it and walked away.

Most lunch hours, I sat with the cheerleaders who shared my late lunch schedule. It seemed to be expected, but I always made it a point to join Mary on Fridays. At least, I could end my week in pleasant company.

On a Tuesday toward the end of football season, I was sitting with Melissa and the others. A few of the football and basketball athletes cracked jokes and threw wads of paper napkins at each other at the far end of the long table. The buzz of fifty conversations punctuated by the occasional outburst of laughter filled the cafeteria.

Bored with Melissa's recitation on the most recent story she'd read from *True Love Magazine* (who really falls in love with their kidnapper?), I wandered into people-watching mode. Marty's hair had grown longer, and he constantly flipped it out of his face. Made me wonder if food ever got mixed in with the tangle. He hardly ever teased me in homeroom anymore. I kind of missed that. Chip munched on a hamburger at the other end of the table, ignoring his buddies, even when a paper wad bounced off his shoulder. How come with guys the strong, silent types were popular, but girls had to be bubbly and all smiles to get people's attention?

A table a few rows away from us held only one person. A guy. He looked kind of familiar, but I hadn't seen him in the cafeteria before. I nudged Melissa, who hadn't yet finished her story.

"Who's that?" I asked.

"What?" Her startled frown should've warned me off.

I rested my hand on the table and pointed toward the guy, trying not to be obvious. "Him." I could count on Melissa for knowing the latest gossip.

She peered across the room. "Oh, yeah. Jimmy Pulizzi. He used to live here. Moved away and now he's back." She returned to her audience.

Jimmy Pulizzi? The bully from sixth grade? Who turned out to *not* be the bully I thought he was? The guy who moved because his dad went to Vietnam? Whose dad was now missing in action? Jimmy, who had tried to make me feel better after my best friend Nancy moved to Arizona?

I stared at the guy. Yeah, that was him. His hair was longer, his face thinner. In fact, he was pretty good-looking. My pulse ticked up a notch. "Let's go talk to him."

No one paid any attention to what I said. They were still hanging on Melissa's every word.

I increased my volume. "Let's go talk to him."

Melissa's voice cut off, and she crinkled her nose at me as if I had bad breath. A one-apple lunch shouldn't have caused that kind of problem. "Talk to who?"

I reached for the beads around my neck. "Jimmy Pulizzi."

The other girls turned around to look behind them. A muffled twitter swept through all three of them to the general tune of "He's cute."

"Yeah, he is," I agreed.

Melissa didn't care for the spotlight shifting to anyone other than herself. "Why would we talk to a guy who used to terrorize the younger kids on the playground?"

"That was years ago. He might've grown up by now." She was really going to hold it against a guy for what he did as a little kid? Besides, before he'd moved to Queens, I'd gotten to know a better side of him, at least for a moment or two.

She stared at me. I squeezed one bead tight, but this time I didn't drop my gaze, not like everyone else who wanted to be accepted in this group. With her audience still whispering to each other about the distant charms of Jimmy Pulizzi, Melissa's ice-blue eyes cooled to subpolar. If anyone had been watching us, they wouldn't have noticed anything amiss by her body language. It was all in the eyes.

"There's no way I'm going to walk over there and

say hi to a person I haven't seen since sixth grade. He's an Air Force kid who left, now he's back, and in a few months, he'll be gone."

The expression on her face implied *good riddance*. And…comprehension dawned. Melissa had *never* forgotten I was an Air Force kid. I'd returned the summer after seventh grade, but she wouldn't let it go. As far as she was concerned, I was *still* in the same category as Jimmy.

I appealed to the girls across from me. "What do you think? Shall we go over there and talk to him? The guy has got to be lonely if it's his first day and nobody bothered to sit with him at lunch." I sure remembered the feeling.

More giggles.

"You can't just go up to a guy and say hi."

"I would die of embarrassment."

"We can't do that."

"Why not?" Pressure built inside my chest like a steam locomotive with an overheated boiler.

Melissa tossed her perfect, silky blond hair behind her shoulder. "Look. If Jimmy has changed, the guys will notice." She nodded toward the flying paper wads." And we'll see him at this table."

I turned to the other three girls and tried one more time. "He's by himself. That's got to be *so* lonely." To release a little of the pressure, I attempted some humor and dangled extra bait. "Who knows? You might get a new boyfriend."

They looked at me, at Jimmy. At Melissa. They shook their heads.

Melissa aimed her perpetual smirk my way.

I was *so tired* of that smirk. *So, what are you going*

to do about it, Debbie? Bow to the queen of the class of 1972 once again?

I had spent almost three years—three *years*—trying to please these people. Three years of groveling, three years of setting aside what *I* thought was important and going along with what *they* dictated. I had worked my tail off to become a cheerleader, just to have an extra edge. I had pushed Mary, a possible good friend, off to the side to get in the good graces of people who "counted," like Melissa.

I doused the fire in my chest with some ice of my own.

Melissa was not my friend. Never had been. Probably never would be.

I didn't need to scream at her. I didn't need her at all.

The beads swung free from my grasp.

In sixth grade, I had faced Jimmy Pulizzi the Bully, looked into his eyes, and I'd seen shame. And pain. Later that summer, Jimmy had told me I was pretty after he heard a girl call me fat. I wished we could have been friends, but he moved away the day after we declared a truce.

I owed him.

Jimmy's dad was missing in action in Vietnam. If my dad hadn't returned from the war, if I hadn't known if he were dead or alive, how would I have survived? Jimmy had to be sad and more lonely than I had ever been.

I stood. Cool. Calm. These girls had no clue. "If you don't want to go with me, then I'll go by myself."

Three girls' mouths dropped open. Melissa's shut into a thin line.

Her disapproval would never have any effect on me again. I stepped away from the group and strode down the aisle toward Jimmy's table.

Chapter 35:
Jimmy

Debbie reads to me.
The duckling is sad until
It becomes a swan.

I hoped I looked confident on the outside, because inside I was terrified. Knowing the other girls were watching, I didn't slow my steps. What if Melissa was wrong? If this guy wasn't really Jimmy, I still wanted to be nice to a new kid. And if he was Jimmy, what if he didn't remember me? I hadn't recognized *him*, at first.

I reached his table and stood behind the chair opposite his. He looked up at me with a squint.

I mustered a smile. "Hi… is this your first day here? I noticed you were sitting by yourself." Was that too direct? Had I embarrassed him?

A smile quirked his lips. "Debbie Hansen?"

He remembered!

I grinned back at him. "Yeah, and I wasn't sure, but you're Jimmy Pulizzi?"

"That's me. Back from the New York City jungle."

He motioned for me to have a seat, and I slid into the chair. "Wow. It's been a long time." *Now* what should I say?

I'd pretty much forced myself into his space, but what would be a safe topic? Asking about his dad would be too raw. Could I get any hint from his eyes? Brown with flecks of green. Yes, I remembered. Remembered that first connection, too. This time I could see sadness.

Or was it my imagination?

He broke the silence. "My mom decided we should get out of the City. She still has a couple of good friends here, so…"

"Yeah, we stayed here, too. My parents decided to keep us in one school for all of high school, so my dad commutes to New Jersey."

Shoot. I'd gone and mentioned my dad.

He nodded, the sadness in his eyes even greater. "So, your dad didn't have to go to 'Nam?"

"He went there. He deployed about a year after your father left." I dropped my gaze. "I heard about your dad being MIA. I'm sorry."

"Thanks."

Awkward silence.

I cleared my throat. "Is this your first day, or have I been totally oblivious all year?"

"Yesterday was my first day back. It's…different from what I remembered."

"It is?"

Was he having to suffer what I suffered almost three years ago?

"Yeah, I hardly know anybody. You're the first person I recognized from the base."

"And that's probably because I came back, too, after we moved to California for four months. Any other Air Force kids have only gotten here since both of us left."

He nodded his understanding. After a moment, the old mischievous grin appeared on his face. "Does that mean Dogface Candi moved?"

I laughed. Maybe he remembered our last conversation, too. "She was gone by the time I returned for eighth grade." I surprised myself by leaning in toward him. "I never got a chance to thank you for what you said the day before you moved."

"You mean when I said, 'You're not fat, and Candi's ugly?'" He shook his head. "I couldn't stand her."

"Yeah, but I was the one who yelled at you and called you names on the bus earlier that summer."

His grin returned. "I deserved it that day."

"Nobody deserves that. I felt terrible as soon as I said it, and I never had the guts to apologize."

The hint of snark left his face. "Apology accepted."

I sucked in a breath and exhaled in relief. "I don't think I realized until just now that's one reason I wanted to talk to you."

"And the other was you really wanted to meet the cute new guy, right?"

Was he flirting with me? I liked it.

"Right. The others at my table were drooling all over you, so I figured I'd better move fast." And I felt comfortable flirting right back. *Amazing.*

A blush accompanied his laugh.

"Anyway," I continued, "on that last day before

you moved, you were the one who had something kind to say. You made me feel better. So, thank you. A couple of years late." My apology had needed a thank-you attached.

His grin reappeared. "I still think you're pretty."

Jimmy *was* flirting with me. And I *liked* it.

"You haven't turned out so bad either. I'm glad I invited myself to your table."

The buzzer sounded to move on to sixth period.

"Where do you head next?" he asked.

"History. You?'

"Geometry. Too bad we don't have any classes together."

"Yeah."

"But I could eat lunch with you sometimes. If you want." He said it carelessly, but I was sure he wanted to.

I knew I did.

I looked back at the table I'd just walked away from. Melissa's laser gaze was still locked on me.

"If you'd rather sit with your friends, I get it," Jimmy said.

I swung back to him. "No. I'd rather sit with you."

When I left Spanish class at the end of the day, Leigh followed me to my locker. "I heard what you did at lunch today."

"Heard what?" As if I didn't know.

"Melissa told you not to talk to him."

I frowned at her. "Melissa isn't my boss."

Usually, her critical attitude would have

browbeaten me into total submission. Not anymore.

Why would she care if I talked to Jimmy? I considered two possibilities, neither of which had me shaking in my shoes. Either Leigh was jealous that a good-looking guy liked me, or she didn't relish the feeling of losing power over me. The control thing was probably the kicker, but I wouldn't rule out envy either.

I pushed my locker door shut with a little more force than necessary. "Welcoming someone new to the school isn't a crime. In fact, consider it my good deed for the day."

She looked startled. Not only was this new Debbie *un*intimidated, but she had already initiated her own game plan.

Leigh gathered up her arrogance once again. "It would've been better for the guys to welcome him than one girl."

"But they didn't, did they?" My hand clenched into a fist. *What was I going to do? Bash her?*

Leigh's chin lifted in defiance at my accusation.

I expelled my frustrations with a sigh. "Have you ever been the new person in school? Or anywhere?"

Her brows rose in surprise at my question, then dipped to a frown as she considered her answer. "Not in school. But maybe my first day of ballet class when I was six." She chuckled at the distant memory.

"Were you scared?"

"Scared I didn't know how to do ballet." She added another chuckle.

I didn't crack a smile. "Scared someone would laugh at you, right? Scared you wouldn't be good enough? Maybe none of the other little ballet dancers would be your friend because you didn't measure up?"

Our eyes met, and I tried that "looking into the eyes of the soul" thing. A glimmer of the scared little girl of memory, then it winked out as if a candle snuffer dropped over it.

Leigh shrugged, a silent refusal to share any further memories. The arrogant grin remained on her face.

I wasn't done. "Do you remember when I came back to Hampton Shores the summer after seventh grade?"

Her grin faltered. "That… was awkward. You thought Chip would still be your boyfriend, but he liked me by then."

"You know what was more awkward for me than that?"

She blinked and didn't respond.

"I came back, and no one welcomed me. It was like they didn't even want to *see* me again. All of a sudden, I had *no* friends."

She shifted from one foot to the other. "We were just…surprised…that you really did come back."

Yeah, that had been obvious. "Did *surprise* mean you should shut me out? When I had been friends with you before?"

"No, that wasn't it."

"So, what was 'it?'" I was sure my suspicions were correct.

"It was…Chip."

Not the answer I expected. "Chip told everybody to ignore me?"

"Of course not." Leigh didn't meet my eyes. "I was afraid Chip would like you again."

I cracked a smile. "I guess back in eighth grade I

would've liked that."

Leigh pulled herself back together. Head cheerleader. Brisk. Efficient. "Any other ancient history questions for me?"

"Yeah. One." Like the real answer to my burning question.

"Go for it." She managed to look bored.

"Chip might have been *your* reason for not wanting to be my friend, but that doesn't explain the others. What did I ever do to all of you?"

She peered at me, eyes hard. "You didn't *do* anything."

What did that mean? "I did plenty. We were in the same classes. I sang in choir with some of you. Played football on Sunday afternoons with you. Stood around at 7th grade dances with you."

She rolled her eyes. "I meant it had nothing to do with what you did. Although sometimes, with all your smarts, you're a bit arrogant. It had everything to do with who you *are*."

"Who I am." Now we were getting somewhere. I stared at her, waiting. I'd make her say it.

"You want me to spell it out for you?"

"Yeah. I do."

"If Chip hadn't chosen you back then, you wouldn't have been part of the group in the first place. Air Force kids never work out. And if you hadn't been part of the group, you wouldn't have expected to be back with us, and your feelings wouldn't have been hurt."

I nodded. Leigh boiled it down to Chip, but I'd known from the first rejection it had to do with my being military. "I guess I was kind of like the ugly duckling."

Leigh had opened her mouth to add something, but shut it at my comment. "*What?* What does a fairytale have to do with anything?"

"Follow me, here. I'm trying to give you a simile. Like we learned about in English?" *Whoa.* That last line made me as snarky as Melissa and Leigh combined. I toned down the attitude. "The swan's egg accidentally got put in with a nest of duck eggs. And once all the eggs hatched, the baby swan didn't look like any of his brothers and sisters. The ducklings thought he was too big and too awkward. He didn't fit in with the rest of them." I opened my eyes wide to appear as harmless as possible. "Do you get it?"

She thought about it. "Yeah. You didn't fit in." She had enough of a guilty conscience to glance away. "Sorry if that hurts your feelings."

"I don't think it does anymore. But I guess you're stuck with seeing me every day through the end of basketball season." I adjusted the purse strap on my shoulder. "See you at practice."

I glided down the hall feeling like the beautiful swan taking flight at the end of the *Ugly Duckling* fairytale. New confidence filled the air beneath my wings.

Chapter 36:
Ronni

I miss Debbie's old
Friend, Wonni. I mean Rrronni.
Talking is so hard…

The next day at lunch, I had some options. If Jimmy was sitting alone again, I'd join him. If not, I'd either sit with Mary's group or with Wendy and her best friend.

I would *not* be at Melissa's table. My choice. All the weight of trying to please those people had lifted off me. It was like I had punched that hovering dragon of fear right in the eye and it fled, defeated.

I entered the cafeteria with my lunch. Not just an orange. Tired of being hungry all the time, I'd added a salami sandwich. Maybe I'd splurge on a slice of pizza the next time the cafeteria offered it. After retrieving a vanilla cream soda from the machine, I scanned the room.

There. Same place as before. Jimmy slid onto the bench of the empty table. Girls at Melissa's table glanced his way, but nobody moved. The guys on the other end of it had their eyes on a mini-skirted figure who sashayed her way out the door. Wendy was in deep conversation with Linda. Mary's back was to Jimmy, so she wouldn't even know he was there. Kids at the tables surrounding his appeared to have no awareness of his presence, as if he were invisible.

Decision made. I approached Jimmy's table, and his eyes lit up in welcome. "Hey! Glad you made it."

"Me too." I sat across from him, the bag crackling as I pulled out my lunch.

He was brown bagging it, too, but his sandwich looked straight out of an Italian deli. About three times the height of my pitiful slices of salami and Wonder Bread, Jimmy unwrapped a hoagie bun filled with all kinds of meats and veggies.

He noticed me staring and grinned. "Having an Italian mama *and* grandma in the same house has definite advantages." He lifted the glorious sandwich and bit off a huge chunk. It took a lot of jaw work before his mouth was empty enough to say anything more. "I never stay hungry for long."

"Guess not." I finished my puny sandwich and peeled the orange while he concentrated on his feast. "How did the rest of your day go yesterday?"

"Not bad. I like having biology at the end of the day. I stayed and talked with Mr. Freiburg after. Didn't have to worry about being late for the next class."

"Mr. Freiburg is pretty nice. A little eccentric, but nice. And fair." I pulled an orange segment from its brothers. "Did you take biology in Queens, or is this new for you?"

"I was taking it. But different book so slightly different order, you know? And the class was a zoo, so

I couldn't learn very much. Too bad because I really like studying that stuff." He took another huge bite of sandwich and chewed away.

"So far, we've only dissected earthworms. But next month, we're supposed to get to frogs." Why was I talking about this subject while eating my lunch?

Jimmy didn't seem to mind. "Cool," he said with his mouth still full. He gulped down what was left. "We didn't get to dissect anything. They said there wasn't enough money. I think it was more like they didn't want scalpels in the hands of some students."

"You could've been stabbed in class?" I'd heard city schools were rough, but…

He shook his head. "Naw. But those things would disappear and get used someplace else." He looked at me to see if I caught his meaning. I did.

"Anyways," he eyed the last inch of his hoagie, "I don't have to deal with it anymore. I've got the beach and a boat. What more could I want?"

Me, maybe? If he loved the beach like I did, he might be the boyfriend of my dreams. As for the boat, I could coach myself out of any seasickness. Mind over matter.

While he finished that last bite of bread, I popped another orange segment into my mouth. I might as well give it something to do, since as usual, not one coherent thought had entered my head so my brain could pass it on to my speech center.

Jimmy washed down his meal with a carton of milk, then wiped his mouth with the back of his hand. He must have had second thoughts about that because he plucked a paper napkin out of his lunch bag and dried off the hand. "So, what do people do around here on the weekend?"

My mind darted to parties like Mary's and parties after football games and I'll-meetcha-at-the-movie nights and occasional dances. "The usual stuff, I guess. Is it any different in the City?"

He rolled his eyes. "I wouldn't know. If I wasn't at school, my mom barely let me out of her sight."

If I were a mom living in a high-crime city, I wouldn't let my baby out of my sight either, no matter how old he was. Jimmy seemed to be waiting for a more detailed answer to his question about Hampton Shores's social life. I changed the subject.

"You have a boat?" Usually, that's all it would take to get a guy waxing eloquent on his seafaring darling. Jimmy didn't prove me wrong.

"It's really just a dinghy." He bobbed his head in apology. "But in the spring, I'll have enough money to add a motor. And she's a sweet little thing. My uncle gave her to me after he knew we were moving back here. Got her a new coat of paint, too."

"What color?"

"Red and white. Like stripes on a flag."

He watched for my reaction like some teachers do when they ask a loaded question. *Would I pass the test?* A lot of kids—like those in the anti-war crowd—might rip right through him for such a patriotic statement.

"So is the lettering in navy blue?" I asked.

His whole body relaxed. "Yeah."

"What's her name?"

"Mia."

M-I-A. Missing In Action. "Oh, Jimmy." I blinked back the sting of tears.

His smile held more sorrow than I could generate

with my sympathy. "You get it."

I kept blinking. "My dad crashed over there. But in safe territory. He survived. He's fine now." What else could I say? "I'm sor—"

"Don't be." He grabbed my hand. "You deal with whatcha got to deal with, y'know?"

I nodded. Yes, I knew.

We stared into each other's eyes, just like we had back in sixth grade, when I caught a glimpse into his soul. But this time neither one of us was angry. Or ashamed. This time we connected in agreement.

And some kind of electrical current flowed from his hand to mine. I gave a little tug to pull away, and he immediately released it.

I returned to the safer subject of fall weekend activities in Hampton Shores. "There's always some kind of party after the game on Saturday. You want to go?"

"With you?"

"Yeah."

"Cool."

I had just asked a guy out on a date. *Was this worse than "I'll meetcha at the party?"*

As I headed for home after cheerleading practice, Ronni ran to catch up with me. *Unusual.* We hadn't walked home together all year. Not since that fateful cheer practice before try-outs.

"Hey," she said, a little breathless.

"Hi."

We walked the familiar path in silence.

She broke it as we approached her house. "Something happened with you, didn't it?"

I stopped walking to stare at her. "Something happened with me?"

"Yeah." Her voice trailed off. "You've been different the last couple of days."

"What do you mean?"

She met my eyes. "Up until yesterday, you were always afraid to speak your mind. Like you didn't want people to be mad at you."

"I guess you've been talking to Melissa or Leigh."

Ronni glanced away. "*They* talked to *me*."

"And I'll bet you got an earful."

She shrugged. "It doesn't matter what they actually said. But yesterday, you acted like you couldn't care less what Leigh or Melissa thought of you. And you've always wanted them to accept you."

I held her gaze but remained silent.

"And you did the same thing today." Another awkward silence, then a nervous giggle. "Leigh was shocked. She actually used the word." Ronni mimicked her in a high British accent. "'I'm *shocked* that quiet little Debbie had the guts to tell me off.'"

Last year, I would have laughed at the imitation, but now, I fired a question instead. "Did Leigh send you to talk to me?"

Ronni stepped back in self-defense. "Why would she do that?"

"To get me back in line. That's why."

"Get you back—"

"In line. Toe the line. Stay in line. The *Line,* according to Leigh and Melissa." I glared at her. "Remember when you used to tell me I should stand up

288

for myself? I shouldn't satisfy Bill's every whim?"

She nodded, eyes large.

"For a long time, I just couldn't do it. And it made you mad."

She nodded again.

"But the other day, everything just got to me." I flipped my hands away from me. DONE, in sign language. "I was sitting there with Melissa and some of the others. And I saw Jimmy Pulizzi sitting all by himself. And nobody would be friendly with him. Why? Because he was Air Force? Because he had been a bully back in *elementary* school? Because he hadn't proved himself *worthy* of Hampton Shores's standards? It was me all over again. Except worse."

Ronni's eyes widened even more, as if what could be worse?

"How would *you* feel if you didn't know if your father was alive or dead? Or tortured? And nobody in this entire school showed an ounce of kindness?"

I glared at her again. "You tell our precious captain that except for cheerleading, I am no longer under her command. I will not be the Earth orbiting her Sun."

Mr. Crane would say I was mixing my metaphors, but I didn't care. "You tell Leigh to think back to what I said about her first-grade ballet class. I *will* be nice to Jimmy. And if that offends Leigh and Melissa, tell them they can go to—" I stopped myself. I would never wish that on anybody. Not even Melissa.

I never knew Ronni's innocent face could look so guilty. She was too nice. But lately? Maybe she was tangled as tightly in Melissa's web as I had been.

"Just tell them there's a new Debbie in town. And she's *not* moving any time soon."

I strode down the road, and I didn't look back. *Oh, that felt good!*

Chapter 37:
Mrs. McNab

Dee-chuh knows my name.
But she calls me the wrong name.
On purpose! Bad girl!

K rista's screeching pierced through the closed front door as I gingerly maneuvered the icy front steps in my smooth-soled shoes. After tapping my feet against the threshold to get rid of wet, February snow, I slipped through the door and followed the noise to the den.

"What do you want, child? What do you need?" Grandma held her hands open in a gesture of helplessness. Her pleading only brought more screams. Poor Grandma got all fluttery like a nervous sparrow whenever Krista went on a rampage.

"Where's Mom?"

Grandma turned my way, startled. No wonder she didn't hear me come in with Krista's yowling. "We're out of coffee. She ran to the store to get some."

Krista didn't notice me either. She pointed upward to the fireplace mantel and screamed. What did the fireplace ever do to her? And where were the boys?

And the dog?

I stood on the brick hearth and checked to see what might be on the mantel that angered her. Aha! A miniature troll doll peeked from under the evergreen garland which had remained there since Christmas.

I plucked the doll from its hiding place and showed it to Krista. "Is this what you want?"

She immediately calmed down and held out her hands. Easy fix, but something told me a brother or two was responsible for the latest outrage. "Who put it up there?"

Krista could see the word *who*.

"Way." She scowled as her lips turned down.

Yeah, Wade would've been my guess.

"You want to punch Wade, don't you?" I made a fist and a punching motion. *Wade* was easy to lipread, too.

With a short nod she made a U-turn, obviously on her way to Wade's bedroom to follow my suggestion. She had seen YOU-PUNCH-WADE but had missed the "want to" part of my sentence.

I grabbed her. "No. Forget it. You have your doll." I pointed to the troll and signed HAVE.

She frowned and ignored me. "Baaa. Way baaa."

I held her in place as she struggled. "Yes. Wade is bad. But you are good." I pointed to her and signed GOOD, then blew her a kiss. "Don't be like Wade."

She shook off my grip and glowered.

"Play a game?" I spoke and signed at the same time.

Holding the troll in one hand, Krista approached the game cupboard and pulled out *Sorry*.

I dropped to the floor and sat cross-legged.

"Okay."

Grandma heaved a sigh. "Thank you. I just didn't know what she wanted."

"I got lucky this time."

"Well, after your father, you seem to be able to calm her down the most."

"More than Mom?"

"Your mother tends to get angry first, *then* tries to solve the problem. You deal with her more like your father does."

Only Daddy had the magic touch. Unfortunately, he still spent the work week in New Jersey, which meant he wasn't around for most of the chaos.

So, Grandma thought I treated Krista like Daddy did. I smiled inside.

As we set up the *Sorry* board, Jimmy rapped lightly on the door frame. I nudged Krista, who looked up, grinned, and filled up the yellow circle with game pieces—his favorite color.

Walking away from Melissa that day back in October proved to be the best move I'd made since starting high school. In the last four months I'd learned that sparks in romance *weren't* pure fiction and having a boyfriend who was fun to be with and who enjoyed my family made life pretty sweet. My parents saw more of Jimmy in one week than they'd ever seen of Bill in a whole year. Black Jack knew he was good for a magnificent scratch behind the ears. Krista figured out quick that Jimmy would do anything to please her. Since he was an only child, he called her his adopted little sister.

Even my brothers seemed to approve once they met him. They also remembered how he used to bully kids on the bus years ago, but unlike my classmates, Paul and Wade had kept an open mind regarding the present-day Jimmy.

"How did the interview go?" I asked him.

Most days, Jimmy walked home with me right after school if I didn't have cheer practice or show choir rehearsals, but he had started a job search for the spring and summer.

"Pretty good, I think." He hunkered down on the carpet in front of the yellow starting circle. "Your dad said I could use him for a reference since he knows the owner. So. Hopeful."

As Krista carefully counted out eight squares forward on the *Sorry* board, Jimmy and I practiced sign language.

"EYES-BLUE-YOU," Jimmy signed.

I smiled. "EYES-BROWN-YOU."

"YOU-PRETTY-YOU." He smiled back. "How do you say *blush*?"

"I never learned that one. Stop embarrassing me." I circled the fingerspelling of R on my cheek. Maybe that was the sign for blush—red cheek.

"Chimmy!"

We looked at Krista, who seemed perturbed with us.

"Chimmy. Oo. Oh." She stabbed her finger at Jimmy, then pointed to the board. "You go," she was trying to say.

He picked up a 4 card, and Krista laughed. "Oh baaa." *Go back.* Her fist circled on her chest for SORRY, but her smirk told us what a little liar she was.

He made his game piece stomp backwards four spaces much to her delight. After I marched twelve spaces around the board, Krista took her next turn.

"Why can't she make the sound for G?" Jimmy asked.

"You can't see a G. It's at the back of your throat. Same problem with K."

"So, she can't say her name?"

"No. And you can't see R, S, or T either. And she hates her speech teacher, so she won't try to say the sounds that are difficult."

"Poor kid."

"My fault, too. It was my idea to name her Krista."

"It's a pretty name."

"Yeah, I thought so. But now I wish we'd named her Molly."

Jimmy mouthed the word *Molly*. "I see what you mean."

"Chimmy!"

Oops. Jimmy's turn again.

After Jimmy left, Krista and I put away the pieces to *Sorry* and pulled out the game of *Trouble* with its dice popper. Krista loved to feel the vibration when she pushed down on the popper, and the dice tumbled all over the place in its bubble globe. Black Jack joined us. The sound of the popper always fascinated him. He'd stare at it with such intensity, he must've thought it was a small, caged animal.

Mom peeked into the family room. "Another game? We'll be eating dinner in about twenty minutes."

I nodded and let Krista go first. She popped a one which allowed her onto the board. When she looked for me to take my turn, I was ready with a question.

"Is Mrs. McNab mean?"

Mrs. McNab was Krista's speech teacher.

Krista could see three of the four words from my question. She shook her head.

"But you don't like her?" I signed NOT-LIKE.

She shook her head again as I popped a four. That wouldn't let me out of my start corner. "Why not?"

Krista didn't respond, and I realized she'd been placing all her attention on the popper and not on my lips. When she looked up, I repeated my question.

"Why not?"

"Oo-iss-uh." She pointed to herself.

Oo-iss-uh? What's an oo-iss-uh? Mystified, I had to ask. "Oo-iss-uh?"

Big sigh. Eyes rolling in disgust. "Me! Oo-iss-uh!"

She acted like I was a big dunce. I mouthed KR. Yeah, Krista could only see the oo shape of my lips. Oo-iss-uh with a K in front would be Koo-iss-uh. So, Oo-iss-uh meant *Krista*.

Mrs. McNab *had* succeeded in getting Krista to make the S sound, but the only time I ever heard her say a T on her own was at that gas station last summer.

"Does Mrs. McNab want you to say *Krista*?" I emphasized the K by spelling it and touching my throat.

Krista growled in response. I'd been warned.

I spelled R and said, "Errrr."

With a sassy sneer, Krista answered, "Uhhhhhr."

I was pushing my luck.

"Tih." I spelled T and let my thumb touch behind my front teeth.

Her sneer still in place, she copied my motion, then flipped her thumb out of her mouth leaving me with the feeling she'd just sent me an obscene message.

"But you say *Oo-iss-uh*?" I spelled W and S and pointed at her.

I'd pushed her over the edge. With a resounding *no*, Krista tossed the board in the air, letting the little pieces sail across the room. Black Jack scrambled to his feet and ran for cover.

I stood. "No more game. *You* pick up the mess."

I turned to walk from the room, but she chased after me and grabbed my hand.

"Deechuh." She signed SAY. "Deena." Her eyes pleaded for me to understand.

Deechuh meant teacher. Krista had tried very hard to get some kind of sound out for the T. But *Deena?* Make the D into a T, and you've got Teena. *Teacher Teena?* Teacher says *Teena.* Mrs. McNab was calling her a different version of her full name, Christina. The *wrong* name, as far as Krista was concerned. "Mrs. McNab says Teena?"

Krista's eyes got big, and she nodded with two swift jerks of her head.

"No problem," I said as I signed and fingerspelled. "Mom will tell Mrs. McNab to call you Krista."

Krista smiled. Problem solved.

Only it wasn't. When Mom told Mrs. McNab, the lady already knew Krista didn't like to be called "Teena."

"I'm trying to get Krista to make the T sound. She can do it, but she doesn't want to. And the K escapes her entirely. I'm waiting for her to get so agitated it will be important enough for her to use the T and work on the K to tell this dumb teacher what her name is."

Mom and Daddy went along with the idea. Almost every day, someone in the family would ask her, "Is your name Teena or Krista?"

"Wissuh" was always her first response when Mom asked.

But if the boys initiated the question, you could be sure of a scream.

Mom told her Mrs. McNab was waiting for Krista to say her name correctly. I told her, too. It only made Krista angrier. The lady knew her name but wouldn't say it.

Chapter 38:
Student Teacher

Debbie is coming
To school with me. Everyone
Watches me and smiles.

Winter dragged into a cold spring, and Krista still wouldn't say a K for Mrs. McNab.

When it came time for Easter break, Krista's school took Holy Week off. My school started vacation on Good Friday and lasted through the *following* week. With Jimmy in Florida visiting his other grandparents and not returning until Thursday, I could only look forward to boredom.

So, I asked if I could spend a couple of days at the deaf school to observe, maybe help. If I planned on becoming a special education teacher, it could be a great experience. And spending time at Krista's school might keep my week of vacation from dragging as slowly as our little Renault used to when it toiled through the Rocky Mountains.

Mom received an enthusiastic yes from Sister Ignatius, but there was a catch. Not sure of the legalities of transporting a nonstudent, Mom would have to drive me herself. Good. While the new driver from the deaf school always kept Charlene and Lucy under control, I'd never said anything to them again. Traveling to school on their bus would make for an uncomfortable ride.

Mom was happy to drive. It meant Krista could leave for school a half hour later and get home quicker.

Student teaching, here I come!

On Tuesday morning, I sat in the back of the classroom and did nothing but observe. First on the agenda was the weather. Ten children sat bunched together on carpet squares. Sister Evangeline and Miss Lynn, the class aide, took turns pointing out the window, then displaying a cut-out of a cloud and a sun and pressing them onto a flannel board. A little boy paper doll was also attached to the board.

Sister Evangeline pointed to one of the little kids. "Diana, what clothes should the little boy wear?" She pointed to several items of paper doll clothing lying on the floor in front of the board.

Diana knew the drill and chose a jacket, making sure the doll was *very* warm—the collar covered his nose. Another child chose a pair of pants which ended up so skewed the doll had one bare leg. The last little girl dressed the doll with a cap. All the little kids clapped at their creation. The cap fell off of the paper doll's head. Giggles.

Following the weather and the calendar, the kids went to their seats, and Miss Lynn handed out wide-lined paper and fat pencils. She and Sister Evangeline wandered the room helping individuals write the letters P and R and B. After fifteen minutes of hard labor, it was time for recess. Out came the dolls, the trucks, the blocks, and the puzzles.

Krista was learning exactly what I had learned in preschool, but something seemed off. The classroom had all the usual items—block letter flashcards and posters, the smells of tempera paints and crayons, but…a lack of sound…no children's voices.

Every school I attended was filled with shrieks of laughter, whispers when you weren't supposed to be talking, or the low hum of conversation as small groups focused on a project. But not here. Plenty of eye contact and hand motions proved they communicated with each other, but the only sounds came from occasional grunts, squeals from the hearing aids, or a scream from a frustrated child. It took me all morning to get used to it.

I often caught the kids peeking at me with sly smiles. Then they'd look toward Krista whose smug expression announced pride in her special status. During lunch, I opened milk cartons and unscrewed lids on thermoses. Everyone wanted a chance to get close to Krista's big sister. One little boy *tightened* his thermos then raised his hand for my assistance.

After outdoor recess and rest time on little mats, the teacher allowed me to help with afternoon activities. Each adult (including me) took a small group, and we practiced phonics. I had the M card, the L card, and the dreaded K card. When I asked my group their names, they told me Michael and Lena. And of course, Krista. Ah, which is why I had the M, L, and K cards.

We started with M. We took turns saying the letter.

"EMMMMM-uh."

We took turns saying the sound: "MMMMMM-uh."

I asked Michael to say his name.

"Mmaii--ngul."

Pretty good. I nodded my approval. He grinned.

I extended my arm and made a sweep of the room. "What starts with M?"

Blank stares.

I pointed to the Magic Marker on a nearby table. "Mmmmarker." I pointed to Lena. "What else starts with M? More M's." I signed MORE but she frowned in confusion. I fingerspelled M and made another sweep of the room.

Lena looked around. She pointed at the piles of sleeping mats. "Maa."

I nodded. "Mat-ih." I made sure she could see my tongue and teeth.

"Maaa-tuh," she repeated.

"Good!" I smiled at her and slid my eyes sideways toward Krista.

Her gaze twitched from me to Lena and Michael. She knew what I was doing and awarded me with a nasty frown. *Would she have a tantrum in school?*

I moved on to L. "What is this letter?"

"ELLL-uh," they chorused.

"Perfect. And what is the L sound?" I cupped my hand around my ear.

"LLLLLL-uh," came the reply from all three.

I turned to Lena. "And what is your name?"

She grinned, delighted to be in the spotlight. "LLena."

I gave a thumbs-up. "What else in the room starts

with L?" Again, I made a sweeping motion with my arm. This time they knew what to do.

"Lie-yuhn," Krista said, pointing to the picture of a lion on the L card posted above the chalkboard.

"Lam," Michael said, pointing to the picture of the lamb next to the classroom altar celebrating Holy Week.

"Lippp-uh," Lena said, putting her finger on her lower lip.

Clever girl. Smiles and hugs all around.

I held up the K card. "What letter?"

"AYYY," they all said.

I shook my head. "Watch me. KKAYYY." I touched my neck just beneath my chin.

Three little faces frowned in concentration. Each put his or her finger beneath their jaw. "NGGGAYYY."

"Yes!" I applauded. It didn't bother me that they voiced the NG sound instead of the K. They'd found *almost* the right spot on the back of their throats.

They grinned at each other.

"And how does K sound?" Again, I cupped my hand around my ear.

They looked confused. Stupid question on my part. You can barely hear a K sound except for the short pressure in the back of your mouth.

I tried to show them. Keeping my mouth as open as I could and still make the correct sound, I about gagged myself as my finger pushed my tongue against my throat. "Kih. KKih."

Krista sprayed spit in her disgust. "Ptuh!" But the others tried hard.

"Nnkh," Michael said.

"Ntuh." From Lena.

Almost nose to nose with each child, I repeated, "Kkih."

"Nkuh." Lena and Michael performed together.

Krista said nothing. I raised my eyebrows. She swiveled a hundred and eighty degrees on her bottom and sat with her back to me. I ignored her.

"What starts with K in this room?" I swept my arm in a grand motion for a third time.

Michael pointed to the K card containing the picture of a man with a crown. "Nking."

Lena pointed to Krista. "Nkwissa." So Krista wasn't the only one who had trouble with R and T.

I gave each of them a quick hug and tapped Krista on the back. "Kih?" I asked, glancing around the room.

She jumped to her feet, and with a snarl said, "Ngihng." And she drew back her foot like she planned to *Kick* me.

I signed STOP and glared at her. She glared back.

Krista noticed Sister Evangeline watching her, and she thudded to a sitting position on the floor.

"Let it go," Sister Evangeline told me. "She controlled herself."

Chapter 39:
My Name is Krista

Debbie told me to
Work hard, so I worked and worked.
And I said my name!

On the way home from school, I peered into the back seat at Krista and held up the fingerspelling of K. "Why do you get so mad?" I touched K to my neck.

Krista's mouth tightened. She could see "mad" on my lips, K on my hand, and she knew what I asked by the expression on my face. She turned toward the window, her back to me. Rude.

After dinner I cornered her again while we played Go Fish. "Why do you hate K?" I signed WHY.

"Harrr." Krista's face dared me to make any further comment, either on the good use of R or the lack of a D at the end.

"'Tina' is easier," I said. "You could *be* Tina. Or Tee." I pointed at her.

Her lips jutted out in a pout, and she shook her head. "No Dee."

"Well, if you want to be Krista, you have to say K." I signed my words. IF—WANT--K-R-I-S-T-A—SAY--K.

"Harr-duh."

"If it's worth being Krista, it's worth the hard work."

Too complicated, and I couldn't sign all those words yet. She stared at me, her face a question mark.

I tried again with signs and voice. "You like 'Krista.'"

She nodded yes.

"Then work hard. Over and over and over. Kih, kih, kih, kih." I signed work over and over. And spelled K-K-K-K against my throat. "You will be happy when you can say 'Krista.'" YOU-HAPPY-SAY-K-R-I-S-T-A-YOU.

"Happy" was an easy word to lipread, too. Her pout softened to a frown of thoughtful concentration.

I put a finger on her lips and repeated my words. "When you say 'Krrr-ih-ssstuh,' you will be happy."

I looked at the cards in my hand and held up two fingers. "Do you have any twos?"

Krista grinned. "Ngo fish."

Wednesday's schedule at the school for the Deaf followed pretty much like Tuesday's except for Krista's speech lesson in the afternoon. Sister Evangeline said I could go with her and watch the speech therapy session. Krista's trudging pace down the corridor reminded me of a prisoner on death row walking to her execution. Mrs. McNab welcomed us at her door.

"Hi Tina. And you're Debbie, right?"

I shook her hand. "Nice to meet you."

We walked into a small room displaying large alphabet cards posted on the walls. Stacks of flashcards showing letters and letter blends lined the counter by the window, and a machine of some sort sat on one of three student desks in the center of the room.

Krista and Mrs. McNab sat next to each other at the remaining two desks, while I was offered a folding chair in a corner opposite them. I watched the two go through their paces. Krista could repeat almost everything Mrs. McNab asked her to, even the K – with some hesitation. Maybe she tried to please me more than the teacher. With each little triumph, she glanced my way with a small grin.

Mrs. McNab held up a picture of a ball. "What is this?"

"Ball."

She held up another card.

"Umbwella."

"Umbrrrella," Mrs. McNab repeated.

"Umbuh-rrrrella."

"Good."

And so it went for almost half an hour. Letters to words to phrases to sentences.

"I like hamburgers," Mrs. McNab said. "What do you like?"

"Ham," said Krista.

"Say 'I like ham.'"

"I lll-i-guh ham."

Mrs. McNab smiled. Not Krista.

"What else do you like, Tina?"

Krista stiffened and didn't answer.

"Tina?"

Krista shook her head. Short, sharp jerks.

"Tina? Is ham the only thing you like?"

I cringed inside, waiting for the inevitable scream of frustration.

Instead, I heard, "No Dee-nah."

Mrs. McNab raised her eyebrows.

Krista stared past my shoulder and took a deep breath. She formed her lips into a small "o." I could see her little tongue practice pushing against the front teeth, but she said nothing out loud.

She continued to mouth each letter of her name, so slowly that nausea began to build in the pit of my stomach with every motion of her lips. A swallow and a frown, purse the lips for an R, open them slightly for "ih," with almost a snarl as upper and lower teeth were revealed, then tongue against the top teeth for a T, and finally open her mouth wider to make an "uh."

For the first time in months, I grabbed Nora Jean's beads and hung onto them, as if my connection with them would spur Krista to victory.

Silence reigned in the speech therapy room as Krista repeated those motions over and over for close to a minute, maybe more. No sign of a tantrum. Krista continued to focus on some spot on the wall behind me. I doubted she was aware of my presence in that moment.

My baby sister had disappeared. A serious young girl took her place. A little girl reminding me of myself from years ago.

Mrs. McNab waited. A small, expectant smile twitched at the corners of her lips. I held absolutely still, not even taking a breath, my fingers gripping the beads but unmoving. In my head, I mouthed each letter right along with Krista.

Krista's voice, harsh with strain, broke the quiet. "Kih-kuh-rrrr-ih-ssss-ttuh. Mah nehm ihss Kuh-rrrr-ih-ssss-ttuh."

She'd done it! The lump in my stomach climbed to my throat.

Gently grasping Krista's chin, Mrs. McNab made sure they faced each other. "Your name is Krista? Not Tina?"

"No Tteena! Wis---" she stopped herself. "K-kuh-rrrr-ih-ssss-ttuh."

Mrs. McNab hugged her, which Krista stiffly accepted. The teacher walked to her desk, opened a drawer and pulled out three candy bars.

"Very good work," she told Krista with a thumbs-up and a broad smile. "Pick one." She held out the candy bars.

For the first time in the entire session, Krista relaxed. After studying her choices, she picked out a Three Musketeers Bar.

We danced down the hall, passing one of the other preschool classes on their way out to recess. The kids stared and the teacher threw me a questioning glance, but she offered no reprimand.

When I caught Krista's eye, I whispered, "You did it! You said your name!"

She nodded, eyes sparkling.

Before we entered her classroom, I stopped and made sure she watched my face. "You, me. Best friends." I signed along with the words.

BEST-SISTERS, she signed back. And we wrapped our arms around each other.

A long time ago, I had dreamed what it would be like to have a best friend in a sister. We would read together, play the piano together, and ride bikes together. Sure, I'd known twelve years' difference in age would allow us limited time. Deafness and cerebral palsy had extended the wait. But we'd become best friends in ways I'd never imagined.

It was Krista who taught me to see the wonder and the beauty of the desert. I had taught her Black Jack was worthy of her trust, even if kittens weren't. We laughed at the same things, and we cried over the same things. As awful as I had been last summer when I constantly ignored her, she had only offered me love.

If God told me He could magically replace her with the sister of my old dreams, I wouldn't trade. How could that girl compare to the beautiful friend beside me?

When Mom came to pick us up, I kept reminding myself to zip my lips. The announcement was Krista's to make. No way would I steal her glory.

As I opened the car door, Mom observed, "You two look pretty happy. Good day?"

"The *best* kind of day," I said. "Krista has something to tell you."

Krista had climbed into the car and was fastening her seatbelt. I tapped her knee, and she looked up.

"Tell Mom." My feet tapped a fast rhythm on the car's floor. If I'd been able to stand, I would have gone into a cheer, complete with jumps and a cartwheel. "K-R-I---S-T-A! GO-OOOH, KRISTA!"

Krista looked toward Mom's expectant face.

"I sehd ma nehm. I sehd K-K-rr-ih-ss-tuh."

Mom squealed like a teenager at a rock concert.

She jumped out of the car, ran around to Krista's door, and leaned in to give her a big squeeze. "I am so proud of you!"

When she finally let go, Krista's face held the same determination I'd seen in the speech therapy room. This kid would go far. She'd work and work and work until she reached the goals she'd set for herself. No matter how long it took.

"Ndonn'tt ttell Fa-thuh." Krista's voice held command.

"Don't tell Father? He will want to know." Mom looked ready to cry.

"I ttell Fa-thuh." Krista jabbed at her chest for emphasis.

"But Father won't be home for two more days." Mom held up two fingers.

It wasn't like Krista could talk to him on the phone.

Krista smiled, and her eyes crinkled with mischief. She nodded.

Mom raised her eyebrows accepting Krista's challenge. "Then let's plan a party for when Father comes home." She even signed PARTY.

Since when had Mom learned sign language?

Chapter 40: Celebrations
We are having
A party! For me! Daddy
Will be so surprised!

When we arrived home from Krista's school on Thursday, Jimmy was there to greet us.

"Guess what?" We spoke at the same time.

"You go first," I said.

"No. You first." He gave me the smile reserved just for me.

Was he going to ask me to go steady? That would be so cool to officially own the status. But he didn't even have a class ring yet. Whatever it was, it must be good if he thought he could top Krista's accomplishment.

By the time I reenacted the whole scene at Krista's school, she had wandered in to say hi to one of her favorite people.

"YOU-SAY-NAME-YOU," he signed to her.

She beamed. "Mah nehm iss Kuh-rriss-ttuh."

That sounded pretty smooth. She'd been

practicing.

As she scampered with a lopsided gait out of the den, I grabbed Jimmy's hand. "Okay. Your turn."

He smiled, started to speak, and…choked up.

But I thought he was going to tell me something happy. "What happened?"

He swallowed and tried again. "My mom." He swallowed once more. "My mom received a letter." His lips pressed together.

Our original "guess whats" should've made for an *exciting* letter. What kind of excitement would cause him to force back tears?

"From my dad." He blinked. "Inside a prison camp." His lips trembled in the midst of an angelic smile.

Jimmy hadn't heard from his dad in two years. MIA, missing in action, usually meant dead. But not this time. The letter immediately moved his dad from MIA to POW. Prisoner of war. Was that good? Or horrible?

If it were *my* dad, the first picture in my mind would be a concentration camp like the one where Anne Frank died. How would he survive? But no, POW was good. POW meant *alive*.

Jimmy's dad was *alive*.

I had no words. I wrapped my arms around his neck and kissed those trembling lips.

Mom entered the room, eyebrows raised, and we stepped away from each other.

"We're celebrating," I said.

The best Mom could do on a minute's notice was to invite Jimmy for dinner, pull a bunch of little American flags from the decorations closet and plant them in a small bowl as a centerpiece. The boys pounded Jimmy on the back when they heard the news, and Grandma offered her best wishes. With Krista's "name celebration" planned for Friday, Mom decided she'd invite Jimmy and his mom and grandma to eat with us on *Saturday* night.

Jimmy and I walked to the village since we had some time yet before dinner. And who should we see walking into the stationery store but Ronni.

Ronni's family never traveled over spring break. It was one more thing we'd had in common. Except for the three times in my entire school life when we visited Aunt Nell, our family didn't go anywhere in the spring either.

Ronni and I had barely spoken all year, but she deserved to know the latest about Krista. She'd been my first friend when I returned to Hampton Shores, and only Ronni and Nora Jean had ever loved my little sister as if she were their own.

"Be right back," I told Jimmy, and I hurried into the store. "Ronni, wait up."

She halted and turned toward me, a quizzical expression on her face.

"I wanted you to be one of the first to know." I smiled. A real one. Not the fake I'd perfected for the last seven months.

She tilted her head to the side.

"Krista said her name! With a K sound and everything!"

"Krista with a *K*?" Ronni's expression moved from

curious to confused to… *comprehension*. Her famous smile lit up her face "I only remember her saying 'Oo-wee-uh.' She couldn't pronounce a K or hardly any other consonants." She nodded in satisfaction. "She's come a long way."

"She's been able to say S for a while, and Rs have been getting better. It's the T and the K that have been the hardest."

Her smile softened, and her gaze seemed to center on the floor behind me. "I miss seeing Krista…" When she looked up at my face again, her eyes were sad. "Thanks for telling me."

Was it possible she missed being friends? Or did she only miss my sister?

"My dad doesn't know yet what Krista can say. She wants to tell him herself when he gets home. So we're having a party tomorrow night to celebrate. Would you like to come? Krista would like it, I'm sure."

I would too. Ronni used to be my "safe place." A serene pool beside a waterfall. The petty torrents of Melissa and Leigh and others like them could splash into our pool, but Ronni and I would paddle around paying no attention to the little waves. I wanted those calm waters back. I wanted Ronni to be my best friend again.

"I know it's a Friday night and you probably have a standing date with Roger, but…" I didn't want to say the obvious stuff.

Ronni caught my eye and looked away. Was she trying to figure out how to say no without hurting my feelings again?

Should I just give it up?

"Roger's in Florida until Sunday. And even if he was in town, I don't think he'd mind." Her dazzling smile returned. "Yeah, I'd love to be there and hear Krista say her name."

That night the whole family except Daddy made a to-do list together: paper chains to string all over the house, signs praising Krista, each one with a big K and the rest in small letters. Krista picked the colors, pink and green. A cake, of course, with the same kind of lettering. A dinner menu that turned out to be a combination of Krista's favorite dinner and Daddy's favorite dinner. Steak – with spaghetti on the side. I informed Mom of our extra guests.

On Friday after Krista got home from school, Jimmy joined us, and we stapled strips of construction paper into connecting loops.

Ronni arrived a short time later. With a shriek, Krista threw herself at my old friend. She'd missed Ronni almost as much as I had. Krista pulled Ronni into the kitchen to show her the special cake. Then she dragged her back to the art supplies table, aka our dining room table.

I finally had a chance to introduce Ronni and Jimmy.

"You're in my art class, aren't you?" Jimmy asked.

"Yeah."

"You do good stuff."

"Thanks." She looked straight at me but kept talking to Jimmy. "Maybe you and Debbie and me and Roger can meet up at the movies some time."

Jimmy knew my history with Ronni and looked my way, questioning. I nodded slightly and smiled.

He twined his fingers around mine as he turned his attention to Ronni. "That would be fun."

We continued to staple strips of paper, and we blew up balloons until we gave ourselves headaches from lack of oxygen. Krista decided where to place every balloon. Once we had all the chains draped through all the rooms and our posters were thumbtacked to all the walls, there was nothing more to do excerpt wait for Daddy.

Paul, Wade, and Jimmy played HORSE using the basketball hoop above our garage. Ronni and I sat on the front steps, the early spring evening so mild I could smell the salt in the air.

Ronni offered me a sly grin. "So, do you think you might have a date for the Beach Bonfires next month?" She glanced Jimmy's way.

"I hope so. I don't think *he'll* stand me up."

"Me neither. He's too nice." The grin faded and she gazed beyond the park across the street. "Who would've thought I'd ever say that about Jimmy Pulizzi? Just goes to show…"

"People change," I finished for her.

"Yeah."

The atmosphere between us turned somber.

"*I* changed." Ronni drew her legs close to her body and rested her chin on her knees. "I'm sorry."

Wow. All this time, I'd wondered how one cheerleading practice could have ruined our friendship. Maybe I'd had no right to expect her to be a best friend forever. Friendships evolved and dissolved. Just the way of nature.

Or maybe it *was* her fault. She'd *chosen* to turn her back on me that day. Then again, blaming her made it easier to excuse myself, especially when *I* hadn't always made time for *her* when Bill was my boyfriend.

She must have taken my silence for anger. "You and Jimmy don't really have to double date with me and Roger. I can understand why you wouldn't want to."

I bumped her shoulder with mine, our old way of saying, *You're kidding, right?* "I think a double date is a great idea. Are you sure Roger won't mind?"

"I'm sure. Guys don't worry about stuff like that. At least, not as much as girls." She rose to her feet, jumped off the steps, and did a handspring into the grass.

My words had pumped her up like an inflatable Tigger.

"Do guys ever come up with the idea of a double date all by themselves?" I asked.

"No way." She ran across the yard. Cartwheel. Roundoff. Flip. Then she ran back to the steps. "Here's how Roger and I do things. He asks me out, and I plan the rest of it—which movie, which restaurant, or just a walk on the beach."

With a happy smirk, she slid into a split and shook her fists as if she were holding pompoms.

"You're as nutty as ever." I stepped toward her and tugged on one of her hands so she could slide back up to a standing position.

The screech of tires on the road grabbed our attention.

Where was Krista? Where was Black Jack? With heart pounding, I scanned the road in the twilight, searching for a small body.

Ronni laughed. "Can you believe those two?"

"Who?" My heart continued to pound, but no one else seemed panicked.

The snappy little Corvair had stopped in front of the house. With its convertible top down, Melissa and Leigh stared back at us, shocked expressions on their faces. Shocked with me? Or Ronni? Or maybe both of us in my front yard had almost given Melissa a heart attack.

Ronni beamed her million-watt smile to them and hugged me. "Let's see what they have to say." She darted across my front lawn to the street.

It had been such a great day. *Did I want to ruin it?* For one short moment, I hesitated. A very short moment. If this was a day of new beginnings, why not try something new with those two as well?

Ronni was talking a mile a minute when I caught up to her leaning on the car's door. "...and since I've known Krista since she was tiny, Debbie invited me over for the party."

Did Ronni feel the need to explain her presence at my house? But she seemed relaxed, not defensive, in front of the boss ladies.

Time to start my experiment. Deep breath. Go.

"Did Ronni tell you the reason for the party?" I hoped my smile looked friendly.

Melissa sniffed. "So, your sister said her name. The kid's six or something. Big deal."

Ronni stiffened beside me. "She's only four."

Before I lost my cool and continued the feud, I ignored Melissa's jab. "It's hard for deaf people to talk, especially when they're little. It's frustrating. They try and try, and people still don't understand them. Failure's scary." I stared directly at Leigh in the passenger seat. "Remember what you said about ballet class?"

Wearing an incredulous scowl, Melissa turned to Leigh. "You two never had ballet class together."

Ronni echoed those thoughts without the attitude. "Yeah, what's so important about ballet all of a sudden?"

Leigh returned my stare. Haughtiness no longer resided in her eyes.

Which allowed me to step away from our past.

"Would you like to join us? Krista is so proud of herself. The more people who come to her party, the happier she'll be."

"Now?" Leigh asked.

"We're just waiting for my dad to get home, and then the party will start."

I glanced at Ronni for her reaction. Her broad grin indicated she liked the idea.

The steady tap of the basketball on the pavement had stopped. The boys probably wondered what we were talking about.

Leigh looked at Melissa as if to say, "What do you think?"

Melissa snorted. "Sorry."

Yeah, right.

"We've already made plans. A bit more exciting than a little kid's party." She sneered at me as her hand reached for the stick shift. "I'll bet you even have balloons all over the house."

Ronni winked at me. "Dang, we should've thought of that."

Melissa jerked the car into first gear and stalled.

"Mercy! Please! Have mercy on that transmission!" Jimmy kneeled in the driveway, his hands clasped in prayer. He hadn't lost his talent for mockery when the occasion begged for it.

My brothers hooted.

The gears growled again, and Melissa jolted down the road for several yards before smoothing out her ride.

Ronni waved goodbye—prom queen style. That cracked me up.

Daddy arrived before seven. He must have left New Jersey a little earlier than usual. Had Mom spilled the beans?

Enticing aromas wafted from the kitchen as he stepped into a house of paper ornaments. Chains of all colors hung from the stair railing, looped around curtain rods, and draped over furniture. "Krista" signs, all with a giant **K**, lined the hall and covered the walls. Balloons were strewn throughout the living room, halls, and dining room. Poor Melissa couldn't understand what makes for fun.

Daddy dropped his bag on the bottom step of the stairs. "What is this all about?" He nodded toward Jimmy and Ronni. "Are we having a party? Did Krista win a million bucks?"

All of us grinned at him like she *had* won the million-dollar sweepstakes. We were on our honor not to say a word. Grandma sat in the living room watching us with a regal smile. I could hear Mom in the kitchen saying Daddy was here. Krista turned the corner from the dining room into the hall a little too quickly for her stilted gait in braces, and she fell headlong onto the hardwood floor.

The smiles left our faces. *Had she hurt herself? Would her surprise get ruined?* We rushed toward her, but she scrambled up again and launched herself into Daddy's arms. The spill didn't affect *her* smile.

Daddy looked at her with a question in his eyes. He pointed at the signs. "It's not your birthday."

Krista shook her head. She pointed to the signs as well. "Nehm pahrdee."

"Name party?" He looked at the rest of us, bewildered, but no one enlightened him. Still holding her in his arms, Daddy asked Krista directly. "Name party?"

Krista nodded in excitement. "Mah nehm."

"I see it's your name," Daddy said.

"I sehd ma nehm."

"You *said* your name?"

He held himself in expectant stillness and looked at Mom, who had followed Krista into the living room. The pure joy on her face made her even more beautiful.

Krista placed her hands on Daddy's cheeks and turned his face back toward hers. "Mah nehm iss K-Kih-rrisss-tuh."

Daddy moved his lips, silently repeating her words. Then he covered her face with kisses until she screeched with laughter and begged to get down.

It was the best party ever. No presents wrapped in fancy paper, but gifts of laughter and peace and family and friends floated around us. After dinner, Mom brought out the large sheet cake ordered from the A&P,

just the way Krista wanted it. Frosted in white and lettered with a green K and all the other letters in pink:

My name is **Krista.**

Nine people could never eat all of that cake. *Oops!* The fork heading for my mouth clattered to the floor. *How did that happen?*

"Debbie. You've got crumbs everywhere." Grandma hurried for the broom.

I called after her. "Don't worry about it."

Several more forks composed a series of clinks and clunks as they hit the maple planks. All the guys grinned.

Krista looked my way. What was so funny?

I pointed under the table where the dog worked his way around the silverware and snuffled up cake crumbs.

Krista grinned. And dropped her cake-filled fork.

Enjoy, Black Jack.

Afterword

Although the **World Without Sound** series is fiction, the Hansen family is based on my own family, and many of the scenes you've read are true.

So, what is the rest of our story? What happened over the last fifty years?

We grew up and got old, of course!

But if I were reading about Debbie and Krista for the first time, I would want to know how it all turned out for them. So here is the history of our family and friends in a nutshell:

Once **Mom** and **Daddy** retired to North Carolina, they spent a lot of time on their boat traveling the Intercoastal Waterway. **Grandma** chose to live nearby in a senior community and have her own apartment. She lived to be ninety-one. Daddy passed away in 2011 shortly before he turned eighty. We miss him. Mom has moved to Florida and lives in her own apartment. She loves visits from her children and grandchildren.

Paul became a fighter pilot in the Navy, and when he returned to civilian life, he continued to fly for a private corporation. As of 2023, he has not yet retired.

Wade stayed in New York where he works in construction. His love for the beach never allowed him to remain inland for long.

Black Jack lived a long and happy dog's life. He may have followed Paul home, but he became Wade's constant companion until the day he lay down for a nap in a sun patch on the lawn and never woke up.

I (Debbie) became a teacher, just as I knew I would. And even though I trained for special education, over the years I taught elementary grades, music, science, and Spanish. And now, I'm a writer.

No, I didn't marry **Jimmy** and live happily ever after. Jimmy is one of the few major characters in this book who is mostly fiction. Although, he and Debbie would've made a perfect love story, wouldn't they? Instead, I married my college sweetheart who is the *true* love of my life. We've raised three sons and love to spend time with our eight grandchildren.

Ronni really was my best friend through junior high, but we drifted apart in high school, and unlike in this book, we were never close again. It's one of the reasons I made her a strong character—what I wish could have been.

Nora Jean was a real friend, too. While her life in the foster care system wasn't a whole lot of fun, and though we never stayed in touch after I left California, I assume she did *not* die a tragic death.

Not only did **Krista** learn to speak, her school also taught sign language to their students starting in the mid-1970s. When she graduated from Cleary School for the Deaf, she attended the local Catholic high school where they set up a program for the large class of Deaf students.

Krista attended college at the National Technological Institute for the Deaf (NTID) in Rochester, New York, and later she received her bachelor's degree from Gallaudet University near Washington, D.C. For many years, she worked as an accountant for the government.

But Krista also has a teacher's heart, so she went back to college and became a teacher for the Deaf, fulfilling *my* original dream. When asked why she wanted to change careers, she said, "Because I want to help people." She moved on to teaching life skills to deaf adults, leading Bible studies for the Deaf at her church, and helping deaf women who were victims of domestic violence.

My most important dream *did* come true. Krista and I share the same love for family and for Jesus, and He granted me the desire of my heart. My sister and I are truly best friends forever.

Forever.

DISCUSSION QUESTIONS

1. Debbie gets weary of Krista's temper tantrums. Do you think she was wrong in getting angry with Krista in Chapter 1? Why or why not? How would you have handled the situation if Krista were *your* sister?

2. What is your opinion about families who sent their toddler children to live at a deaf school?

3. Now that Debbie is in high school, she has the opportunity for many new experiences in school and in her social life. What does she enjoy doing? What is she afraid of? How are you like Debbie? How are you different?

4. Ronni doesn't like Bill. Do you think she's right, or do you think she's too hard on him?

5. Ronni makes the cheerleading squad in ninth grade but Debbie doesn't. How would you react if your best friend succeeded in something that you both wanted to do, but you did *not* succeed?

6. In the chapters where Debbie wants a pet, she tells three main stories about animals, two about cats and one about dogs. Which of her stories did you find most entertaining? Why?

7. In Chapters 10-12, Debbie describes her aunt's ranch, her extended family, and the action among all the cousins. What was your favorite part of those chapters? Why?

8. The family isn't supposed to use sign language with Krista, and she can't read lips very well. What might have happened if Krista hadn't been able to communicate what happened on the station wagon-bus?

(Chapter 13)

9. When Bill doesn't show up after he asks Debbie out, life gets messy! Name at least two things that Debbie did wrong after Bill stood her up. Name something she did right.

10. As time goes on, Krista learns to say some words. Name a word she could say correctly. Name a word she always had trouble saying. What letters are hardest for deaf people to both see and say?

11. Think about Debbie's summer job babysitting the Smythe-Halsey children. How was she a good babysitter? Would you have kept working at such a thankless job, or would you have quit?

12. Do you think a real angel visited Debbie, Krista, and their mom at the beach?

13. Sometimes Krista seems to know things that no one else knows. How is that possible?

14. Debbie finally becomes a cheerleader in tenth grade. Why isn't she all that happy about it?

15. For writers, "a turning point" is when a character recognizes the truth about herself or about a situation and begins to go in a new direction. When Debbie attends Mary's party, something happens that is a "turning point" for Debbie. What was the turning point?

16. What happened to break the friendship between Debbie and Ronni?

17. What were you thinking as Debbie turned her back on Melissa and walked toward Jimmy's table? (Chapter 34)

18. What things do Jimmy and Debbie have in common?

19. Why was Krista so angry with Mrs. McNab?

20. By the end of the book, almost everyone is happy about Krista's ability to say her name. Who is the one person who doesn't care? How has Debbie's attitude changed toward that person?